THE AWAKENING OF DHARAVI

Atul Arjun Mohite

NU VOICE PRESS

First published by NU VOICE PRESS 2025
An imprint of Hubhawks Pvt. Ltd
www.nuvoicepress.com

The characters and events portrayed in this book are fictitious. Any similarity to real persons, living or dead, is coincidental and not intended by the author.

ISBN: 978-81-990481-4-0

Printed at Manipal Technologies Limited, Manipal
Published by: Nu Voice Press

Chapter 1

ASH IN THE GUTTERS

THE TASTE OF ASH HAD been on Nisha Patel's tongue for three days now. Metallic and bitter, like licking copper pennies in the monsoon heat. She ran her tongue across her teeth again, trying to scrape away the phantom flavour that had no earthly source. The pre-monsoon air hung thick and oppressive over Dharavi, pressing down on the narrow alleys like a weight she could feel in her bones.

"*Paagal ladki*," she muttered to herself, adjusting the strap of her canvas bag as she navigated the familiar maze of corrugated metal roofs and brick walls. Crazy girl, indeed. Three days of tasting ash when there was no fire and no smoke, but the usual cocktail of exhaust fumes, cooking spices, and the eternal dampness that never quite left Mumbai's largest slum.

Nisha paused at the junction of two alleys, where Mrs. Sharma's tea stall competed for space with a cobbler's workshop and a narrow passage that led deeper into the heart of Dharavi. The old woman looked up from her bubbling kettle, her weathered face creasing into a smile.

"*Chai*, *beta*?" she called out, already reaching for a glass.

"Not today, aunty," Nisha replied, though her throat felt parched. Every rupee counted, and she had exactly forty-three rupees left in her pocket, which had been carefully counted that morning and recounted twice. Forty-three rupees stood between her and the engineering textbook she needed for next week's entrance exam preparation.

The engineering scholarship. Her ticket out of this labyrinth of dreams deferred and possibilities constrained by circumstance. Nisha had been preparing for the Joint Entrance Examination for two years now, studying by candlelight when the power failed, solving equations on the backs of discarded newspapers, memorising formulas while helping her mother sort recyclables. If she could just score high enough, if she could just prove herself worthy, she could build bridges and design systems that would lift entire communities out of poverty. She could become the engineer who finally brought reliable electricity and clean water to places like Dharavi. The future she dreamed of was specific and tangible—concrete and steel and mathematical precision applied to human problems that had waited too long for solutions.

She continued down the main passage, her feet knowing every pothole, every loose stone, every place where the drainage backed up during heavy rains. A group of children ran past her, chasing a makeshift kite made from plastic bags and bamboo sticks, their laughter echoing off the walls.

"Nisha *didi*!" called eight-year-old Arjun from the group, his gap-toothed grin bright in his dirt-smudged face. "Come fly kites with us!"

"Later, *chotu*," she called back, ruffling his hair as he bounced on his toes. "After I finish my work."

Arjun's face fell slightly, but he nodded with the resigned understanding of a child who had learned early that work came before play in Dharavi. The other children had already moved on, their attention captured by a new game involving bottle caps and a circle drawn in the dust.

Nisha felt the familiar tug of guilt in her chest. When was the last time she had simply played? When had she stopped seeing the narrow alleys as an adventure playground and started seeing them as obstacles to navigate, problems to solve, systems to escape?

The taste of ash intensified as she approached her family's modest dwelling—two rooms and a shared courtyard, home to three generations of Patels. The air shimmered with heat, and something else. Something that made her skin prickle and her spine straighten instinctively.

"*Ma*!" she called as she ducked through the low doorway, immediately enveloped by the familiar scents of turmeric, cumin, and the slight mustiness of clothes that never quite dried completely in the humid air.

Priya Patel looked up from where she sat cross-legged on a worn cotton mat, sorting through a pile of plastic bottles by colour and size. At forty-two, her hands moved with practiced efficiency, but Nisha noticed the way her mother's dark eyes immediately fixed on her face, searching.

"You look pale," Priya said without preamble, setting down a blue bottle and reaching toward Nisha's forehead. "And you haven't been eating properly."

"I'm fine, Ma." Nisha caught her mother's hand, noting the roughness of her palms, the small cuts from handling sharp plastic edges. "Just tired from studying."

It wasn't entirely a lie. She had been studying—Advanced Engineering Mathematics until two in the morning, Chemistry formulas scrawled across every available surface in their small room. But the tiredness ran deeper than academic exhaustion. It settled in her bones like the monsoon humidity, persistent and inexplicable.

Priya's eyes narrowed. "The headaches?"

"They're getting better."

Another partial truth. The headaches had indeed diminished over the past day, but they'd been replaced by something stranger. A restless energy that made her want to pace, to move, to push against the walls of their small world with her bare hands.

"*Beti*," her mother said softly, using the endearment that always made Nisha's resolve crack slightly. "I know you think I worry too much, but …"

A low rumble of thunder cut through her words, though the sky visible through their small window remained a pale, washed-out grey. Nisha glanced up, frowning. The weather reports had mentioned possible rain, but this sounded different. Deeper. More urgent.

"The monsoon's early this year," Priya murmured, but there was something in her voice that made Nisha look at her sharply. Her mother's face had gone very still, her hands frozen mid-motion over the plastic bottles.

"Ma? What's wrong?"

Before Priya could answer, the thunder came again. Except this time, Nisha felt it in the ground beneath her feet, a vibration that seemed to pulse in rhythm with her heartbeat. The taste of ash exploded across her tongue, so strong she gasped and pressed her hand to her mouth.

"*Kya hua?*" Priya was on her feet instantly, her hands gripping Nisha's shoulders.

"Nothing, just ..." Nisha shook her head, trying to clear the sudden dizziness. "The taste is back. Stronger."

The look that crossed her mother's face was one Nisha had never seen before—a flash of something that might have been recognition, followed immediately by fear so profound it made Priya's hands tremble against Nisha's arms.

"What taste?" Priya's voice was barely above a whisper.

Before Nisha could answer, the rain began.

But this wasn't the usual progression of monsoon weather—first the wind, then scattered drops, building gradually to the steady drumbeat of tropical rain. This came all at once, as if someone had torn a hole in the sky. Water poured down in sheets so thick that visibility dropped to mere meters within seconds.

The sound was deafening. Not just the rain itself, but the way it struck every surface in Dharavi—metal roofs, plastic sheeting, packed earth—creating a cacophony that made conversation impossible. Nisha and her mother stood frozen, watching through their window as the familiar world outside dissolved into a wall of grey water.

Then came the wind.

It hit like a physical blow, rattling their walls and sending anything not nailed down into chaotic flight. A piece of corrugated metal flew past their window with a shriek of tortured steel. Nisha heard shouts from neighbouring dwellings, though the words were lost in the overwhelming roar of the storm.

"We need to get to higher ground," Priya shouted, her voice barely audible, even though she was standing right next to Nisha.

Nisha nodded, already moving toward their small bundle of emergency supplies, a habit learned from years of monsoon seasons that brought both life-giving water and devastating floods. But as she reached for the waterproof bag containing their important documents and small savings, the world outside their window changed in a way that stopped her cold.

The rain wasn't just falling. It was rising.

The drainage channels that normally carried away the monsoon floods were backing up, but too quickly, too dramatically. Water was pouring out of gutters and storm drains, flowing uphill in defiance of gravity, creating rivers where none should exist.

"That's not possible," Nisha breathed, pressing her face to the glass.

But Priya had gone very still beside her, and when Nisha glanced at her mother's reflection in the window, she saw that Priya's lips were moving in what looked like a prayer, or a protection charm.

The water continued to rise, transforming the familiar paths of Dharavi into something alien and treacherous. Nisha watched a motorbike get swept away like a toy, watched people struggling to move through currents that should have been ankle-deep but reached their waists.

And through it all, the taste of ash grew stronger, until it felt like breathing smoke.

"We have to go," Priya said urgently, grabbing their emergency bag. "Now."

They pushed out into the storm together, immediately soaked to the skin despite the short overhang that provided nominal shelter outside their door. The rain was warm, but it struck with surprising force, each drop feeling like a small impact. Nisha had to squint to see even a few feet ahead.

The normal sounds of Dharavi—the calls of vendors, the hum of machinery, the constant background chatter of thousands of people living in close proximity—had been swallowed entirely by the storm. In their place was something else, something that made Nisha's skin crawl with its wrongness.

Whispers.

Not human voices, but something that sounded almost like language carried on the wind and rain. Words she couldn't quite catch, in a rhythm that seemed to match the pulsing in her temples.

"Do you hear that?" she called to her mother.

"Hear what?" Priya's response was sharp, worried.

Before Nisha could explain, a child's scream cut through the storm noise—high, terrified, and heartbreakingly familiar.

"Arjun!" Nisha spun toward the sound, trying to locate its source in the wall of rain.

The small boy she'd spoken to earlier was trapped in a shallow drainage channel, which had now become a raging torrent of muddy water. He was clinging to a piece of rebar that had jutted from the concrete, his small body being pulled by the current, his face a mask of terror.

Without thinking, Nisha plunged toward the water.

"*Nahi*!" Priya's scream followed her, but Nisha was already waist-deep in the flood, fighting against a current that was far stronger than any natural rain runoff should have been.

The water was shockingly cold despite the warm rain, and it pulled at her with what felt like deliberate intent. Each step was a struggle, the muddy bottom sucking at her feet, debris striking her legs and arms as the current carried it past.

"Hold on!" she shouted to Arjun, though she wasn't sure he could hear her over the storm.

The whispers were louder now and more insistent. With a chill that had nothing to do with the cold water, Nisha realised they seemed to be coming from the flood itself, from the churning, muddy water that surrounded her.

She was still three meters away from Arjun when her foot slipped on something slick and she went under.

The world went silent.

Underwater, the whispers became words. Words not in Hindi or English or any other language that she recognised, but, she somehow understood them. They spoke of depth and darkness, of ancient currents and patient waiting. They spoke of power that ran in bloodlines like underground rivers, surfacing only when the barriers grew thin.

They spoke her name.

Panic flared in her chest as she struggled toward the surface, but the current was too strong, the debris-filled water too chaotic. Her lungs burned with the effort of holding her breath, and her vision began to darken at the edges as oxygen deprivation made her movements sluggish and uncoordinated. She could feel her chest wanting to spasm, to force her to breathe in the muddy water that surrounded her. Pressure built behind her eyes until it felt like her skull might crack.

In that moment of desperate need, as consciousness began to slip away, Nisha did something she had never done before.

She stopped fighting the water and instead spoke to the earth beneath it.

Not with words, but with something deeper—a desperate plea that came from the same place as breath, as heartbeat, as the electric impulse that sparked through nerve and synapse. She called to the solid ground below the chaos, to the foundations that held up their precarious world, to the bones of the city itself.

And the earth answered.

Power erupted through her like lightning through water. It was raw, uncontrolled, and utterly impossible. The muddy bottom of the drainage channel heaved upward, forming a column of earth and debris that lifted her toward the surface. The water around her suddenly obeyed laws that had nothing to do with gravity or fluid dynamics, carving new channels that flowed around Arjun instead of threatening to sweep him away.

Nisha broke the surface gasping, standing on a pillar of earth that definitely hadn't been there moments before. The whispers had stopped, replaced by a silence that felt expectant, waiting.

Arjun was safe, and somehow transported to the edge of the channel by currents that now flowed gently instead of rushing toward destruction. He stared at her with wide eyes, his small hands still gripping the rebar but no longer in danger of losing his hold.

The rain continued to fall, but the water around them had calmed, flowing in patterns that looked almost deliberate, almost artful. As if someone had redesigned the entire drainage system of this small section of Dharavi to better serve its inhabitants.

Nisha looked down at her hands, still raised from her desperate underwater gesture, and saw something that made her heart stop.

On her right forearm, just below the elbow, a perfect spiral mark glowed with soft, warm light—not a tattoo or a scar, but something that seemed to be made of light itself, visible even through her soaked sleeve.

She was still staring at it in shock when a voice spoke behind her.

"Well," the voice said calmly, as if commenting on the weather rather than addressing a teenager standing on an impossible pillar of earth in the middle of a supernatural storm. "That's certainly an interesting way to awaken."

Nisha spun around, nearly losing her balance on her earthen platform, and found herself looking at a woman in her fifties with silver-streaked hair and the kind of calm, penetrating gaze that suggested she had seen far stranger things than this.

The woman stood at the edge of the drainage channel, completely dry despite the ongoing downpour, wearing simple cotton clothes that should have been soaked through but somehow remained untouched by the rain.

"Who are you?" Nisha called, her voice shaky with shock and adrenaline.

"My name is *Guru* Chanda," the woman replied, stepping forward with no apparent concern for the flooded ground that somehow supported her weight as if it were solid. "And I've been waiting for you to wake up, Nisha Patel."

The way she said it, not as if she had been expecting this specific moment, but as if she had been waiting for years, made Nisha's newly awakened power pulse beneath her skin like a second heartbeat.

"I don't understand," Nisha whispered.

Chanda's expression softened slightly, though her eyes remained alert and watchful. "The mark on your arm is called the spiral of Mumbadevi. It indicates that you carry the blood of the city's patron goddess. A power that has been dormant in your family line for generations."

Nisha glanced down at the glowing spiral, then back at the impossible woman standing in the flood as if it were a sidewalk. "That's not possible. Magic isn't real. There has to be a scientific explanation for …"

"For what? For the way you commanded the earth to rise? For the way the water obeyed your will?" Chanda stepped closer, and Nisha could see genuine compassion in her dark eyes alongside the watchfulness. "Child, you just saved a life using power that had been sleeping in your bloodline for three centuries. The scientific explanation is that some forces in this world operate according to laws that your textbooks haven't discovered yet."

Behind them, the sounds of Dharavi were slowly returning as the unnatural storm began to subside. Nisha could hear voices calling out, people checking on neighbours, the gradual resumption of normal life in the wake of the inexplicable weather.

But she could also hear something else—her mother's voice, calling her name with a note of desperate fear.

"Nisha! *Beta*, where are you?"

Priya appeared at the edge of the channel, and when her eyes found her daughter standing on the impossible pillar of earth, her face went white. But it wasn't shock at the miracle that Nisha read in her mother's expression. It was recognition, and beneath that, a terror so profound it made Nisha's newly awakened power recoil.

"*Nahi*," Priya whispered, her gaze fixed on the spiral mark that was now clearly visible on Nisha's arm. "*Nahi, nahi, nahi...*"

She was shaking her head, backing away as if the sight of her own daughter had become something too terrible to bear.

"Ma?" Nisha's voice cracked. "Ma, what's wrong? What's happening to me?"

Priya pressed her hands to her mouth, tears streaming down her face. When she spoke, her voice was so quiet that Nisha had to strain to hear her over the settling sounds of the storm.

"I hoped it would skip you," she whispered. "I prayed every day that the old blood would sleep for another generation. That you could have a normal life, a safe life ..."

"What old blood?" Nisha demanded, stepping down from her earthen pillar onto the muddy ground. The spiral mark pulsed brighter as her feet touched the earth, and she felt power flowing through her like electricity through copper wire.

But before Priya could answer, a new sound cut through the air. A low, rumbling growl that definitely didn't come from any animal native to Mumbai.

All three women turned toward the source of the sound, and Nisha felt her blood turn to ice.

Something was rising from the deepest part of the flooded drainage channel. Something with too many teeth and eyes like black holes, something that moved through the muddy water as if it belonged there, as if the flood had been specifically designed to provide it with a pathway into their world.

The creature fixed its alien gaze on Nisha, and when it spoke, its voice was like the sound of waves breaking against rocks, layered with harmonics that suggested vast depths and patient hunger.

"Sister," it said, and the word sent ice through Nisha's veins. "You're finally awake. He's been waiting for you."

Chanda stepped between Nisha and the creature, her calm demeanour shifting into something harder, more dangerous. "She's under protection," she said firmly. "The awakening is too recent. She needs time to understand…"

"Time?" The creature's laugh was like the sound of drowning. "Time is what mortals worry about. She carries the old blood, the deep blood. She belongs with us now."

The spiral mark on Nisha's arm flared brighter, and she felt the creature's words pulling at something deep in her chest—a recognition she didn't want to acknowledge, a calling she didn't want to answer.

"I don't belong to anyone," she said, surprised by the steadiness of her own voice.

The creature's many eyes fixed on her with what might have been amusement. "We'll see, little sister. When the tides rise and the barriers fall, you'll understand what you really are."

It began to sink back into the muddy water, its form dissolving like smoke. But its final words reached them clearly, carrying the weight of a prophecy and a threat.

"The convergence comes. The deep calls to the deep. And blood will answer blood."

Then it was gone, leaving only the normal sounds of a Mumbai afternoon after rain—the splash of people moving through puddles, the distant honk of traffic resuming its usual chaos, the calls of vendors whose wares had survived the downpour.

Nisha stood frozen, staring at the water where the impossible creature had disappeared. The spiral mark on her arm continued to glow, though fainter now, like the afterimage of staring at a bright light.

"What was that thing?" she whispered.

Chanda's expression was grim. "A messenger. And unfortunately, not the last one you'll encounter." She turned to face Nisha fully, her dark eyes serious. "You're in considerable danger, child. More than you can possibly understand right now. The awakening of a Spiral Bearer draws attention from forces that have been waiting centuries for this moment."

"Spiral Bearer?" Nisha touched the mark on her arm, feeling warmth pulse beneath her fingers.

"Later," Chanda said firmly. "Right now, you need to make a choice. You can come with me to a place where you can learn to control your power safely, where you can understand what you're becoming ..."

"No." Priya's voice was sharp, desperate. She stepped forward, reaching for Nisha. "She's just a child. She has exams and a planned future. This isn't her world."

Chanda's expression softened with sympathy, but her voice remained firm. "I'm afraid that choice was made for her the moment she awakened. The power can't be ignored or suppressed, it will only grow stronger and more dangerous without proper training."

Nisha looked between the two older women, feeling as if her life had split into before and after in the space of a single afternoon. Before: dreams of engineering school, a normal future, problems that could be solved with equations and hard work. After: glowing marks on her skin, creatures from nightmares, and powers that defied every law of physics she had ever learned.

But as she stood there, still tasting ash on her tongue, still feeling the impossible warmth of divine power flowing beneath her skin, she realised that 'before' had been an illusion. The headaches, the restless energy, the growing sense that something was calling to her from just beyond her understanding—this had been building for weeks, maybe months.

The only real choice was whether to step into the unknown willingly or wait for it to drag her in anyway.

"If I come with you," she said to Chanda, "will I be able to protect people? Like I protected Arjun?"

The older woman nodded slowly. "Among other things. Though the path is neither easy nor safe."

Nisha glanced back at her mother, seeing the fear and love warring in Priya's dark eyes. She thought of their small room, of the textbooks stacked beside her sleeping mat, of the engineering scholarship that had been her goal for so long.

Then she thought of the creature's black eyes, of its promise that others would come, of the way her power had responded to Arjun's danger without conscious thought or control.

"I'm sorry, Ma," she whispered, and stepped toward Chanda.

Priya's sob was like a physical blow, but before Nisha could reconsider, Chanda grasped her hand. The world exploded into light and motion, folding around them like paper, carrying them away from everything Nisha had ever known and toward a destiny she was only beginning to understand.

The last thing she heard before the translation swept her away was her mother's voice, calling prayers to gods both ancient and merciful, begging them to bring her daughter home safely.

Chapter 2

THE MARK AND THE WHISPER

"THE TRANSLATION", THAT WAS WHAT *Guru* Chanda called it later. It felt like being turned inside out while falling through a kaleidoscope. Nisha's stomach lurched as reality folded around them, the familiar chaos of Dharavi dissolving into streaks of colour and impossible angles. For a terrifying moment, she felt herself scattered across multiple dimensions, her consciousness stretched thin as spider silk.

Then, with a jarring thud that knocked the breath from her lungs, they materialised in what appeared to be a shallow cave carved from living rock.

Nisha collapsed to her knees, retching, her body rejecting the violation of every natural law she'd ever understood. The stone beneath her palms was cool and smooth, worn by countless years of use, and she focused on its solidity to anchor herself as the world stopped spinning.

"The first translation is always difficult," Chanda said, her voice gentle but distant. "Your body isn't accustomed to moving through folded space."

"Folded space?" Nisha gasped, wiping her mouth with the back of her hand. "That's…that's theoretical physics. Einstein's equations don't allow for..."

"Einstein's equations," Chanda interrupted with what might have been amusement, "describe only one layer of reality. There are others."

Nisha struggled to her feet, taking in their surroundings with the desperate focus of someone clinging to rationality. The cave was larger than it had first appeared, its walls carved with intricate patterns that seemed to shift and flow in her peripheral vision. Soft light emanated from the stone itself, casting no shadows, but somehow providing perfect illumination.

"Where are we?" she asked, though part of her wasn't sure she wanted to know.

"In safety," Chanda replied simply. "For now."

The older woman moved with practiced ease through what Nisha now realised was not a natural cave, but some kind of antechamber. Corridors branched off in several directions, and the air carried scents of sandalwood and something else—something ancient and patient, like libraries full of old books or temples where prayers had been offered for centuries.

But even as Nisha tried to process the new environment, her attention was drawn inexorably to her right arm. The spiral mark continued to glow beneath her wet sleeve, pulsing gently in rhythm with her heartbeat. When she pushed back the fabric to examine it more closely, she had to bite back a gasp.

The mark was beautiful and terrifying in equal measure. It looked as if someone had drawn a perfect spiral on her skin using liquid moonlight, each curve flowing seamlessly into the next. But it wasn't just a surface marking. The light seemed to emanate from within her arm, as if her very blood had been transformed into something luminous.

"How is this possible?" she whispered, tracing the edge of the spiral with one finger. The touch sent warmth racing up her arm and down her spine, carrying with it an echo of the power she'd wielded in the drainage channel.

"Your bloodline carries a gift," Chanda explained, settling onto a stone bench that seemed to have grown naturally from the cave floor. "A connection to forces that most humans cannot perceive, let alone command. What you did today—calling the earth to rise, reshaping the flow of water—these are manifestations of divine essence channelled through mortal form."

"Divine essence?" Nisha's scientific mind recoiled from the terminology even as she felt the truth of it thrumming in her bones. "You're talking about magic. Actual magic."

"I'm talking about power that flows from the same source as the gods themselves," Chanda corrected. "Call it magic if you must, but understand that it follows laws just as rigid as those governing gravity or electromagnetism. You simply haven't learned to perceive those laws yet."

The spiral mark pulsed brighter, as if responding to their conversation, and Nisha felt something stirring in the depths of her mind, not quite a voice, but a presence that seemed vast and patient and utterly alien to her human consciousness.

"Something's happening," she said, pressing her hand to her temple as pressure built behind her eyes. "I can feel ... there's something else here. Something trying to …"

The presence exploded outward from the spiral mark like a dam bursting, flooding her awareness with images and sensations that definitely didn't belong to her. She saw vast underwater palaces built from coral and pearl, felt the weight of oceanic depths pressing down on her lungs, tasted salt water that carried the flavour of centuries.

And through it all, a voice which was ancient, patient, and unmistakably not human, whispered her name.

Nisha. Sister. Child of two worlds.

"No," she gasped, stumbling backward until her shoulders hit the cave wall. Her heart pounded with terror at the invasion of her most private mental space. The foreign consciousness felt massive and alien, pressing against the boundaries of her individual identity with casual strength that could crush her sense of self without effort. "Get out of my head!"

The presence withdrew slightly, but didn't disappear entirely. Instead, it settled in the back of her mind like a weight she could feel but couldn't dislodge, watching her with what felt like amused patience.

Chanda was on her feet instantly, her earlier calm replaced by sharp concern. "What did you see?"

"I saw... underwater cities. And someone was calling me sister." Nisha's voice was shaky, and she couldn't stop touching the spiral mark as if she could somehow scrub it away. "The same voice as that creature in the drainage channel."

The older woman's expression darkened. "The connection is stronger than I anticipated. That's ... concerning."

"Concerning how?" Nisha demanded. "What aren't you telling me?"

Before Chanda could answer, the sound of running footsteps echoed through the corridors, growing rapidly closer. Nisha tensed, her newly awakened power stirring in response to potential threat, but Chanda merely sighed.

"Your mother," she explained. "I wondered how long it would take her to follow us."

Priya Patel burst into the antechamber like an avenging angel, her *sari* torn and muddy, her dark hair streaming with water from the rain that was apparently still falling in the world above. Her eyes were wild with fear and desperate determination as they fixed on Nisha.

"*Beta*!" she cried, rushing forward to pull Nisha into a fierce embrace. "Are you hurt? Did they ..." She stopped mid-sentence as her gaze fell on the exposed spiral mark, and all the colour drained from her face.

"Ma, how did you find us?" Nisha asked, returning the embrace but watching her mother's expression with growing unease.

"I followed the translation trace," Priya said absently, her voice hollow. Then, as if registering her own words, she looked up sharply at Chanda. "You knew. You knew I could follow."

"I suspected," Chanda admitted. "Few mortals can perceive translation traces, let alone follow them. It suggests you have some familiarity with these forces."

Priya's laugh was bitter and desperate. "Familiarity? I've spent seventeen years trying to forget everything I learned about these forces. Seventeen years hoping the old blood would sleep in my daughter's veins."

"The old blood?" Nisha pulled back from her mother's embrace, studying Priya's face with new understanding. "Ma, you knew this would happen. You knew what I was."

"I knew what you might become," Priya corrected, her voice barely above a whisper. "What all the women in our family line might become, if the spiral chose to manifest. My grandmother carried the mark. She died screaming when I was twelve years old, her mind shattered by voices from the deep."

The weight in Nisha's mind stirred at the mention of voices, and she felt an echo of alien amusement that definitely didn't belong to her.

Your grandmother was weak, the presence whispered. *She fought what she should have embraced. You are stronger.*

"Get out," Nisha hissed, pressing both hands to her temples. "I said get out of my head!"

"What's wrong?" Priya grabbed Nisha's shoulders, her eyes wide with terror. "What's happening to her?"

"The connection is already strong," Chanda observed, her tone clinical despite the obvious concern in her expression. "The spiral has awakened something that was sleeping in her bloodline. Something that doesn't want to go back to sleep."

Sleep is for the weak, the voice agreed. *For those who deny their true nature. You are daughter of the depths, child of the ancient waters. Why do you cling to these surface dwellers who can never understand what you are?*

"Because they're my family!" Nisha shouted, though she wasn't entirely sure if she was speaking aloud or directing the words at the presence in her mind.

The alien consciousness recoiled slightly at the vehemence in her mental voice, and in that moment of withdrawal, Nisha felt something else—a vast network of similar presences, all connected to the same source, all carrying the same patient hunger. And at the centre of that network, a consciousness so vast and ancient that touching it even briefly made her feel like an ant trying to comprehend a mountain.

That consciousness noticed her attention, and when it focused on her in return, she felt herself drowning in depths that had nothing to do with water.

So young, it mused, its voice like the sound of waves against distant shores. *So much potential. Come home, little sister. Let me show you what you could become.*

"No!" Nisha wrenched herself away from the mental contact, gasping as if she'd been holding her breath underwater. The sudden disconnection left her dizzy and nauseous, but blessedly alone in her own mind.

Both Priya and Chanda were staring at her with expressions of alarm and something that might have been fear.

"The Sea King," Chanda said quietly. "You made contact with the Sea King."

"The what now?" Nisha asked, though even as she spoke, she felt the rightness of the name resonating in her bones.

"An ancient entity that sleeps beneath the Arabian Sea," Chanda explained. "The source of the power that runs in your bloodline. For centuries, he has been bound by seals and barriers, but the convergence of tides weakens his prison. And he calls to his children."

"His children," Nisha repeated, touching the spiral mark that continued to pulse with alien light. "You're saying I'm related to some kind of sea monster?"

"Not related," Priya said, her voice breaking. "Claimed. The spiral mark doesn't just indicate power, it indicates ownership. You belong to him now, whether you want to or not."

The presence stirred again in the back of Nisha's mind, and this time its amusement was clear and cold.

She begins to understand, it whispered. *Tell them about the others, little sister. Tell them about what awaits those who deny their heritage.*

Images flooded Nisha's awareness without her permission—brief flashes of other spiral bearers throughout history, women and men who had tried to resist the call of the depths. She saw them driven mad by voices they couldn't silence, consumed by power they couldn't control, eventually dying alone and broken while the sea sang lullabies in their ears.

"Stop," she whispered, but the images continued. A woman in British-era Mumbai throwing herself from a cliff into the Arabian Sea; a man in the 1960s found dead in his apartment, his body desiccated as if all the water had been drawn from his cells.

This is the fate of those who resist, the presence explained with detached patience. *But for those who embrace their nature, there are other possibilities.*

The images shifted, showing underwater palaces filled with transformed humans who moved through the depths with fluid grace, their eyes black as the deepest trenches but their faces serene with otherworldly contentment. They were beautiful and terrible and utterly inhuman, and Nisha felt a treacherous part of herself drawn to their alien perfection.

"I can see it on your face," Priya said, tears streaming down her cheeks. "The same expression my grandmother wore before the madness took her completely. Please, *beta*, fight it. Don't let it define you."

"How?" Nisha asked desperately. "How do I fight something that's literally in my blood?"

"You learn," Chanda said firmly. "You come with me to the Pathshala, where others have faced similar challenges. Where you can discover what you're truly capable of."

"The Pathshala?"

"A school," explained. "Hidden beneath the Siddhivinayak Temple, where those touched by divine essence have learned to master their gifts for over eight hundred years. Not everyone there carries the spiral mark, but they all face similar struggles with forces beyond ordinary human comprehension."

Priya shook her head violently. "No. I won't lose her to that place. I know what happens to spiral bearers who try to train their power. They burn themselves out, consumed by forces too vast for mortal minds to contain."

"And what's the alternative?" Chanda asked gently. "Let her face this alone? Allow the Sea King's influence to grow unchecked until she loses herself entirely?"

Before Priya could answer, a new sound echoed through the antechamber. A wet, slithering noise that seemed to come from the stone walls themselves. The temperature dropped noticeably, and Nisha felt her breath misting in the suddenly frigid air.

"It's here," she said, recognising the presence she'd felt in the drainage channel. "The creature from before."

Chanda's expression sharpened, and she moved to place herself between Nisha and the nearest corridor entrance. "Impossible. The translation should have severed any tracking connections."

But even as she spoke, water began to seep through cracks in the stone walls. Not ordinary water, but the same phosphorescent fluid that had filled the drainage channel during the flood. It pooled on the cave floor, spreading outward in patterns that looked almost deliberate.

From the largest pool, the creature began to emerge.

It was even more unsettling here than it had been in the chaos of the storm. In the soft light of the cave, Nisha could see details that her adrenaline-flooded mind had missed before—the way its form seemed to shift between solid matter and flowing liquid, the intricate patterns of bioluminescence that danced across its skin, the intelligence that gleamed in its too-many eyes.

When it spoke, its voice carried harmonics that made the cave walls vibrate in sympathy.

"Sister," it said, addressing Nisha directly while ignoring the two older women entirely. "You have felt his touch. You know what you are."

"I know I'm human," Nisha replied, though the words felt less certain than they had an hour ago.

The creature's laugh was like the sound of waves breaking against rocks. "Human? Child, your blood carries the deep currents. Your power flows from sources that predate humanity by eons. You are no more human than I am."

It gestured toward the spiral mark with something that might have been a hand or a tentacle, and the symbol flared brighter in response.

"The change has already begun," it observed. "Can you feel it? The cold in your bones that no surface warmth can touch? The way your lungs long for water instead of air? These are gifts, sister. Signs of your true heritage awakening."

Nisha wanted to deny it, but she couldn't ignore the chill that had settled in her chest since the mark had appeared, or the way she'd been unconsciously holding her breath for longer and longer periods without discomfort.

"What do you want?" she asked.

"To bring you home," the creature replied simply. "To the depths where you belong, where others of your kind wait to welcome you. The surface world will only bring you pain and madness. Come with me, and I will show you wonders beyond imagining."

"She's not going anywhere with you," Priya said fiercely, stepping forward despite her obvious terror.

The creature's multiple eyes fixed on her with something that might have been pity. "Ah, the surface mother. Tell me, woman of small understanding, what can you offer her? A life of hiding from her true nature? Years of fighting against forces that will ultimately consume her anyway?"

"I can offer her love," Priya said simply. "A family. A chance to choose her own path."

"Love?" The creature's amusement was evident. "What is love compared to belonging? She will never truly fit in your world. She has already grown cold, distant, alien to your warm-blooded kind. But in the depths, she will find others like herself. She will find peace."

Nisha felt the truth of those words like a knife between her ribs. Even now, surrounded by people who claimed to care about her, she felt isolated by the strange new awareness flowing through her consciousness. The spiral mark pulsed in rhythm with the creature's voice, and she found herself taking an involuntary step toward the phosphorescent pool.

"Nisha, no," Chanda said sharply. "Don't listen to it. The choice it offers isn't freedom. It's surrender."

"Is it?" the creature asked. "Or is resistance the true surrender? Fighting against your nature until it tears you apart from within?"

Come, whispered the vast consciousness at the back of Nisha's mind. *Let me show you what awaits those who embrace their heritage.*

And suddenly, Nisha was elsewhere. Not physically, but in a vision so vivid it might as well have been reality. She stood in a vast underwater city built from living coral and cultivated pearl, its bioluminescent architecture pulsing with organic light. Figures moved through the water-filled streets with fluid grace—humans transformed by deep magic, their original forms still recognisable but enhanced, perfected, freed from the limitations of air-breathing biology.

They looked at her with eyes like dark stars and smiled with genuine welcome. Here, their expressions seemed to say, "you will never be alone. Here, you will never have to hide what you are."

This could be your reality, the Sea King's voice explained. *No more pretending to be something you're not. No more watching your loved ones fear the power that flows in your veins. Only acceptance, understanding, and the tranquillity of finally coming home.*

The vision was beautiful and terrifying and utterly seductive. For a moment, Nisha felt herself wavering, drawn by the promise of belonging, of never again feeling like an outsider in her own life.

But then she thought of Arjun, clinging to that piece of rebar while the flood tried to sweep him away. She thought of her mother's tears, of Chanda's offer to teach her control, of all the people in Dharavi who might need someone with her power to stand between them and the incomprehensible forces that were awakening in the world.

"No," she said, both to the creature and to the vast presence in her mind. "I won't abandon the people I love for the promise of easy belonging."

The creature's form rippled with what might have been disappointment or admiration. "Interesting. Most of your kind are not so ... resistant to logical persuasion."

"Maybe that's because most of my kind haven't spent their whole lives believing that any problem can be solved if you understand it well enough," Nisha replied. "I don't understand you yet. I don't understand what I'm becoming. But I understand that running away from difficult questions has never led to good answers."

The presence in her mind pulled back with something that felt like respect. *You are indeed stronger than your grandmother,* it admitted. *Very well. We will wait. But know this, little sister—the convergence comes whether you embrace it or resist it. When the barriers fall and the deep rises to meet the surface, you will face a choice that no amount of courage or stubbornness can avoid.*

The creature began to sink back into the phosphorescent pool, its form dissolving like mist. But its final words reached them clearly:

"The old powers wake. The city bleeds. And those who carry the spiral mark will choose their allegiance when the tides rise highest."

Then it was gone, taking the unnatural water with it, leaving only slightly damp stone and the lingering scent of deep ocean to prove it had ever been there.

In the silence that followed, Nisha became aware that she was shaking. Not from cold, though the chill in her bones seemed to have deepened, but from the magnitude of what she had just experienced.

"That," Chanda said quietly, "was a test. And I'm not entirely certain you passed it."

"What do you mean?" Nisha asked.

"You resisted the immediate temptation, which shows strength of will. But you also made contact with forces that will not forget your defiance. The Sea King now knows you exist, and that you carry active spiral mark blood. He will try again, and the next time, his approach will be more…sophisticated."

Priya moved to Nisha's side, taking her daughter's cold hands in her own warm ones. "There has to be another way. Some path that doesn't lead to madness or transformation."

"Perhaps," Chanda admitted. "But it will require training, understanding, and allies who comprehend the forces at work. The Pathshala can provide all three."

Nisha looked down at the spiral mark, still glowing softly on her arm, then up at her mother's tear-stained face. The choice should have been easy—stay with family, pursue her normal dreams, pretend this had never happened.

But she could feel the alien presence still lurking at the edges of her consciousness, patient and hungry. She could feel power flowing through her bloodstream like a second heartbeat. And she could remember the creature's words about the convergence, about barriers falling and old powers waking.

"If I go to this school," she said carefully, "will I learn how to protect people? How to use this power to help instead of just ... survive it?"

"Among other things," Chanda replied. "Though the path will not be easy, and there are no guarantees of success."

"There never are," Nisha said, thinking of all the entrance exams she'd studied for, all the scholarship applications she'd submitted without knowing if they would lead anywhere. "But doing nothing isn't actually an option, is it?"

She looked at her mother, seeing the fear and love warring in Priya's dark eyes. "Ma, I have to try. I can't pretend this isn't happening, and I can't face it alone."

Priya closed her eyes, tears spilling down her cheeks. When she opened them again, her expression held a terrible kind of resolution.

"Then I'm coming with you," she said firmly. "If my daughter is walking into danger, she won't face it without her family."

Chanda looked surprised. "The Pathshala isn't typically open to …"

"To mothers who've spent years learning to recognise the signs of spiral mark awakening?" Priya interrupted. "To women whose grandmothers carried the old blood and who know exactly what happens to families that try to ignore these forces?"

There was something in her voice that made Chanda study her more carefully. "You've had training."

"Enough to know that sending a newly awakened spiral bearer into that place alone is asking for tragedy," Priya replied. "My daughter goes nowhere without me."

Nisha felt a surge of gratitude so intense it made her chest tight. Whatever came next, at least she wouldn't face it completely alone.

"Very well," Chanda said after a long moment. "But understand that the Pathshala has its own rules, its own dangers. And what your daughter is becoming…it's unlike anything we've seen in three centuries."

"We'll learn together," Nisha said, squeezing her mother's hands. The spiral mark pulsed brighter, as if responding to her decision, and she felt the alien presence stir with what might have been approval.

Interesting choice, it whispered. *We shall see where this path leads you, little sister.*

Nisha didn't respond, but as Chanda began preparing for another translation, she found herself wondering if she had just chosen salvation or simply a more complicated form of doom. The power in her blood sang with alien harmonies, and in the distance, she could swear she heard the sound of rising tides.

Chapter 3:

THE PATHSHALA'S VEIL

THE SECOND TRANSLATION WAS, IF anything, worse than the first.

Nisha felt herself scattered across impossible geometries, her consciousness stretched through dimensions that her mind couldn't properly process. Reality became a kaleidoscope of folding space and twisted time, where up and down lost all meaning and the concept of 'self' became dangerously fluid. She was dimly aware of Priya's hand clutched in hers, an anchor of warmth in the chaos, but even that sensation felt distant and dreamlike.

When they finally materialised, Nisha collapsed immediately, her body rejecting the violation of natural law with violent nausea. She found herself on hands and knees, retching onto polished stone that felt impossibly smooth beneath her palms. The surface was cool and somehow comforting, carved from what looked like a single piece of granite but with veins of some luminescent mineral threading through it like captured starlight.

"The disorientation will pass," *Guru* Chanda said gently, though her own voice carried a slight tremor of exhaustion. "Translation through multiple dimensional barriers is taxing even for experienced practitioners."

Nisha struggled to focus on their surroundings, desperate to ground herself in observable reality. They were in a vast chamber that defied her understanding of architectural engineering. The ceiling soared impossibly high, lost in shadows that seemed to move independently of any light source. Massive columns of the same luminescent stone supported archways that led off in all directions, and everywhere she looked, intricate carvings covered the walls. They were not mere decoration, but complex patterns that seemed to shift and flow when she wasn't looking directly at them.

"This is impossible," she whispered, her engineer's mind reeling. "The load-bearing requirements alone…you can't have a chamber this size carved from solid rock without internal supports, and the foundation would need…"

"The Pathshala exists in a space between spaces," Chanda explained with patient amusement. "The normal rules of physics apply only when they're convenient."

The air was different here. It was cooler than the humid heat of Mumbai above, but not uncomfortably so. It carried scents that Nisha couldn't quite identify: sandalwood and ancient stone, yes, but also something that reminded her of libraries full of old books and the particular stillness that settled around places where many people had come to learn over the course of centuries.

Priya had recovered more quickly than Nisha, though her face was pale and her hands shook slightly as she helped her daughter to her feet. "How far beneath the temple are we?" she asked, her voice echoing strangely in the vast space.

"Distance is relative here," Guru Chanda replied. "We are beneath the Siddhivinayak Temple, yes, but also adjacent to it, and in some ways, above it. The Pathshala occupies a pocket of folded space that intersects with the surface world at multiple points."

Nisha felt the spiral mark on her arm pulse gently, as if responding to the ambient energy of the place. The sensation was both comforting and unsettling, like having a second heartbeat that didn't quite match the rhythm of the first.

As her eyes adjusted to the strange, source-less illumination, she began to notice details that her initial shock had missed. The carvings on the walls weren't static. They were moving, flowing like slow water, telling stories in a visual language she didn't recognise but somehow found partially comprehensible. Figures appeared and dissolved in the stone, acting out what looked like historical scenes or mythological events.

"Those are the Chronicle Walls," Chanda explained, following Nisha's fascinated gaze. "Devotees of Saraswati have been inscribing the Pathshala's history there for eight centuries. The murals are imbued with fragments of consciousness—memories preserved in stone and mineral, creating a living record of everyone who has studied here."

"Living record?" Nisha moved closer to one of the walls, drawn by a section that seemed to depict figures manipulating elements of earth and water, fire and air, forces that looked remarkably similar to what she had done in the drainage channel. "You mean these are actual memories?"

"In a sense. Touch the wall gently, and you may catch echoes of past students, past lessons, past discoveries."

Nisha hesitated, remembering the alien presence that had invaded her thoughts during the creature's visit. The last thing she wanted was more foreign consciousness in her head. But her curiosity was stronger than her caution, and she placed her palm lightly against the carved stone.

The sensation was nothing like the Sea King's invasive whispers. Instead, she felt a warm flutter of human consciousness. Brief glimpses of other students who had stood in this same spot, experiencing their own wonder and confusion. A boy from decades past, struggling to control flames that danced around his fingers. A girl whose touch could make plants grow with impossible speed. A young man who could see through solid objects, overwhelmed by the constant visual noise until he learned to filter his perception.

All of them seemed afraid. All of them seemed amazed. All of them were desperately trying to understand what they were becoming.

"They were like me," Nisha whispered, her hand still pressed to the stone.

"In some ways," Chanda agreed. "Though your particular manifestation is…unique. The spiral mark has not appeared in the Pathshala for over three hundred years."

The mention of the spiral mark sent a chill through Nisha that had nothing to do with the cool air. She pulled her hand away from the Chronicle Wall, unconsciously covering the glowing symbol on her arm with her other hand.

"What happened to the last person who had it?"

Chanda's expression grew carefully neutral. "That is a conversation for later, when you have had time to understand more about divine essence and its manifestations. For now, let me show you how the Pathshala functions."

They walked deeper into the complex, their footsteps echoing softly off the polished stone floors. Nisha tried to map their route in her mind, but the corridors seemed to curve in ways that defied three-dimensional geometry. Passages that should have led them in circles instead opened onto entirely new areas, and doorways appeared where none had been visible moments before.

"The architecture adapts," Chanda explained, noticing Nisha's confusion. "The Pathshala grows and shifts to accommodate the needs of its inhabitants. Rooms appear when they are required, passages open to provide efficient routes, and dangerous areas seal themselves when students are unprepared for their challenges."

"It's alive?" Priya asked, her voice tight with unease.

"Not in any biological sense. But eight centuries of accumulated devotion and divine essence have given it a form of awareness. The Pathshala wants its students to succeed, so it helps them navigate both its physical and metaphysical challenges."

They passed through a circular chamber where water flowed up the walls in spiraling patterns, defying gravity as it formed intricate geometric shapes in the air before falling back into channels carved in the floor. Beyond that, a library where books floated freely through the air, organising themselves according to some logic that became clear only when a reader approached with a specific question in mind.

"How many students are here?" Nisha asked, though they had seen remarkably few people during their tour.

"Currently? Perhaps forty. The Pathshala never houses more than it can properly teach, and divine essence manifestation is rare enough that we are seldom at capacity."

As if summoned by her question, they encountered their first group of students in what Chanda called the Harmony Hall, a space where multiple practice sessions could occur simultaneously without interference. Nisha watched in fascination as a girl about her own age stood in the centre of a circle of floating crystals, her eyes closed in concentration. The crystals chimed in complex harmonies as they moved, creating music that seemed to reshape the very air around them.

Nearby, a boy was working with what looked like living equations. Mathematical symbols that moved through three-dimensional space, rearranging themselves into increasingly complex formulas that glowed with soft blue light.

"Saraswati devotion," Chanda explained quietly. "The girl creates healing frequencies through crystal resonance. The boy works with what he calls 'divine mathematics', using numerical relationships to understand and predict divine essence flows."

"Divine mathematics?" Nisha's engineering background made her lean forward with interest despite her general overwhelm.

The boy, who looked a year or two older than herself, heard her question and turned. He had kind eyes behind wire-rimmed glasses and the ink-stained fingers of someone who spent most of his time taking notes.

"It's not as mystical as it sounds," he said with a slight smile. "Divine essence follows patterns, just like any other form of energy. Once you learn to recognise the mathematical relationships governing those patterns, you can predict how they'll behave and sometimes influence their flow."

"He's Dev Sharma," Chanda introduced. "One of our most promising students in the theoretical applications of divine essence."

Dev's smile widened. "And you must be the new arrival everyone's been talking about. I heard you manifested spontaneously during the storm this afternoon. No training, no preparation, just pure instinctive response to crisis."

"You heard about that?" Nisha felt heat rising in her cheeks.

"News travels fast in the Pathshala," the crystal-working girl said, opening her eyes and letting her floating stones settle gently to the floor. "Especially when it involves someone pulling off earth-shaping on their first manifestation."

She was strikingly beautiful, with long black hair and eyes that seemed to hold flecks of gold, but there was something about her expression that made Nisha cautious. It wasn't hostility, exactly, but a kind of assessing curiosity that felt uncomfortably intense.

"Kritika Sood," she introduced herself. "Mahalaxmi devotion, specialising in harmony and influence." Her gaze lingered on Nisha's covered arm. "Is it true you carry the spiral mark?"

The question sent a ripple of tension through the hall. Nisha noticed that other students had stopped their practice sessions and were listening with poorly concealed interest.

"Kritika," Chanda's voice carried a note of warning.

"I'm sorry, but it's a reasonable question," Kritika replied, though her tone remained carefully respectful. "The spiral mark hasn't appeared in living memory. Naturally we're curious about what it means for the Pathshala."

"What it means," Chanda said firmly, "is that we have much work to do. Dev, would you mind showing Nisha the theoretical framework for divine essence manifestation? I believe her scientific background would benefit from understanding the underlying principles."

Dev nodded eagerly. "Of course. Would you like to see how divine mathematics maps onto traditional physics? The relationships are actually quite elegant once you adjust for multi-dimensional energy flows."

Despite everything that had happened, Nisha found herself genuinely interested. Here, finally, was someone trying to approach these impossible phenomena with systematic thinking rather than mystical acceptance.

"Yes, please," she said. "I've been trying to understand how any of this is possible within the laws of physics as I know them."

"Ah, well, that's your first problem," Dev said with enthusiasm, already beginning to manifest new equation-symbols in the air. "The laws of physics as most people know them describe only the most obvious layer of reality. But if you extend Maxwell's equations to account for divine essence fields, add some corrections for dimensional folding, and factor in consciousness as a fundamental force rather than an emergent property ..."

As Dev launched into an explanation that was equal parts advanced physics and metaphysical theory, Nisha felt some of her tension ease for the first time since the spiral mark had appeared. Here was something she could work with—not mystical mumbo-jumbo, but actual mathematical relationships that could be studied, understood, and applied systematically.

She was so focused on Dev's floating equations that she almost missed the soft chime that echoed through the Harmony Hall. But the immediate way every student stopped what they were doing and turned toward the sound told her it was significant.

"Dinner assembly," Kritika explained. "The Pathshala maintains regular meal times as anchor points for students who might otherwise lose track of time entirely."

"Time moves differently here," Dev added, dismissing his equations with a gesture. "It's easy to spend what feels like an hour studying and discover that three days have passed in the surface world. The bells help keep us synchronised."

As they moved with the other students toward what Chanda called the Sustenance Hall, Nisha couldn't help but notice the way conversations quieted when she passed. Word of her arrival had indeed spread quickly, and she could feel curious eyes following her progress.

The Sustenance Hall was another impossibly large chamber; its ceiling lost in shadows that moved like slow clouds. Long tables made from the same luminescent stone as everything else were arranged in a pattern that seemed random but felt somehow harmonious. Food appeared on the tables as students approached. It wasn't materializing from nothing, but emerging from the recesses in the stone as if the tables themselves were producing it.

"How does this work?" Nisha asked, staring at a plate of what looked like perfectly prepared dal and rice that had simply risen from the table surface when she sat down. Her scientific mind struggled to process what she was seeing—matter didn't just spontaneously organise itself into complex forms, especially not hot, freshly cooked food that somehow maintained perfect temperature and flavour.

"Accumulated devotion," Chanda explained. "For eight centuries, students and teachers have offered thanks for their meals here. That gratitude, combined with divine essence manipulation, has created a self-sustaining system that provides nourishment based on individual need."

The food was delicious. Better than delicious, actually. Each bite seemed perfectly calibrated to provide not just flavour but a sense of satisfaction that went beyond mere physical hunger. Nisha found herself eating more than she had intended, her body apparently craving the strange nourishment in ways she didn't fully understand.

"The mark is changing you," Priya said quietly, speaking for the first time since they had entered the hall. She was studying Nisha's face with the worried intensity of a mother noticing new symptoms in a sick child. "You're eating like someone who hasn't had a proper meal in days."

Nisha paused mid-bite, suddenly aware that her mother was right. She had been wolfing down the food with an urgency that felt out of proportion to her actual hunger. The spiral mark pulsed gently against her arm, and she felt that strange chill in her bones that had been growing stronger since the mark appeared.

"The manifestation of divine essence is taxing," Chanda said. "Especially spontaneous manifestation under stress. Your body is trying to replenish resources that were depleted during your awakening."

But even as she spoke, Nisha caught something in the older woman's expression. A flicker of concern that suggested there might be more to her hunger than simple energy depletion.

Before she could ask about it, a new voice interrupted her thoughts.

"So, you're the one with the spiral mark."

Nisha looked up to see a girl about her own age standing beside their table. She was compact and athletic, with short-cropped hair and callused hands that spoke of serious physical training. Her eyes were sharp and assessing, but not unfriendly.

"Mira Nair," she introduced herself. "Kartikeya devotion. I specialize in protection and combat applications."

"Combat applications?" Nisha repeated.

Mira's smile was grim. "Divine essence isn't just for healing crystals and floating books. Sometimes we need to fight things that conventional weapons can't touch." Her gaze grew more serious. "And if what I'm hearing about increased sea-spawn activity is true, we're going to need every capable fighter we can get."

"Sea-spawn?" The term sent a chill down Nisha's spine that had nothing to do with the mark on her arm.

"Creatures from the deep places," Mira explained. "They've been testing our perimeter defences for weeks now, growing bolder each time. Today's storm seems to have emboldened them even further."

Chanda's expression tightened. "Mira, this is neither the time nor the place for such discussions."

"Isn't it?" Mira's voice was respectful but firm. "If the spiral mark has awakened, if the barriers are weakening, shouldn't our newest student understand what she's walking into?"

The Sustenance Hall had grown quieter, and Nisha realised that their conversation was drawing attention from nearby tables. She could feel the weight of curious and worried gazes, the sense that her presence had disturbed some equilibrium that the Pathshala had maintained for years.

"What barriers?" she asked, though part of her was afraid to hear the answer.

Chanda sighed, clearly realising that the conversation had moved beyond her control. "There are ancient seals and wards that keep certain…entities…from freely accessing the surface world. The convergence of tides weakens those barriers, and creatures that have been contained for centuries begin to test their boundaries."

"The creature in the cave," Nisha said, understanding flooding through her. "And the one in the drainage channel. They're not just random appearances."

"No," Chanda confirmed. "They are scouts, testing the strength of our defences and searching for weaknesses they can exploit."

"Searching for spiral bearers," Mira added bluntly. "Because you're connected to the same power source as their master. You're either a potential ally or a threat that needs to be eliminated."

The spiral mark pulsed more strongly, and Nisha felt that alien presence stir in the back of her mind—not intrusively, but like a cat stretching in sunlight, aware and watchful.

They speak truly, the Sea King's voice whispered. *The barriers weaken with each passing day. Soon, the choice will come whether you are ready or not.*

"Get out of my head," Nisha muttered, pressing her hand to her temple.

"What's wrong?" Dev asked, concern clear in his voice.

"The connection," Priya said, her face pale with fear. "It's getting stronger, isn't it? You can hear him even here, in this protected place."

Before Nisha could answer, a deep, resonant hum began to emanate from the walls themselves. It was barely audible at first, more felt than heard, but it quickly grew stronger. The luminescent veins in the stone began to pulse in rhythm with the sound, and the Chronicle Walls flickered with urgent, rapidly-changing images.

Every student in the hall was on their feet within seconds, their expressions ranging from confused to alarmed. Chanda's face had gone completely white.

"What is that?" Nisha asked, though the spiral mark was pulsing in perfect synchronisation with the hum, and she had a sick feeling she already knew.

"A calling," Chanda said quietly. "Something is trying to reach through the barriers that protect this place. Something powerful enough to make the Pathshala itself resonate with its presence."

The hum grew deeper, more insistent, and Nisha felt it in her bones like a second heartbeat. Around the hall, other students were looking at each other with growing alarm, but their gazes kept returning to her, as if they instinctively understood that this disturbance was connected to her arrival.

Do you hear it, little sister? the Sea King's voice was clearer now, stronger, as if the mysterious hum had opened a clearer channel between them. *The deep calls to the deep. The convergence begins, and the ancient pacts that have kept our realms separate grow thin.*

"How long?" Nisha asked aloud, not caring who heard her. "How long before these barriers fail completely?"

The answering silence was more terrifying than any words could have been.

Time grows short, the Sea King confirmed. *Days, perhaps. Weeks if the surface dwellers are fortunate. But the tide rises regardless of mortal will, and when it reaches its peak, you will face the choice that has been waiting in your blood for generations.*

The hum reached a crescendo that made the stone tables vibrate, then gradually faded back to barely perceptible levels. But it didn't disappear entirely. It settled into the background like tinnitus, a constant reminder that something vast and patient was pressing against the boundaries of their reality.

"Well," Mira said into the stunned silence that followed. "I think we can safely say that your arrival has been noticed."

Nisha looked around the hall at the faces of her new fellow students. Some were frightened, some curious, some grimly determined. These were people who had learned to channel impossible forces, who had dedicated their lives to understanding and protecting against threats that most humans couldn't even conceive of.

And they were all looking at her as if she might be either their salvation or their doom.

The spiral mark pulsed gently against her arm, warm and cold at the same time, and Nisha realised that her old life, with her dreams of engineering school and normal problems with predictable solutions, was truly over. Whatever came next, it would be shaped by forces far older and more dangerous than anything she had ever imagined.

But as she looked at Dev's earnest face, at Mira's determined expression, at Kritika's thoughtful assessment and her mother's fierce protectiveness, she felt something that might have been hope. She wasn't facing this alone. Whatever the spiral mark meant, whatever the Sea King wanted, whatever these failing barriers portended—she had allies now, people who understood at least some of what she was going through.

It would have to be enough.

The hum continued its patient rhythm, and in the distance, she could swear she heard the sound of rising water.

Chapter 4:

FIRST ENCOUNTERS

NISHA WOKE TO THE SOUND of water dripping in perfect, measured intervals—*drip, drip, drip*—like a metronome counting time that moved differently than the world above. She lay still for a moment, disoriented by the absence of familiar sounds: no traffic noise, no vendors calling their wares, no children playing in the alleys. Instead, there was only the soft whisper of air moving through stone corridors and the distant hum that had settled into the Pathshala's bones the night before.

The room *Guru* Chanda had assigned her was simple but comfortable. It was carved from the same luminescent stone as everything else, with a sleeping alcove that seemed to have grown naturally from the floor and walls. A small basin filled itself with clean water as she approached, and when she looked into it, her reflection showed the spiral mark still glowing softly on her arm, visible even through the sleeve of the simple cotton tunic that had been provided for her.

She had slept deeply, which surprised her. Given everything that had happened in the past day, with the awakening of impossible power, the encounter with creatures from nightmares, the discovery of an entire hidden world beneath Mumbai, she expected to lie awake wrestling with the implications. Instead, she had fallen asleep almost immediately after her head touched the pillow, as if the Pathshala itself had somehow encouraged rest.

Now, however, her mind was spinning with questions. How exactly did the food-producing tables work? What were the mathematical principles governing dimensional folding? How many other students were there, and what kinds of abilities did they manifest? The engineer in her needed to understand the systems at work here, to map the logical structures underlying what appeared to be pure magic.

A soft chime echoed through her room. Not the dinner bell from the previous evening, but something gentler, more like a suggestion than a command. When she emerged into the corridor, she found other students moving in the same direction, their conversations quiet and purposeful.

Dev appeared at her elbow as if he had been waiting for her. "Morning assembly," he explained, his wire-rimmed glasses slightly fogged from what looked like an early practice session. "*Guru* Chanda likes to start each day with an overview of planned activities and any…developments that might affect our studies."

"Developments?" Nisha asked, though she suspected she knew what he meant.

"Yesterday's disturbance has everyone on edge," Dev admitted. "The Pathshala hasn't experienced anything like that resonant hum in decades. The Chronicle Walls have been flickering all night, showing fragmented images that don't make sense to most of us."

They joined the stream of students moving toward what turned out to be another impossibly large chamber, this one with tiers of stone seating arranged in concentric circles around a central platform. As they found seats, Nisha counted roughly forty students, ranging in age from what looked like early teens to people in their twenties. All of them had the slightly otherworldly quality she was beginning to associate with divine essence manipulation—a particular kind of awareness in their eyes, as if they were seeing layers of reality invisible to ordinary perception.

Chanda stood on the central platform, but she wasn't alone. Several other adults flanked her, their ages and bearing suggesting they were senior teachers. Nisha noticed that one of them. A thin man with prematurely white hair, who kept glancing in her direction with an expression that might have been concern or calculation.

"Before we begin today's instruction," Chanda announced, her voice carrying clearly through the chamber without apparent amplification, "I want to address the disturbance that occurred during last night's meal. The resonance you felt was a probe—an attempt by external forces to test the strength of our protective barriers."

A ripple of whispered conversation ran through the assembled students. Nisha felt dozens of gazes settling on her, and the spiral mark began to pulse gently in response to the attention.

"The probe was unsuccessful," Chanda continued firmly. "Our defences held, and the Pathshala remains secure. However, the attempt itself indicates that the convergence of tides is accelerating more rapidly than our previous calculations suggested."

The white-haired teacher stepped forward. "I am Master Varun," he said, his voice carrying the authority of long experience. "I oversee combat readiness and protective protocols. Given recent developments, all students will participate in enhanced defensive training over the coming days."

"Enhanced how?" asked a girl from the upper tiers.

"Practical application under simulated stress conditions," Varun replied. "And for our more advanced students, patrol duty in the outer sections of the Pathshala, where the barriers are thinnest."

This announcement generated more serious discussion among the students. Nisha could sense undercurrents of excitement and apprehension in equal measure—these were young people who had been training for theoretical applications of their abilities, now facing the possibility of real danger.

"What about the new student?" The question came from Kritika, who was seated a few rows away. Her tone was carefully neutral, but Nisha caught the undercurrent of challenge in it. "Should someone with an untrained spiral mark be participating in defensive activities?"

The question hung in the air like a blade, and Nisha felt every eye in the chamber focus on her with laser intensity. The spiral mark grew warmer against her arm, responding to the attention and the implied criticism.

"That," Chanda said carefully, "is precisely why Nisha will require intensive individual instruction before joining group activities. The spiral mark represents a form of divine essence manifestation that we have not encountered in the Pathshala for over three centuries. We must proceed cautiously."

"But not too cautiously," Mira interjected from across the chamber. "If external forces are actively probing our defences, we need every capable practitioner we can get. And from what I heard about yesterday's spontaneous earth-shaping, capability isn't the issue."

"Control is always the issue," Varun said sharply. "Uncontrolled power is as dangerous to allies as it is to enemies."

The words stung, partly because Nisha suspected they were true. She thought of the way the earth had erupted around her in the drainage channel, responding to desperation rather than conscious direction. How many people could have been hurt if her power had manifested differently?

"Which is why," Chanda said, regaining control of the conversation, "today's schedule will include assessment sessions for Nisha. We need to understand the scope and nature of her abilities before we can design appropriate training protocols."

As the assembly broke up and students began moving toward their various classes and practice sessions, Dev lingered beside Nisha's seat.

"Don't let Kritika get to you," he said quietly. "She's not trying to be cruel. She's just…cautious about changes to the established order. The Mahalaxmi devotion emphasises harmony and balance, and your arrival has definitely disrupted the equilibrium here."

"And Master Varun?" Nisha asked, watching the white-haired teacher deep in conversation with Chanda.

"He's seen what uncontrolled power can do," Dev replied. "Lost friends to manifestation accidents, fought creatures that broke through our defences because someone couldn't maintain proper ward discipline. His caution comes from experience, not prejudice."

They were interrupted by Mira's approach. Up close, her compact build was even more impressive. She moved with the fluid precision of someone who had trained their body as rigorously as their mind, and her dark eyes missed nothing as they assessed Nisha's posture and expression.

"Ready for your first real lesson?" she asked without preamble.

"I thought assessment came first," Nisha replied.

Mira's grin was sharp. "Assessment *is* the first lesson. You can't evaluate someone's capabilities in a sterile environment—you need to see how they respond under pressure, how their instincts guide their power when conscious thought isn't enough."

She led them through corridors that Nisha hadn't seen the previous day, past chambers where other students practiced their various devotions. Through one doorway, she glimpsed a boy about her own age standing motionless while blue electricity danced around his fingers, his face serene with concentration. In another room, a girl was working with what looked like living shadows, shaping them into complex three-dimensional forms that moved independently through the air.

"Indra devotion and Kali devotion," Dev explained, following her gaze. "Lightning manipulation and shadow-work respectively. Both require incredible focus and emotional discipline."

"What happens if they lose control?" Nisha asked.

"Depends on the nature of the loss," Mira answered. "Indra devotees who lose focus usually just give themselves a nasty shock. Kali practitioners…" She paused. "Well, shadows have a way of reflecting the darker aspects of their wielder's psyche. Lose control there, and you might find yourself facing parts of yourself you'd rather not acknowledge."

They arrived at a circular chamber that was notably different from the others Nisha had seen. Instead of smooth, polished stone, the walls here were rough and scarred, marked by burns, gouges, and impact craters that spoke of serious combat practice. The floor was covered with a thick mat that looked like it had been repaired multiple times.

"Combat assessment chamber," Mira announced. "Don't worry, we're not throwing you into actual fighting on your first day. But I want to see how your power responds to different types of stress and stimulus."

Kritika appeared in the doorway, carrying what looked like a collection of precisely cut crystals in a cloth pouch. "Guru Chanda asked me to assist with the assessment," she explained. "My crystals can monitor and record the harmonic frequencies of divine essence manifestation."

She began placing the crystals around the chamber in a pattern that looked random but felt purposeful, each stone humming softly as it settled into position. The sound reminded Nisha uncomfortably of the resonant hum from the previous evening, though these tones were clearly benevolent.

"What exactly are you planning to do to me?" Nisha asked, a note of apprehension creeping into her voice.

"Nothing harmful," Mira assured her. "I'm going to create various scenarios that might trigger your power response, and Kritika will monitor how your divine essence flows react. Dev will track the mathematical patterns underlying your manifestations."

Dev had already begun summoning his floating equations, complex formulas that hung in the air like luminous spiderwebs. "I'm particularly interested in seeing how your power draws from multiple devotional streams simultaneously," he said. "The theoretical implications are fascinating."

"Multiple streams?" Nisha asked.

"Most practitioners channel divine essence through a single devotional focus," Kritika explained, her crystals beginning to emit a soft, coordinated hum. "Ganesha for analytical problem-solving, Kartikeya for protection and combat, Mahalaxmi for harmony and influence, and so on. But the spiral mark suggests you can access several streams at once."

"Is that good or bad?"

"Unprecedented," Dev replied. "Which makes it potentially either."

Mira stepped back to give Nisha room in the centre of the chamber. "Let's start simple. I want you to try lifting this." She gestured to a stone block about the size of a table, clearly too heavy for normal human strength to move.

Nisha approached the block, the spiral mark beginning to warm against her arm. She placed her hands on the rough stone and tried to remember the feeling from the drainage channel. It wasn't panic and desperation, but the deeper sensation of connection to the earth itself.

For a moment, nothing happened. Then, gradually, she felt power flowing through her like warm honey, connecting her to the stone beneath her feet, the walls around her, the vast foundational structure of the Pathshala itself. The block began to rise, lifting smoothly into the air as if it weighed nothing.

"Impressive control for someone with no formal training," Mira observed. "Now, can you shape it while it's suspended?"

Nisha focused on the floating stone, trying to extend her connection beyond simple levitation. Slowly, carefully, she began to reshape it, smoothing the rough edges, carving simple geometric patterns into its surface. The work was intuitive rather than conscious. Her hands moved in gestures that felt right, and the stone responded as if it were clay rather than solid rock.

Kritika's crystals chimed in complex harmonies, and Dev's equations flickered with increasing activity. "Fascinating," he murmured. "You're simultaneously drawing from Mumbadevi earth-work, Ganesha analytical structure, and…" He paused, his expression growing puzzled. "There's a third stream I don't recognise. Something much older."

The mention of an unknown power source sent a chill through Nisha that had nothing to do with the Pathshala's cool air. She set the sculpted stone block gently on the floor, stepping back as the spiral mark pulsed more brightly.

"Unknown how?" she asked.

"The mathematical signature doesn't match any of the established devotional patterns," Dev explained, his floating equations rearranging themselves into new configurations as he tried to analyse what he'd observed. "It's definitely divine essence, but it's ... wilder. More primal. Like something from before the current pantheon was established."

Before the current pantheon. The phrase resonated in Nisha's mind, and she felt that alien presence stir in the depths of her consciousness—not intrusively, but with satisfied awareness, as if something long dormant was finally beginning to wake.

"Let's try something more challenging," Mira said, apparently oblivious to Nisha's internal turmoil. "I want to see how you respond to multiple simultaneous stimuli."

She began moving around the chamber, creating obstacles that required different types of responses. Stone projectiles that had to be deflected, sudden changes in the floor level that demanded quick adaptation, barriers that appeared without warning and had to be bypassed or overcome.

Nisha found herself responding instinctively, her power flowing through multiple channels simultaneously. Earth rose to block projectiles, the floor reshaped itself to provide stable footing, and barriers crumbled at her touch. But with each manifestation, she felt something else. It was a growing sense of connection to forces that had nothing to do with the established devotional traditions.

"Stop," Kritika said suddenly, her voice sharp with alarm. "Something's wrong."

The crystals around the chamber had changed their harmonic pattern, their gentle humming replaced by discordant tones that set Nisha's teeth on edge. Dev's equations were flickering erratically, their stable patterns dissolving into chaos.

"What's happening?" Nisha asked, though she could feel the answer in the increasing warmth of the spiral mark and the growing pressure in her mind.

"You're resonating with something external," Kritika said, moving quickly to adjust her crystal placements. "Something that's not part of the Pathshala's protected space."

The alien presence in Nisha's mind stirred more actively, and she felt the edges of another consciousness pressing against her awareness. Something vast, patient, and utterly inhuman.

You grow stronger, the Sea King's voice whispered. *Each use of power opens the channel wider, makes the connection clearer. Soon, the barriers will mean nothing.*

"No," Nisha said aloud, pressing her hands to her temples. "Not here. Not now."

But the presence was already withdrawing, leaving behind only an echo of alien amusement and a promise that it would return when she was ready to listen.

The discordant humming of Kritika's crystals gradually settled back into harmony, and Dev's equations stabilised into recognisable patterns. But the damage was done. All three of her new companions were looking at her with expressions ranging from concern to barely concealed fear.

"That," Mira said quietly, "was not just divine essence manifestation."

"No," Kritika agreed, her face pale as she gathered her still-trembling crystals. "That was contact with something actively hostile to the Pathshala's protective systems."

Dev was studying his equations with the focused intensity of someone trying to solve a problem that might determine all their fates. "The third power stream," he said slowly. "It's not unknown because it's ancient—it's unknown because it's been actively sealed away. The mathematical signatures suggest bindings, containment protocols, barriers designed to prevent exactly this kind of manifestation."

"Which means," Mira concluded grimly, "that your awakening isn't just unusual, it's actively dangerous to everyone here."

The words hit Nisha like a physical blow. She thought of her fellow students going about their studies, trusting in the Pathshala's protection, unaware that her very presence might be undermining the barriers that kept them safe.

"I should leave," she said, the decision forming even as she spoke the words. "If my being here puts everyone at risk …"

"Absolutely not," Dev interrupted with surprising firmness. "Running away won't change what you are or make the connection weaker. If anything, it would leave you vulnerable to external influence without any support system."

"Dev's right," Kritika added, though her expression remained troubled. "The resonance we just witnessed, happened because you're fighting the connection, not because you're embracing it. The internal conflict is creating instabilities that external forces can exploit."

"So, what do I do?" Nisha asked desperately.

"You learn," Mira said simply. "You train. You figure out how to control power that nobody fully understands, because the alternative is letting it control you."

As if summoned by their conversation, Chanda appeared in the chamber doorway. Her expression was grim as she took in the scarred walls, the still-trembling crystals, and the shaken faces of the students.

"I felt the disturbance from three levels away," she said quietly. "How bad was it?"

"Contact with the external entity," Kritika reported. "Brief but definite. The protective barriers held, but they were definitely tested."

Chanda's gaze settled on Nisha with a weight that felt like judgment and compassion in equal measure. "The acceleration continues," she murmured. "We have less time than I hoped."

"Time for what?" Nisha asked.

"To prepare you for what's coming," Chanda replied. "The spiral mark isn't just a sign of power, it's a beacon. And every time you use your abilities, every time you make contact with the entity that claims you, you make it easier for things far worse than probing consciousness to find their way here."

The chamber fell silent except for the soft humming of Kritika's crystals and the gentle whisper of air through stone corridors. Nisha felt the weight of forty lives suddenly resting on her shoulders—students and teachers who had dedicated themselves to learning and protecting others, now potentially at risk because of powers she didn't understand and couldn't fully control.

"How long do we have?" she asked quietly.

"Days," Chanda replied. "Perhaps weeks if we're fortunate. But the convergence accelerates with each passing hour, and the barriers that have protected both the Pathshala and the surface world for centuries grow thinner."

"Then we'd better get started," Dev said, his quiet determination somehow more reassuring than any dramatic declaration. "Nisha, I know this is overwhelming, but you're not facing it alone. We'll figure out the mathematical principles governing your power, develop control techniques, create safeguards against external influence."

"And I'll make sure you know how to fight if control isn't enough," Mira added. "The spiral mark gives you power, but power without training is just dangerous chaos."

"The crystals can help monitor your emotional state and warn us if the external connection tries to strengthen," Kritika offered. "Influence manipulation works both ways—if something is trying to affect your mind, we can create counter-harmonics to disrupt the attempt."

Looking at their faces, worried but determined, frightened but committed, Nisha felt something she hadn't experienced since the spiral mark had first appeared: hope. Not the desperate hope for a return to normalcy, but the harder hope that came with accepting impossible circumstances and choosing to face them with allies who understood the stakes.

"All right," she said. "Teach me."

As they began planning her accelerated training schedule, the spiral mark pulsed gently against her arm, and in the depths of her mind, she felt the Sea King's presence settle into patient watchfulness. He would wait, she realised. He had been waiting for centuries, and he could wait a little longer while she learned to understand the power that connected them.

But his patience wouldn't last forever, and when it ran out, all the training in the world might not be enough to protect the people she was growing to care about.

The Pathshala hummed around them, its ancient stones holding back forces that grew stronger with each passing hour. And in the combat assessment chamber, four young people began the desperate work of preparing for a war that none of them fully understood, but all of them were determined to survive.

Chapter 5:

HALLS OF DEVOTION

THE SPIRAL MARK PULSED GENTLY against Nisha's arm as she followed Dev through corridors that seemed to reshape themselves with each step. After yesterday's alarming assessment session, Chanda had decided that Nisha needed to understand the full scope of divine essence manifestation before they could design appropriate training protocols. The best way to do that, apparently, was a comprehensive tour of the six accessible Devotion Halls.

"Think of it as a survey course," Dev explained, his floating equations flickering around him like luminous companions. "Each hall represents a different approach to channelling divine essence, a different relationship between human consciousness and the fundamental forces of creation."

"And the seventh hall?" Nisha asked, though she suspected she already knew the answer.

Dev's expression grew uncomfortable. "The Mumbadevi Hall has been sealed for three centuries. After what happened yesterday, I don't think anyone's eager to discuss reopening it."

They paused at the entrance to the first hall, where carved symbols above the doorway depicted an elephant-headed figure surrounded by geometric patterns of impossible complexity. The Ganesha Devotion Hall, Dev explained, was dedicated to the removal of obstacles through understanding and optimisation.

"My specialty," he said with a slight smile, gesturing for her to enter ahead of him.

The hall was unlike anything Nisha had seen in the Pathshala so far. Instead of the flowing, organic architecture that characterized most of the complex, this space was precisely geometric—perfect circles, exact angles, crystalline formations that seemed to embody mathematical principles in physical form. Students sat in meditation poses before intricate mandalas that shifted and evolved as they watched, their eyes tracking patterns that revealed hidden connections between seemingly unrelated phenomena.

"Divine mathematics," Dev explained, leading her to where a senior student was working with what looked like a three-dimensional equation that hung in the air like a sculpture made of light. "We identify the underlying patterns that govern both divine essence and physical reality, then find ways to optimize those patterns for maximum beneficial effect."

The senior student, a girl who looked to be in her early twenties, glanced up from her work. "Surface world application," she said, indicating her glowing equation. "Traffic flow optimisation for the morning rush. If we can adjust the timing of just twelve traffic lights in South Mumbai, we can reduce average commute time by fifteen percent while improving air quality through reduced idle emissions."

Nisha stared at the floating mathematics, her engineering background allowing her to follow some of the logic. "You're using divine essence to solve urban planning problems?"

"Divine essence, properly applied, can solve any problem," the senior student replied. "The key is understanding that magic isn't separate from science, it's science operating on a broader spectrum of natural laws."

Dev nodded enthusiastically. "That's exactly what I was trying to explain yesterday. Divine essence follows mathematical principles just like any other form of energy. Once you understand the equations, you can predict and direct its behaviour with precision."

As they watched, the girl's equation completed its optimization sequence, and she made a small gesture that sent the solution flowing outward through the walls. Somewhere above them, Nisha realised, traffic lights were adjusting their timing patterns based on divine mathematical calculations.

"Ganesha devotees work behind the scenes," Dev explained as they moved deeper into the hall. "We identify systemic inefficiencies and optimise them, usually without anyone in the surface world realising that problems they've struggled with for years have suddenly become manageable."

They passed students working on a variety of projects—someone optimizing the nutritional distribution in school lunch programs, another mapping the most efficient emergency response routes for monsoon flooding, a third calculating the precise adjustments needed to improve the structural integrity of aging apartment buildings.

"This is incredible," Nisha murmured, watching a boy about her own age manipulate a complex three-dimensional model that seemed to represent Mumbai's entire power grid. "You're actually making the city work better."

"That's the idea," Dev said. "Divine essence isn't just about personal power, it's about using that power to improve life for everyone. The Ganesha approach emphasises service through understanding."

When they moved to examine the practice areas, Nisha felt the spiral mark grow warmer. Here, students were working with geometric constructs that required them to channel divine essence through precisely defined patterns. She watched one girl create a perfect dodecahedron of glowing energy, then gradually transform it into increasingly complex polyhedral.

"Want to try?" Dev asked, noticing her fascination.

Nisha approached the practice area cautiously, remembering yesterday's dangerous resonance. She placed her hands in the position Dev demonstrated and tried to channel her power through a simple geometric pattern.

The result was immediate and chaotic. Instead of a clean geometric form, her divine essence manifested as something organic and flowing. Not the precise mathematics of Ganesha devotion, but the wild, primal patterns of something much older. The spiral mark flared brightly, and several nearby students looked up in alarm as her power disrupted their careful geometric constructs.

"Interesting," Dev murmured, his analytical mind clearly fascinated despite the disruption. "Your power simply doesn't align with structured geometric channelling. It's like trying to force a river through a precisely machined pipe—the fundamental natures are incompatible."

As they left the Ganesha Hall, Nisha felt a mixture of admiration and frustration. The systematic approach appealed to her engineering background, but her power seemed to resist every attempt at precise control.

The Kartikeya Devotion Hall was dramatically different. Where the Ganesha Hall had been all about order and optimisation, this space thrummed with barely contained energy. Students sparred with weapons made of solidified divine essence, their movements fluid and precise as they practiced combat forms that had been refined over centuries.

Mira appeared at their side as if she had been waiting for them. "Welcome to the warrior's domain," she said with a grin that was equal parts welcoming and challenging. "Here we learn that sometimes the best way to remove an obstacle is to cut through it."

The hall's architecture reflected its purpose—high ceilings provided space for aerial manoeuvres, reinforced walls bore the scars of countless practice sessions, and the floor was marked with training circles that glowed softly to define sparring areas. The air itself seemed to vibrate with the energy of disciplined violence, though Nisha could sense the ethical framework underlying every technique.

"Kartikeya devotion isn't about mindless aggression," Mira explained, leading them to where two advanced students were engaged in a spectacular display of energy-weapon combat. "It's about the precise application of force to protect those who cannot protect themselves."

One of the sparring students wielded a spear of crystallized lightning, its blade crackling with barely contained electrical energy. Her opponent fought with twin daggers that seemed to be made of solid flame, their edges leaving trails of golden fire in the air. Both moved with the fluid grace of dancers, their combat a deadly ballet of attack and defence.

"The weapons are extensions of their will," Mira continued. "Divine essence shaped by intent and refined through discipline. Watch how they never commit to an attack that would leave them unable to defend their partner if a real threat appeared."

Nisha studied the sparring session, beginning to understand the deeper philosophy. These weren't just warriors. They were guardians, their every technique developed with the assumption that their primary purpose was to stand between danger and those they had sworn to protect.

"Try this," Mira said, leading Nisha to a practice area where weapons hung in the air like deadly constellations. "Choose something that feels right, and see if you can maintain its form for more than a few seconds."

Nisha approached the floating weapons hesitantly. Her hand passed through several before settling on what looked like a simple staff, not glamorous like the lightning spear or flame daggers, but somehow more suited to her nature. She grasped it, feeling the divine essence respond to her touch.

For a moment, the weapon held its form, solid and reassuring in her hands. Then the spiral mark pulsed, and the staff began to change. Instead of the clean, geometric lines of a traditional Kartikeya weapon, it became something organic. Root-like extensions sprouting from the main shaft, the entire construct flowing and shifting like a living thing.

"Fascinating," Mira murmured, circling around to examine the transformed weapon. "It's still functional, possibly more so than the original design, but it's following completely different principles."

The weapon felt natural in Nisha's hands, responsive to her intentions in ways that the geometric constructs of the Ganesha Hall had not. When she moved it through basic defensive patterns, it seemed to anticipate her needs, extending tendrils to block attacks from unexpected angles.

"Your power definitely has a mind of its own," Mira observed. "That could be either a tremendous advantage or a serious liability, depending on whether you can learn to work with it instead of trying to control it."

Their next stop was the Mahalaxmi Devotion Hall, where Kritika met them with her usual assessing gaze. This space was perhaps the most beautiful they had seen—walls that seemed to be made of crystallised music, floors that reflected not just images but emotions, and an atmosphere that felt like being inside a living symphony.

"Mahalaxmi devotion is about harmony," Kritika explained, gesturing to where students sat in circles, their combined efforts creating complex patterns of light and sound that pulsed with synchronised rhythm. "We learn to perceive the connections between all things and to adjust those connections to create more beneficial outcomes."

The applications were subtler than the direct problem-solving of Ganesha devotion or the protective combat of Kartikeya practice. Here, students worked on projects like reducing conflict in overcrowded neighbourhoods by subtly adjusting the emotional resonances of public spaces, or helping traumatised individuals heal by creating harmonic environments that encouraged psychological recovery.

"Social engineering," Kritika said, noting Nisha's expression. "But always with consent and always for beneficial purposes. We can't force people to change, but we can create conditions that make positive change easier."

When Nisha tried to participate in a group harmony exercise, the results were predictably chaotic. Her divine essence carried those same wild, primal undertones that had disrupted the geometric patterns in the Ganesha Hall. But instead of being purely disruptive, her energy seemed to add a deeper foundation to the group's work—a bass note that gave their harmonies more resonance and power.

"Intriguing," Kritika murmured, her crystals chiming softly as they analyzed the interaction. "You're not harmonising with our established patterns, but you're creating a new pattern that encompasses and amplifies what we're doing."

The Varuna Chamber, dedicated to water manipulation, proved to be the most unsettling environment yet. The moment Nisha entered the space, a vast cavern where waterfalls flowed upward and pools reflected skies that definitely weren't above Mumbai, the spiral mark began to pulse with uncomfortable intensity.

Students worked with rain patterns, water purification systems, and weather management on a scale that made Nisha's head spin. One advanced practitioner was actually communicating with the monsoon clouds, gently adjusting their formation to ensure optimal rainfall distribution across the city.

But as they moved deeper into the chamber, Nisha felt that familiar alien presence stirring in the back of her mind. The water here carried undertones that reminded her of the phosphorescent fluid that had manifested during her encounters with the Sea King's creatures.

"We should move on," she said quickly, backing toward the exit.

"But you haven't tried any of the exercises," Dev protested.

"Trust me," Nisha replied, the spiral mark now pulsing so brightly it was visible through her sleeve. "Water manipulation is definitely not compatible with whatever I'm becoming."

The Saraswati Hall provided a welcome contrast; its atmosphere filled with the gentle creativity of divine essence channelled through artistic expression. Students painted with light, sculpted with music, and wrote poetry that literally came alive on the page. The hall itself seemed to breathe with inspiration, its walls shifting to display the most beautiful moments of creative breakthrough from generations of practitioners.

Here, Nisha found something approaching compatibility. When she tried to participate in a collaborative story-telling exercise, her contributions added depth and mythic resonance to the narrative. Her divine essence manifested as words that carried multiple layers of meaning, creating stories that spoke to both conscious and unconscious understanding.

"Poetry as power," the supervising teacher explained. "Language that reaches beyond mere communication to touch the fundamental structures of reality itself."

But even here, Nisha's contributions carried those same wild undertones. Her stories spoke of deep waters and ancient powers, of connections between realms that mortals were not meant to perceive. Beautiful, but unsettling.

The final stop was the Kali Chamber, and from the moment they approached its entrance, Nisha knew this would be the most challenging. The doorway seemed to absorb light rather than reflect it, and the corridor leading to the chamber proper was lined with mirrors that showed not reflections but truths—fragments of hidden knowledge and suppressed understanding that most people preferred not to confront.

"Shadow work," explained the senior student who met them at the entrance. "Kali devotion is about perceiving what is hidden, understanding what is denied, and sometimes destroying what cannot be reformed."

The chamber itself was a study in contrasts. Brilliant light alternating with absolute darkness, creating spaces where truth could be examined without the comfortable illusions that most people relied on. Students worked alone, confronting aspects of themselves and the world that required solitary courage to face.

"We are the seekers of uncomfortable truths," the senior student continued. "We learn to see through deception, to navigate the spaces between what is said and what is meant, to understand the shadow aspects of both divine and human nature."

When Nisha tried to participate in a truth-seeing exercise, the results were immediate and overwhelming. The spiral mark flared to brilliant intensity, and suddenly she could see the hidden connections threading through the entire Pathshala—lines of power and influence, currents of divine essence, and beneath it all, a growing network of cracks where something vast and patient was pressing against the barriers that contained it.

"Stop," the senior student said sharply, her hand gripping Nisha's shoulder. "You're seeing too much, too fast. The truth can destroy an unprepared mind."

As they left the Kali Chamber, Nisha felt shaken by the glimpse of underlying reality she had received. The Pathshala's protective barriers were indeed weakening, and something was systematically probing for weaknesses.

"Six different approaches to divine essence," Dev summarised as they walked back toward the main halls. "And your power seems to interact with all of them, but never in the expected way."

"It's like you're channelling from a completely different source," Kritika added thoughtfully. "Similar energy, but filtered through a different paradigm entirely."

"The question is," Mira said grimly, "whether that different source is something we can work with, or something we need to defend against."

As if summoned by her words, that familiar hum began to resonate through the Pathshala's stone walls—the same deep, rhythmic pulse that had marked the Sea King's attempt to breach their defences. But this time, instead of fading after a few minutes, it continued, growing stronger with each pulse.

"That's not a probe," Dev said, his face pale as his floating equations began to flicker with alarm. "That's a sustained attempt at contact."

The spiral mark on Nisha's arm was now glowing so brightly that it cast shadows on the walls around them. And in the depths of her mind, she felt that vast alien consciousness pressing against her awareness with newfound urgency.

The barriers weaken faster than anticipated, the Sea King's voice whispered. *The convergence accelerates. Soon, little sister, you will need to choose your allegiance. And choose it quickly.*

"Everyone needs to get to the central chamber," Kritika said, her crystals beginning to resonate with the external pulse. "Whatever's happening, it's affecting the entire Pathshala."

As they hurried through corridors that seemed to stretch and compress with each pulse of alien rhythm, Nisha found herself thinking about the six halls they had visited. Six different approaches to divine power, each with its own philosophy and methodology. Six different ways of understanding the forces that shaped reality.

But her power didn't fit any of them. It was older, wilder, more connected to sources that predated the organised devotional traditions. And if the Sea King was to be believed, it was also connected to forces that the Pathshala had been specifically designed to contain.

The hum grew louder as they approached the central chamber, and with it came the sound that had haunted her dreams since her first encounter with the creature in the drainage channel: the distant crash of waves against shores that existed in realms far from any earthly ocean.

The convergence was accelerating, the barriers were weakening, and somewhere in the depths of her mind, an ancient power was stirring to wakefulness. The tour of the Devotion Halls had shown her the full spectrum of human approaches to divine essence, but it had also made one thing clear: whatever she was becoming, it was something that lay outside the bounds of human understanding.

And that, she realised with growing dread, might make her more dangerous to her new friends than any external threat they might face.

Chapter 6:

THE MUMBADEVI ENIGMA

THE PERSISTENT HUM THAT HAD followed them through the Devotion Halls grew stronger as they approached the central chamber, its rhythm now matching the urgent pulse of the spiral mark on Nisha's arm. Other students emerged from various corridors, their faces tight with concern as they felt the Pathshala itself resonating with whatever force was pressing against its ancient defences.

"The frequency is increasing," Kritika observed, her crystals chiming discordantly as they struggled to analyse the alien resonance. "Whatever's causing this, it's not backing down like the previous probes."

Dev's floating equations flickered erratically around him, their usually stable patterns dissolving and reforming in configurations that hurt to look at directly. "The mathematical harmonics are completely scrambled," he reported. "I've never seen divine essence patterns this chaotic."

As they reached the central chamber, Nisha saw that nearly the entire Pathshala population had gathered. Students and teachers alike, their faces reflecting varying degrees of alarm and determination. *Guru* Chanda stood at the chamber's heart, her hands pressed against what looked like a living map of the complex, its surface pulsing with networks of light that showed the status of various protective barriers.

"The outer defences are holding," she announced, her voice carrying clearly despite the underlying hum. "But something is systematically testing every ward, every seal, every protective protocol we have in place."

Master Varun stepped forward, his weathered face grim. "This isn't random probing. Whatever's out there has detailed knowledge of our defensive systems. Knowledge that should be impossible for any external entity to possess."

The spiral mark on Nisha's arm suddenly flared to painful intensity, and she felt that vast alien consciousness press against her awareness with unprecedented force. The contact was so strong that she stumbled, her vision blurring as images flooded her mind—not her own memories, but fragments of knowledge that belonged to something far older and more patient than any human mind could comprehend.

You see, the Sea King's voice whispered with satisfaction. *The barriers were never meant to contain me indefinitely. They were a temporary measure, a delay while the surface dwellers prepared for the inevitable integration. But they have grown complacent, and now the time of choosing has arrived.*

"Nisha!" Dev's voice seemed to come from very far away, though she could see him reaching toward her with concern. "What's happening?"

Before she could answer, the living map under Chanda's hands flared brilliant white, and suddenly everyone in the chamber could see what Nisha was experiencing. The Sea King's consciousness had somehow used her as a conduit, projecting his awareness into the Pathshala's own systems.

And what he showed them made several students cry out in fear.

The image that filled the air above the central chamber was of the Pathshala itself, but seen from a perspective that no human eye could achieve. Instead of stone corridors and carved chambers, they saw the complex as it truly was—a multidimensional structure existing in folded space, held together by centuries of accumulated faith and divine essence. And throughout that structure, like cracks spreading through stressed glass, ran fissures of something that definitely didn't belong.

"Corruption vectors," Master Varun breathed, his face pale as he studied the projection. "The barriers aren't just weakening, they're actively being subverted from within."

Corruption? The Sea King's amusement was palpable. *I prefer to think of it as…renovation. Your precious sanctuary has served its purpose, but its time of isolation is ending. The convergence cannot be prevented, only embraced or resisted. And resistance will only make the transition more painful for all involved.*

"Get out of our systems," Chanda demanded, her hands moving in complex patterns over the living map as she tried to sever the unauthorised connection.

I am not in your systems, the Sea King replied with patient amusement. *I am speaking through one who belongs to me by right of blood and binding. Every word she hears, every image she sees, becomes part of your precious sanctuary's experience. Did you think the spiral mark was merely decorative?*

All eyes in the chamber turned to Nisha, and she felt the weight of forty frightened and accusatory gazes. She wanted to protest, to explain that she wasn't choosing to serve as a conduit for alien consciousness, but the spiral mark pulsed again and more images flooded the chamber.

This time, they saw the history of the Pathshala from the Sea King's perspective. It was not the noble institution dedicated to training divine essence practitioners, but a prison designed to contain forces that had once moved freely between realms. They saw the original construction, built not just to protect the surface world, but to actively suppress the old connections between depths and heights, water and earth, the primal powers that had shaped the world before human civilization imposed its artificial categories.

Your founders were wise in their way, the Sea King continued. *They understood that the age of open communion between realms was ending, that humanity needed time to develop its own relationship with divine essence. The Pathshala was their compromise—a place where the old ways could be preserved while the new ways took root.*

The images shifted, showing the early years of the Pathshala when it had been very different from its current form. Instead of the organised devotional halls, there had been wilder spaces where students learned to channel forces that had no names in human language. And in the center of it all, a hall that pulsed with power that made even the Sea King's consciousness seem diminished by comparison.

The Mumbadevi Hall, he identified. *Where the children of two worlds learned to bridge the gap between surface and depth, between mortal understanding and eternal truth. Where the Spiral Bearers discovered what they truly were.*

"Stop this," Mira said, her voice tight with anger as she stepped protectively near Nisha. "Whatever you're trying to accomplish, leave her out of it."

Leave her out of it? The Sea King's laughter rippled through the chamber like a wave breaking against stone. *Child, she is not separate from this. She is the key to it all. Every Spiral Bearer carries within them the power to open the sealed ways, to restore the connections that your ancestors severed out of fear.*

The projection shifted again, and now they were seeing the Mumbadevi Hall as it existed in the present—not the sealed, empty chamber that everyone assumed it to be, but a space teeming with suppressed energy. Ancient symbols covered every surface, pulsing with light that suggested something vast and alive was contained within. And at the centre of it all, a pool of water that definitely didn't belong in an underground chamber carved from solid stone.

"Impossible," Master Varun whispered. "The hall was sealed three centuries ago. Nothing should be able to survive in there."

Survive? The Sea King's amusement deepened. *The Spiral Bearers did not simply die, surface dweller. They transformed, evolved, became something greater than your limited understanding could comprehend. And they have been waiting, patient as stone, for one of their kind to awaken and open the way.*

The image focused on the pool of water at the hall's center, and suddenly Nisha could see figures moving within it—not drowning, but swimming with fluid grace, their forms beautiful and terrible and utterly inhuman. Their eyes were the same black as the deepest ocean trenches, but their faces were serene with otherworldly contentment.

One of them looked directly at the projection, her gaze meeting Nisha's across impossible distances, and spoke in a voice like whale song:

"Sister. We have been waiting so long for you to wake."

The voice was familiar, carrying harmonics that resonated with something deep in Nisha's genetic memory. And as the figure moved closer to the pool's surface, her features became clearer. They were recognisably human in origin, but transformed by centuries of exposure to forces that existed beyond the boundaries of mortal flesh.

"Kavita Devi," Chanda whispered, her face white with shock. "But that's impossible. She died fighting to contain the convergence, three centuries ago."

Died? The transformed figure's laughter bubbled up through the water with crystalline clarity. *I suppose that is one way to describe transformation. Yes, Kavita Devi died—the frightened girl who thought she could resist her true nature, who believed that fighting the spiral mark would somehow preserve her humanity. But from that death was born something infinitely more beautiful.*

The projection showed Kavita as she moved through the sealed hall, her form shifting fluidly between human and something more elemental. Other figures accompanied her—dozens of them, all carrying the same serene transformation, all moving with the confidence of beings who had found their true nature.

The Spiral Bearers, the Sea King explained. *Not consumed by their power, as your histories claim, but freed by it. Released from the limitations of purely mortal flesh to become bridges between realms, mediators between the surface world and the eternal depths.*

"They're beautiful," Kritika whispered, her crystals singing in harmony with some frequency emanating from the projection.

"They're not human anymore," Master Varun countered grimly. "Whatever they've become, it's not what any of us would choose."

Choice? Kavita's voice carried gentle mockery. *Child, I spent decades fighting the choice that had already been made for me by blood and birth. The spiral mark is not a curse to be resisted—it is a gift to be embraced. And the sister who stands among you now will face the same choice that I did: fight her nature until it destroys her, or accept transformation and discover what she was truly meant to become.*

All eyes turned to Nisha again, and she felt the spiral mark pulse with increasing intensity. The alien consciousness in her mind was stronger now, more insistent, and she could feel her own sense of self beginning to blur at the edges.

"I won't let you take her," Priya's voice cut through the chamber like a blade. Nisha's mother pushed through the crowd of students, her face set with fierce determination. "I know what you are, what you offer. My grandmother heard the same promises before the madness took her."

Madness? Kavita's expression grew sad. *Your grandmother fought the transformation, clung to mortality when she should have embraced evolution. The madness was not caused by the spiral mark. Iit was caused by rejecting what the spiral mark offered.*

The projection shifted again, showing not the serene figures in the sealed hall, but flashes of other Spiral Bearers throughout history. Men and women who had tried to resist their awakening power, fighting against the changes in their bodies and minds until the internal conflict had literally torn them apart.

This is the fate of those who deny their heritage, the Sea King explained with clinical detachment. *The spiral mark connects its bearer to forces that cannot be contained indefinitely. Attempt to suppress that connection, and it will find other outlets—usually through the slow dissolution of sanity and self.*

"But there's another way," Kavita added, her voice gentle but implacable. "Acceptance. Transformation. The choice to become what you were always meant to be."

The images shifted once more, showing the transformed Spiral Bearers not as isolated figures in a sealed chamber, but as part of a vast community that existed in the spaces between realms. They moved through underwater cities of impossible beauty, worked alongside creatures that seemed to be made of living light, participated in forms of existence that transcended every limitation of purely human life.

This could be your reality, the Sea King offered. *No more struggling against forces you cannot control. No more watching your loved ones fear the power that flows in your veins. Only peace, understanding, and the deep satisfaction of finally coming home.*

For a moment, the offer was overwhelmingly tempting. Nisha felt the spiral mark pulse with warmth, felt her consciousness expand to touch the edges of that vast underwater realm where she would never again be alone or misunderstood. The transformation looked not like death, but like the ultimate expression of what she was meant to become.

But then she looked at the faces around her. Dev's quiet concern, Mira's protective determination, Kritika's analytical fascination, her mother's desperate love. These were people who cared about her not because of what she might become, but because of who she was right now, in this moment, spiral mark and all.

"No," she said, her voice quiet but firm. "I won't abandon the people I love for the promise of belonging somewhere else."

The projection flickered with what might have been surprise. *Interesting,* the Sea King mused. *Most of your predecessors required much more...persuasion.*

"Then they weren't as stubborn as I am," Nisha replied.

Kavita's transformed features showed something that might have been approval. *Stubborn indeed. Very well, sister. We will not force what should be freely chosen. But understand this, the convergence continues whether you embrace it or resist it. The barriers between realms grow thinner with each passing day, and when they finally fail, you will face forces that make our gentle offer seem like the greatest kindness.*

The projection began to fade, but not before showing one final image—the sealed doors of the Mumbadevi Hall, their ancient bindings beginning to crack and glow with phosphorescent light.

The seals weaken, the Sea King observed. *Soon, the choice will be made for you, whether you are ready or not.*

Then the projection vanished entirely, leaving the central chamber in relative silence except for the continued hum that had now become part of the Pathshala's background ambiance. Students and teachers looked around at each other with expressions ranging from terror to fascination, trying to process what they had just witnessed.

"Well," Master Varun said finally, his voice carefully controlled. "That was illuminating."

"The sealed hall," Chanda said, her hands still pressed against the living map, "If what we saw is true, if the previous Spiral Bearers are still alive in there ..."

"Then everything we thought we knew about the Mumbadevi tradition is wrong," Dev finished, his floating equations finally stabilising into recognisable patterns. "They weren't consumed by their power. They were transformed by it."

"Into something that's not human anymore," Mira pointed out grimly. "Beautiful or not, those figures we saw…they've given up everything that makes them part of our world."

"Have they?" Kritika asked thoughtfully, her crystals humming with residual energy from the projection. "Or have they simply found a way to exist in multiple worlds simultaneously?"

The debate continued around her, but Nisha found her attention drawn to the sealed entrance that led to the

Mumbadevi Hall. Even from a distance, she could see that the doors were indeed beginning to crack, ancient bindings failing under pressure that had been building for centuries.

And from beyond those doors, she could hear the sound of water—not the gentle flow of the fountain systems throughout the Pathshala, but the rhythmic pulse of waves against distant shores.

Soon, the Sea King's voice whispered in her mind, fainter now but still present. *The choice approaches, little sister. And when it comes, remember that we offer not just transformation, but belonging. The surface world will never truly accept what you are becoming.*

As if to emphasise his point, Nisha became aware of the way some of the students were looking at her. Not with the friendly curiosity of the past few days, but with the wariness reserved for something that might be dangerous. The projection had made it clear that she was the key to whatever was coming, and not everyone was comfortable with that knowledge.

"We need to accelerate your training," Chanda said, approaching with an expression of grim determination. "If the seals on the Mumbadevi Hall are indeed failing, we may have very little time to prepare you for what's coming."

"Prepare me for what, exactly?" Nisha asked.

"To choose," Chanda replied simply. "And to live with the consequences of that choice, whatever they might be."

As they began discussing modified training protocols and emergency procedures, the hum continued its patient rhythm, and the cracks in the sealed doors grew imperceptibly wider. The convergence was accelerating, the barriers were failing, and somewhere in the depths of a chamber that had been sealed for three centuries, transformed figures moved through phosphorescent water, waiting for their sister to join them in the spaces between worlds.

The Mumbadevi enigma was no longer a mystery buried in ancient history—it was a living choice that demanded to be made, and the consequences would reshape not just Nisha's life, but the entire relationship between the surface world and the powers that slept beneath it.

Time was running out, and the spiral mark on her arm pulsed with the rhythm of tides that had been rising for three hundred years, finally ready to reach their peak.

Chapter 7:
THE RIVER'S MIRROR

THE REVELATIONS ABOUT THE SPIRAL Bearers left Nisha in a state of profound unease that no amount of sleep could cure. She lay in her alcove, staring at the luminescent ceiling while the spiral mark pulsed gently against her arm, its rhythm now synchronised with the persistent hum that had settled into the Pathshala's bones. Every few minutes, she caught fragments of alien consciousness pressing against her awareness—not the invasive force of the Sea King's direct contact, but something subtler, like whispers at the edge of hearing.

You cannot run from what you are, the voices seemed to say. *The choice approaches whether you will it or not.*

When morning came, though the concept of morning was largely theoretical in the Pathshala's timeless environment, *Guru* Chanda appeared at her doorway with an expression that mixed determination with something that might have been dread.

"Today you undergo the trial of the River of Whispers," she announced without preamble. "Given recent… developments, we can no longer afford to follow the traditional progression of training. You need to understand what you're truly facing, and the River is the only reliable way to show you."

"The River of Whispers?" Nisha asked, though the name sent an inexplicable chill through her.

"An ancient test that has been part of the Pathshala's curriculum for seven centuries," Chanda explained as they walked through corridors that seemed to shift to accommodate their journey. "It shows initiates what they most need to understand about themselves and their path. Some see their greatest desires, others their deepest fears. All see truth, though not always the truth they expect."

They descended through levels of the Pathshala that Nisha hadn't known existed, past chambers filled with artifacts from ages when the boundary between the mundane and magical worlds had been far more permeable. The air grew cooler as they went deeper, carrying scents of water and stone and something indefinably ancient.

"What exactly am I supposed to do?" Nisha asked as they approached a heavy door marked with symbols that seemed to shift when she wasn't looking directly at them.

"Enter the River. Let it show you what it will. Try not to lose yourself in what you see." Chanda's voice carried a note of warning that made Nisha's anxiety spike higher. "And remember, whatever the River shows you, it is showing you truth. But truth can be interpreted many ways, and not all interpretations lead to wisdom."

Before they entered the River chamber, Chanda led her to a smaller room where Dev, Mira, and Kritika waited with expressions of mixed concern and curiosity.

"We wanted to share our experiences," Dev explained, his floating equations dim and stable for once. "The River affects everyone differently, but knowing what others have seen might help you understand your own visions."

Mira spoke first, her usually confident demeanour showing cracks of vulnerability. "I saw myself living a normal life," she said quietly. "Working in an office, married to someone who didn't know about divine essence, raising children who would never need to fight monsters or stand guard against impossible threats. It was…peaceful. Safe. Everything I thought I wanted before I understood what the world really needed from me."

"The temptation of ordinary happiness," Kritika observed. "I faced something similar, though mine was more complicated. I saw myself using my influence abilities not to help people, but to control them. To remake society according to my vision of what it should be. The power to fix everything wrong with the world, but only by imposing my will on others."

Dev adjusted his glasses nervously. "Mine was different. I saw the Library of All Knowledge—every secret of the universe laid out in perfect mathematical formulas, every mystery solved, every question answered. I could have spent eternity there, learning everything that could be learned. But I realised that knowledge without application is just another form of selfishness."

"Each of us had to choose," Mira continued. "Between what we wanted and what we knew was right. Between the easy path and the necessary one."

"What if I don't make the right choice?" Nisha asked.

"Then you learn from the mistake and choose again," Kritika said simply. "The River doesn't judge. It just shows you the options and lets you decide what kind of person you want to be."

The River chamber was unlike anything Nisha had seen in the Pathshala. Instead of carved stone, the walls appeared to be made of living water held in impossible vertical sheets. The floor was polished black stone that reflected not the chamber above, but what looked like a night sky filled with unfamiliar constellations. And through the centre of it all flowed a river that glowed with phosphorescent light, its waters moving in patterns that suggested intelligence rather than mere current.

"The River of Whispers," Guru Chanda said, her voice hushed with reverence. "Fed by springs that emerge from the spaces between worlds, carrying not just water but fragments of possibility, echoes of choice, reflections of what could be."

The river's glow was mesmerising, shifting through spectrums of colour that had no names in any human language. As Nisha approached the bank, she could hear the whispers that gave the river its name. They were not quite voices, but something that carried meaning at a level deeper than conscious thought.

"Step into the water when you're ready," Chanda instructed. "Let it carry you where it will. When the visions come, remember that you are still yourself. The River shows you possibilities, not inevitabilities."

Nisha took a deep breath and stepped into the phosphorescent water. It was neither warm nor cold, but something else entirely—a temperature that seemed to exist outside normal sensation. The moment her feet touched the riverbed, the world around her began to shift and blur.

The first vision came gradually, like dawn breaking over a familiar landscape. She stood in the narrow alleys of Dharavi, but they were transformed—clean, well-lit, with proper drainage systems and electrical infrastructure that actually worked. The air was clear of the usual cocktail of exhaust and industrial fumes, replaced by the scents of thriving gardens and efficiently managed waste systems.

She was older in this vision, perhaps in her thirties, wearing the practical clothes of a successful engineer. In her hands were blueprints for another infrastructure project, another systematic improvement to the lives of people who had been forgotten by the broader world's development plans.

"Nisha?" A familiar voice called her name, and she turned to see her mother approaching—but a version of Priya who looked younger, healthier, unburdened by the constant worry that had marked her features in reality. "The municipal committee approved your proposal for the water treatment facility. Construction begins next month."

The vision-Nisha smiled, feeling a deep satisfaction that had nothing to do with divine essence or spiral marks or the weight of impossible choices. This was the life she had always wanted—using her skills to solve real problems, improving the world through systematic application of engineering principles, making a difference without having to grapple with forces beyond human comprehension.

"You've done so much good," her mother continued, pride evident in every word. "The scholarship program, the infrastructure improvements, the community health initiatives. You've proven that one person with the right knowledge and determination can change everything."

As the vision continued, Nisha saw the fruits of her imagined labour. Children playing in safe, clean spaces. Families with reliable access to clean water and electricity. A community that had been systematically neglected finally receiving the resources and attention it deserved.

It was beautiful. It was everything she had ever dreamed of accomplishing.

But as the vision deepened, she began to notice details that made her stomach clench with unease. The Siddhivinayak Temple was closed, its ancient architecture showing signs of neglect. The narrow spaces where street vendors had once sold their wares were empty, replaced by more efficient but somehow soulless commercial structures.

And in the distance, barely visible through the improved air quality, she could see the ocean. But the water was wrong—too dark, too still, reflecting not the sky above but something else entirely.

An elderly woman approached, her face familiar though aged beyond what should have been possible in the years since Nisha's awakening. It took a moment for her to recognise Chanda, but this version was diminished, her eyes holding a haunted quality that spoke of terrible losses.

"You chose well," the aged teacher said, her voice carrying the weight of decades. "The normal life, the simple path. You avoided the madness that claimed the others."

"Others?" the vision-Nisha asked, though part of her already knew she didn't want to hear the answer.

"Your friends from the Pathshala. They tried to hold the barriers when the convergence reached its peak. They fought bravely, but…" Chanda's voice trailed off, and she gestured toward the too-still ocean. "The deep waters rose, and the old powers awakened. Without the Spiral Bearer to bridge the gap between worlds, the conflict consumed everything it touched."

The vision began to fracture at the edges, showing glimpses of what lay beyond the carefully maintained normalcy. Cities swallowed by impossible tides. Creatures from the deepest trenches walking through streets that had never known sunlight. And in the centre of it all, a figure of terrible beauty whose black eyes held the patience of geological ages.

"But you were safe," Chanda continued. "You chose mortality over transformation, simplicity over complexity. You lived a good life, helped many people, died peacefully in your sleep. The cost was only the world."

The vision shattered like glass, plunging Nisha into darkness that felt like drowning. But before she could panic, a new environment materialised around her—the same chamber of pearl and bioluminescent coral that she had seen in her previous encounters with the Sea King's consciousness.

This time, however, she was not alone. The chamber was filled with figures of impossible beauty, their forms shifting fluidly between human and something more elemental. At their centre stood the Sea King himself, no longer the vast, incomprehensible presence she had felt in her mind, but taking a form that was almost human. He was tall, graceful, with sea-green skin and eyes like black stars.

"Welcome, daughter," he said, his voice carrying harmonics that spoke of depths beyond human understanding. "I wondered when you would tire of fighting the inevitable."

The transformed Spiral Bearers moved around her in patterns that suggested both welcome and worship, their movements graceful as dancing kelp. Among them, she recognised Kavita Devi, but this version was more fully transformed than the figure she had seen in the sealed hall—beautiful beyond description, but utterly alien to everything that had once been human.

"You have seen the cost of denial," Kavita said, her voice like whale song given human words. "The surface world cannot survive the convergence without a bridge between realms. Refuse your transformation, and you condemn both worlds to conflict that will destroy all you claim to love."

The Sea King gestured, and the chamber's walls became transparent, revealing the vast underwater city that served as his domain. It was magnificent—spires of living coral that pulsed with bioluminescent light, gardens of sea plants that had evolved beyond any earthly species, creatures that seemed to be made of living water itself moving through the currents with purpose and intelligence.

"This is what awaits," he said. "Not death, not the loss of self, but evolution into something greater than human limitations can conceive. You would retain your essential nature while gaining capabilities that transcend every boundary that currently confines you."

As she watched, Nisha saw other transformed beings working alongside creatures that defied classification—projects that spanned not just the ocean depths but the spaces between dimensions, architectures that existed in multiple realms simultaneously, art forms that incorporated concepts no human language could express.

"You could help both worlds," the Sea King continued. "Bridge the gap between surface and depth, mediate between mortal understanding and eternal truth. The surface dwellers need not be conquered. They could be guided, helped to evolve at their own pace while the deeper waters provide stability and wisdom."

The vision showed her possibilities that made her breath catch. Not the violent conquest that Master Varun and others feared, but genuine cooperation between realms. Surface technology integrated with deep wisdom, human creativity enhanced by perspectives that spanned millennia, conflicts resolved through understanding rather than force.

And at the centre of it all, herself. She was not lost to transformation, but expanded by it, capable of existing simultaneously in multiple worlds, serving as a living bridge between different forms of consciousness.

"The choice is yours," the Sea King said gently. "But choose knowing the full scope of what you accept or reject. Mortality is not automatically virtue, and transformation is not automatically corruption."

The underwater city faded, leaving Nisha floating in phosphorescent water that carried her gently toward the riverbank. As she climbed out, dripping with light that gradually faded from her skin, she found Guru Chanda waiting with an expression of intense concern.

"How long was I in there?" Nisha asked, surprised to find her voice hoarse as if she had been screaming.

"Three hours," Guru Chanda replied. "Unusually long for a first trial. What did you see?"

Nisha described both visions in detail, watching Guru Chanda's expression grow increasingly troubled as she spoke. When she finished, the older woman was quiet for a long moment, staring at the now-still waters of the River of Whispers.

"Both visions carry truth," she said finally. "The normal life you saw, it could be achieved, but the cost would indeed be catastrophic. The convergence cannot be stopped, only guided. Without a Spiral Bearer to serve as a bridge, the clash between realms would devastate both worlds."

"And the transformation?"

"Also truth, though perhaps not the complete truth. The Sea King's offer is genuine—you could retain your essential self while gaining capabilities beyond human limits. But transformation always carries costs that are not apparent until after the change is complete."

They walked back through the Pathshala's corridors in contemplative silence, but as they approached the central levels, the familiar hum that had become part of the complex's background ambiance suddenly intensified. The spiral mark on Nisha's arm flared to brilliant intensity, and she felt the Sea King's consciousness press against her awareness with renewed urgency.

The barriers weaken faster than anticipated, his voice whispered. *The convergence accelerates beyond all previous calculations. The choice approaches, little sister, whether you will it or not.*

And as if to emphasise his words, a deep, resonant crack echoed through the Pathshala's stone walls. The sound of something ancient finally giving way under pressure that had been building for centuries.

"The sealed doors," Chanda said, her face pale with understanding. "The Mumbadevi Hall is opening."

They ran through corridors that seemed to stretch and compress around them, following the source of the sound to the chamber where the sealed entrance had stood for three hundred years. What they found there made both of them stop in their tracks.

The ancient doors, bound with protections that had been maintained by generations of practitioners, were cracked from top to bottom. Through the gaps, phosphorescent water was beginning to seep, pooling on the stone floor in patterns that looked almost like writing.

And from beyond the damaged barriers came the sound of voices—not the alien whale song of the transformed Spiral Bearers, but something achingly familiar: the sound of someone calling Nisha's name.

"Sister," the voice called, clear as crystal despite the massive stone doors that separated them. "The time has come. The choice cannot be delayed any longer."

It was Kavita Devi, but not the transformed figure from the visions. This voice carried the accents and inflections of someone who had been born and raised in Mumbai, someone who had once been as human as Nisha herself.

"Join us," the voice continued. "Learn what you were meant to become. The surface world needs its bridge, and we need our sister."

The spiral mark pulsed so brightly that it cast shadows on the walls around them, and Nisha felt her consciousness pulled toward the sealed chamber with a force that was becoming increasingly difficult to resist.

"I have to go in there," she said, the words coming from some deeper certainty than conscious thought. "I have to face whatever's behind those doors."

"Not alone," Chanda said firmly. "And not yet. You need more preparation, more understanding of what you're choosing between."

But even as she spoke, another crack appeared in the ancient doors, and more phosphorescent water began to flow through the gaps. The convergence was accelerating beyond anyone's ability to control, and the choice that the River of Whispers had shown her was approaching whether she was ready for it or not.

In the distance, the sound of rising water echoed through the Pathshala's corridors, and the spiral mark on her arm pulsed in rhythm with tides that had been rising for three centuries, finally ready to reach their peak.

The time for preparation was ending. Soon, very soon, she would have to choose between the safety of the known world and the terrifying possibilities of transformation. And whatever she chose, the consequences would reshape not just her own existence, but the relationship between surface and depth, between mortal understanding and forces too vast for human comprehension.

The River of Whispers had shown her the truth, and the truth was this: there were no safe choices left, only necessary ones. The question was whether she would have the courage to make the choice that served something greater than her own fear.

Chapter 8:

VANARAJA'S OFFER

THE PHOSPHORESCENT WATER CONTINUED TO seep through the cracks in the ancient doors, spreading across the stone floor in patterns that pulsed with their own rhythm. Nisha found herself unable to look away from the growing pool, her spiral mark responding to its presence with increasingly urgent pulses of light. The voice of Kavita Devi had fallen silent, but the sense of presence beyond the barriers had only grown stronger.

"We need to evacuate the students," *Guru* Chanda said, her voice tight with controlled panic. "If the seals fail completely…"

Her words were cut off by a sound that seemed to come from the water itself—not the crack of breaking stone, but something more organic, like the slow exhalation of something vast finally stirring to wakefulness. The phosphorescent pool began to swirl, forming spirals that matched the mark on Nisha's arm with uncomfortable precision.

"It's too late for evacuation," Master Varun's voice came from behind them as he approached with several other senior teachers, their faces grim with understanding. "The convergence has reached critical phase. The barriers between realms are dissolving whether we're ready or not."

As if to confirm his words, the very air in the chamber began to shimmer, reality bending like heat distortion as forces that had been contained for centuries finally found expression. The walls themselves seemed to become permeable, showing glimpses of impossible vistas—underwater cities, forests of coral that grew in air instead of water, skies filled with creatures that had never known the touch of sunlight.

"Nisha," Chanda said urgently, "whatever happens, remember that you still have a choice. The visions you saw in the River, they were possibilities, not inevitabilities."

But even as she spoke, the phosphorescent water began to rise, defying gravity as it flowed upward along the cracked doors. Where it touched the ancient seals, the protective symbols flared briefly and then went dark, their power finally exhausted after three centuries of containment.

The spiral mark on Nisha's arm grew so bright that it cast dancing shadows on the walls, and she felt her consciousness being pulled inexorably toward the sealed chamber. Not the violent intrusion she had experienced during the Sea King's previous contacts, but something gentler—an invitation rather than a summons.

Come, a voice whispered in her mind, but this time it wasn't the vast alien consciousness of the Sea King. This was unmistakably human, carrying the warmth and accent of someone who had once walked the same streets of Mumbai that Nisha knew so well. *Come and see what we truly are, sister. Let me show you the choice you're really being asked to make.*

The water had now reached the top of the doors, and as it completed its circuit around the frame, the ancient barriers simply...opened. Not with the violent crash that everyone had expected, but with the quiet dignity of doors that had finally received permission to fulfil their intended purpose.

Beyond the threshold lay not the empty chamber that everyone had assumed, but a space that seemed to exist in multiple dimensions simultaneously. The floor was covered with that same phosphorescent water, but it was only ankle-deep, warm against the skin and somehow more substantial than ordinary liquid. The walls were carved with symbols that moved and flowed like living text, telling stories in languages that predated human writing but somehow remained comprehensible to anyone who looked upon them.

And in the centre of the chamber, rising like an island from the glowing water, stood a figure that was recognisably human despite the changes that transformation had wrought.

Kavita Devi looked exactly as she had in the historical paintings Nisha had glimpsed in the Chronicle Walls, but she was also something more. Her dark hair moved as if she were underwater, even though she stood in air. Her eyes held depths that reflected not the chamber around them, but vast oceanic distances. Her skin carried a subtle luminescence that spoke of centuries spent in communion with forces that existed beyond the boundaries of mortal flesh.

But her smile was purely human—warm, welcoming, and tinged with the gentle humour of someone who had finally found peace after a long struggle.

"Hello, sister," she said, her voice carrying both the accent of old Mumbai and harmonics that resonated in dimensions human ears couldn't quite perceive. "I've been waiting so long to meet you properly."

"You're really Kavita Devi," Nisha said, stepping into the chamber despite Guru Chanda's restraining hand on her shoulder. The warm water lapped at her feet, and she felt the spiral mark respond with a pulse of recognition. "You're really alive."

"Alive?" Kavita's laugh was like music played on instruments of pearl and flowing water. "That's a limited way to think about existence, don't you think? I am what I chose to become. I am not dead, not unchanged, but transformed into something that can exist in multiple realms simultaneously."

Around the chamber, other figures began to materialise—not the full gathering that Nisha had seen in her River vision, but a small group of the transformed Spiral Bearers who had chosen to remain close to the surface world. Each carried the same serene beauty, the same sense of having transcended ordinary human limitations while retaining their essential selves.

"The Pathshala's histories call us consumed," one of them said, a man whose features suggested he had been transformed sometime in the early colonial period. "They say we died fighting forces too vast for mortal minds to contain."

"And in a sense, they're not wrong," Kavita added gently. "The people we were did die. They were consumed not by external forces, but by the choice to become something greater than our original limitations allowed."

"But why?" Nisha asked, studying the faces around her. They were beautiful, alien, filled with a peace that spoke of profound understanding, but they were also no longer entirely human. "Why choose transformation over fighting to remain what you were?"

"Because fighting our nature was killing us slowly," Kavita replied. "Come, let me show you what really happened, three centuries ago."

She gestured, and the moving symbols on the walls began to coalesce into recognisable images—a visual history that told a story very different from the one preserved in the Pathshala's official records.

The images showed a younger Kavita, recognisably the same person but carrying the desperate tension of someone at war with forces in her own blood. She was thin to the point of emaciation, her eyes haunted by visions she couldn't shut out, her hands shaking with the effort of containing power that grew stronger every day.

"I tried everything," the present-day Kavita narrated as they watched her younger self attempt various containment rituals. "Meditation, binding ceremonies, even attempting to surgically remove the spiral mark from my arm. Nothing worked. The power was part of me at a cellular level, trying to suppress it was like trying to suppress my own heartbeat."

The images shifted, showing the physical and psychological toll of prolonged resistance. The younger Kavita grew weaker, more disoriented, sometimes speaking to people who weren't there or responding to sounds that only she could hear.

"The madness wasn't caused by the spiral mark," Kavita explained. "It was caused by fighting the spiral mark. The power needed expression, needed to flow through established channels. When I denied it that outlet, it found others. Usually through dreams, hallucinations, and the gradual dissolution of the boundary between my consciousness and the collective awareness of the depths."

"So, you gave up fighting?" Nisha asked.

"I chose to stop viewing transformation as surrender," Kavita corrected. "The Sea King—Vanaraja, as he was known in the oldest traditions—offered not conquest but partnership. Not the loss of self, but the expansion of self beyond the boundaries that pure mortality imposed."

The images changed again, showing the chamber as it had been three centuries ago. Instead of the empty, sealed space that everyone believed it to be, it had been a thriving centre of learning where surface dwellers and transformed beings worked together to understand the deeper mysteries of divine essence.

"The final confrontation," Kavita continued, "was not between the Pathshala and external invaders. It was between those who believed that transformation was inevitable and those who viewed it as corruption to be resisted at all costs."

Nisha watched as the images showed the argument that had torn the Pathshala apart—teachers and students choosing sides in a conflict that had no clear moral boundaries. Those who supported Kavita's transformation spoke of evolution and expanded consciousness. Those who opposed it spoke of preserving humanity and protecting the surface world from forces it couldn't understand.

"In the end," Kavita said sadly, "I chose transformation not to abandon the surface world, but to save it. The convergence was happening whether we resisted or not. The question was whether it would be guided by wisdom or driven by fear."

The final images showed Kavita's transformation. IT was not the desperate, consuming process that the Pathshala's histories described, but a serene acceptance of expanded existence. As she allowed her consciousness to merge with the deeper currents of divine essence, her physical form began to change, becoming something that could exist comfortably in multiple realms simultaneously.

"And the other Spiral Bearers?" Nisha asked, gesturing to the transformed figures around them.

"Some chose transformation immediately," Kavita replied. "Others fought it for decades or centuries before finally accepting what they were becoming. A few..." Her expression grew sad. "A few chose to fight until their minds shattered entirely, becoming the cautionary tales that your teachers speak of today."

As the historical images faded, new visions began to form on the chamber walls. They were not memories of the past, but glimpses of the present and possible futures. Nisha saw the underwater cities she had glimpsed in the River of Whispers, but now she could understand their true purpose.

They weren't conquering forces waiting to overwhelm the surface world, but research centres where transformed beings worked to solve problems that spanned multiple realms. Climate management projects that operated on a planetary scale. Conflict resolution techniques that addressed the root causes of discord between different forms of consciousness. Art and architecture that incorporated perspectives from species that had never known the limitations of purely physical existence.

"This is what we offer," Kavita said gently. "Not the end of human civilisation, but its expansion into something greater than anyone currently imagines possible."

"And the cost?" Nisha asked, though she suspected she already knew the answer.

"The cost is becoming something that the purely human world cannot fully understand or accept," Kavita admitted. "You would gain capabilities beyond current human limits, but you would also become responsible for mediating between realms that most people prefer to pretend don't exist."

The spiral mark pulsed more insistently, and Nisha felt a new presence entering the chamber—not another transformed Spiral Bearer, but the consciousness she had come to recognise as Vanaraja himself. He materialised slowly, his form shifting between the almost-human appearance she had seen in her visions and something vast and oceanic that her eyes couldn't quite process.

"Daughter," he said, his voice carrying the patience of geological ages and the warmth of currents that had circled the earth for millions of years. "You have seen the choice in its full complexity. What is your decision?"

Looking around the chamber, Nisha felt the weight of possibilities pressing against her awareness. She could see the paths stretching out from this moment. The transformation that would give her the power to bridge realms but would also separate her from everything she had ever known as purely human experience. Or continued resistance that would preserve her current form but potentially condemn both worlds to a chaotic convergence driven by fear rather than wisdom.

"I need to understand something," she said, surprised by the steadiness of her own voice. "If I choose transformation, what happens to the people I care about? My mother, my friends, the students in the Pathshala?"

"They would be safe," Vanaraja assured her. "More than safe, they would be protected by beings who understand both realms and can navigate the challenges of the convergence with wisdom rather than panic."

"And if I refuse?"

Kavita's expression grew troubled. "The convergence continues regardless. But without a bridge between realms, without someone who can translate between different forms of consciousness, the process becomes chaotic. Both worlds suffer, and eventually, both are diminished by the conflict."

Nisha closed her eyes, feeling the spiral mark pulse in rhythm with her heartbeat. In her mind, she could sense the vast network of consciousness that connected all the transformed Spiral Bearers—not a hive mind that would subsume her individuality, but a community of expanded beings who had learned to exist in harmony with forces beyond ordinary human comprehension.

It was beautiful. It was terrifying. It was utterly unlike anything she had ever imagined for her life.

But when she opened her eyes, what she saw was not the transformed figures around her or the magnificent visions of expanded possibility. What she saw was the entrance to the chamber, where *Guru* Chanda, Dev, Mira, and Kritika stood watching with expressions of fear and desperate love.

They couldn't enter the chamber—the phosphorescent water would not support purely human consciousness without preparation—but they had come as close as they could, ready to face whatever emerged from the ancient space.

Dev's floating equations were more active than she had ever seen them, clearly trying to analyse and understand the forces at work in the chamber. Mira stood ready for combat, her hand on a weapon that glowed with Kartikeya energy, prepared to fight even forces she couldn't comprehend if they threatened her friend. Kritika's crystals sang with harmonies designed to provide emotional support and clarity, offering what help she could across the barrier that separated them.

And her mother…Priya stood among them, her face streaked with tears but her expression resolute, ready to accept whatever choice her daughter made as long as Nisha remained true to herself.

"I understand the offer," Nisha said finally, turning back to Vanaraja and Kavita. "And I'm grateful for the choice. But I need more time to consider what it means, not just for me, but for everyone I care about."

Vanaraja's expression showed what might have been respect. "Time is a luxury that grows scarce, daughter. The convergence accelerates beyond our ability to guide it gently. Soon, the choice will be made for you by circumstances beyond anyone's control."

"How long?" Nisha asked.

"Days," Kavita replied sadly. "Perhaps hours. The barriers that have separated the realms for centuries are dissolving faster than even we anticipated."

As if to emphasise her words, a new sound began to echo through the Pathshala. It wasn't the hum of alien consciousness or the crack of failing seals, but something that made everyone's blood turn to ice. The sound of water rising, distant but inexorable, as if the ocean itself was preparing to reclaim land that had been dry since the foundations of the world were laid.

"The deep tides rise," Vanaraja observed with detached interest. "Whether guided by wisdom or driven by chaos, the convergence reaches its culmination. Choose quickly, daughter. The luxury of extended contemplation is ending."

The transformed figures began to fade, becoming translucent as they withdrew to whatever realm they inhabited when not manifesting in the physical world. But Kavita remained solid, her expression kind but urgent.

"Remember," she said, "transformation is not death. It is not the loss of self. It is the expansion of self beyond the boundaries that seemed permanent but were only temporary limitations."

Then she too began to fade, leaving Nisha alone in the chamber with only the phosphorescent water and the weight of the most important decision any human being had ever been asked to make.

The sound of rising water grew louder, and the spiral mark on her arm pulsed with the rhythm of tides that had been building for three centuries, finally ready to reach their peak. In the distance, she could hear voices—her friends calling her name, her mother's whispered prayers, the urgent discussions of teachers trying to comprehend forces beyond their traditional understanding.

The choice was hers to make, but time was running out. Soon, very soon, the convergence would reach a point where choice became irrelevant, and transformation or resistance would be decided by forces beyond anyone's ability to control.

Standing in the warm phosphorescent water, feeling the pulse of ancient power in her blood and the weight of two worlds' fate on her shoulders, Nisha prepared to make the decision that would define not just her own existence, but the relationship between surface and depth, between mortal understanding and forces too vast for purely human consciousness to comprehend.

The deep tides rose, and the spiral mark burned bright against her skin, and somewhere in the distance, the sound of her friends' voices reminded her that whatever she chose, she would not face the consequences alone.

Chapter 9:

UNCONTROLLED RESONANCE

THE URGENCY IN VANARAJA'S WORDS echoed through Nisha's mind as she emerged from the Mumbadevi Hall, the phosphorescent water still clinging to her feet like liquid starlight. The chamber behind her remained open, its ancient seals permanently breached, but the transformed figures had withdrawn to whatever realm they inhabited when not manifesting in physical space. Only the sound of distant rising water remained, growing steadily louder with each passing hour.

"Days, perhaps hours," Nisha repeated to herself, the timeline creating a knot of anxiety in her chest. The weight of the choice she had been shown—transformation or chaos—pressed against her awareness like a physical burden.

Chanda approached cautiously, her expression mixing relief at seeing Nisha emerge unchanged with deep concern about what she had witnessed in the sealed chamber. "What did they show you?"

"Truth," Nisha replied simply. "Or at least, their version of it. The question is whether I have enough time to understand what that truth means before I have to act on it."

Dev stepped forward, his floating equations more agitated than usual, their stable patterns flickering with chaotic energy. "The mathematical harmonics throughout the Pathshala have been destabilising since the doors opened," he reported. "Whatever force that chamber was containing, its release is affecting every divine essence manifestation in the complex."

As if to demonstrate his point, a student's practice crystal exploded in a shower of harmless but alarming sparks at the far end of the corridor. Another student lost control of a water-shaping exercise, sending a geyser shooting up to splash against the ceiling before falling in an uncontrolled torrent.

"The resonance is cascade-failing," Kritika observed, her own crystals chiming discordantly as they struggled to maintain harmony in the increasingly chaotic environment. "Without proper stabilisation, the entire Pathshala could become uninhabitable within hours."

"Which means," Mira said grimly, her hand still resting on her energy weapon, "that we can't afford the luxury of extended contemplation. Whatever you're going to do, Nisha, it needs to happen soon."

The spiral mark pulsed against Nisha's arm, and she felt the alien consciousness in her mind stir with what might have been approval. The Sea King's presence was stronger now, no longer filtered through the barriers that had contained his influence for centuries.

You begin to understand the true timeline, his voice whispered. *The convergence cannot be delayed, only guided. Choose quickly, daughter—chaos approaches whether you will it or not.*

"I need to understand my power first," Nisha said, pushing the alien voice to the back of her mind. "Really understand it, not just react to crisis situations. If I'm going to make a choice that affects two worlds, I need to know what I'm actually capable of."

Chanda nodded, though her expression remained troubled. "Accelerated training, then. We'll start with basic control exercises and advance as quickly as your abilities allow."

"No," Nisha said, surprising herself with the firmness in her voice. "Not basic exercises. I need to understand why my power doesn't work the way everyone expects it to. Why it disrupts your geometric patterns, why it transforms your weapons, why it resonates with forces that predate your established devotional traditions."

Dev adjusted his glasses, his analytical mind already working on the problem. "You want to map the fundamental differences between spiral bearer manifestation and traditional divine essence channelling."

"Exactly. I need to understand what I am before I can decide what I want to become."

They moved to a practice chamber that had been hastily evacuated due to the increasing instability, its walls scarred by the efforts of students who had lost control of their abilities as the Pathshala's harmonic balance deteriorated. The space felt different now—charged with potential energy that made the hair on Nisha's arms stand up and caused her spiral mark to pulse with uncomfortable intensity.

"Let's start with the most basic manifestation," Guru Chanda suggested. "Simple earth-shaping, but with full monitoring so we can analyse exactly how your power flows through different channels."

Dev began summoning his floating equations, creating a three-dimensional matrix that would track every aspect of Nisha's divine essence usage. Kritika placed her crystals in a careful pattern around the chamber, their harmonics designed to provide both monitoring and stabilisation. Mira took position near the door, ready to evacuate everyone if the experiment went dangerously wrong.

"Just lift that stone block," Chanda instructed, indicating the same practice weight that Nisha had worked with during her initial assessment. "But this time, I want you to pay attention to where the power is coming from, how it flows through your consciousness, what it feels like in your bones."

Nisha approached the block, placing her hands on its rough surface. Instead of immediately attempting to lift it, she closed her eyes and tried to sense the deeper currents of power that the spiral mark connected her to.

The first sensation was familiar. The warm flow of earth-based divine essence that she had learned to associate with Mumbadevi energy. It felt like the patient strength of stone, the slow wisdom of soil, the deep stability of bedrock that anchored continents.

But as she extended her awareness deeper, she felt other currents—streams of power that definitely did not match the Pathshala's established categories. There was something that felt like water, but not the controlled, purposeful flow of Varuna devotion. This was wilder, more primal, carrying the restless energy of tides and storms and depths that no human had ever explored.

And beneath that, something even stranger. A current of power that seemed to exist outside the normal categories entirely, ancient and patient and utterly alien to human consciousness.

"Interesting," she murmured, opening her eyes. "It's not just earth-work. There are at least three different power sources, and they're…braided together somehow."

"Show us," Dev said, his equations flickering with anticipation.

Nisha focused on the stone block, but instead of trying to force her power through established patterns, she let it flow according to its own nature. The result was immediate and spectacular.

The block didn't simply rise—it transformed. Stone flowed like clay, reshaping itself into something organic and alive. Roots of crystallized earth spread across the chamber floor, connecting to the walls and ceiling in patterns that suggested not human architecture but the growth patterns of some impossible tree.

"Fascinating," Dev breathed, his equations dancing around the manifestation as they tried to analyse what they were seeing. "You're not just channelling earth energy—you're channelling something that treats stone as if it were living matter."

But as the manifestation continued, something went wrong. The power flowing through Nisha began to resonate with something external, something vast and patient that was pressing against the Pathshala's weakened barriers. The spiral mark flared to painful brightness, and suddenly she could feel the Sea King's consciousness flowing through her connection to the earth itself.

"Stop," Kritika called out, her crystals shrieking in harmonies that hurt to hear. "Something's using your manifestation as a conduit!"

But it was too late. The alien consciousness had already established a foothold, using Nisha's power as a bridge to extend its influence directly into the Pathshala's foundation.

Through her connection to the stone, she could feel the Sea King's awareness spreading through the complex's structural elements, testing weak points, probing for vulnerabilities.

Excellent, his voice whispered, no longer confined to her mind but speaking through the stone itself. *You provide such a clear pathway, daughter. Through you, I can touch every part of this sanctuary that has held me at bay for so long.*

The chamber began to change around them. Where the crystallised roots had spread, the walls started to seep with phosphorescent water. The air grew thick with the scent of deep ocean, and shadows that moved independently of any light source began to flicker in the corners.

"Sever the connection!" Chanda shouted, her hands moving in complex patterns as she tried to disrupt Nisha's link to the alien consciousness.

"I can't!" Nisha gasped, her awareness trapped in the expanding network of stone and water that the Sea King was using as his manifestation medium. "He's using my power to anchor himself here!"

Through her unwilling connection, she could feel the Sea King's satisfaction as he tested the limits of his new foothold in the physical realm. The Pathshala's protective barriers, weakened by centuries of stress and the recent opening of the Mumbadevi Hall, offered little resistance to a consciousness that was now operating from within the complex's own structure.

Dev's equations exploded into chaotic fractals as they tried to map the invasion, their mathematical patterns dissolving under the influence of forces that operated according to entirely different logical principles. "The harmonic cascade is accelerating!" he called out. "If this continues, the entire Pathshala could become uninhabitable!"

"Worse than that," Mira said grimly, her energy weapon blazing as she tried to cut through the phosphorescent water that was now ankle-deep throughout the chamber. "He's not just invading the Pathshala. He's using it as a staging ground for something larger."

Through her connection to the Sea King's consciousness, Nisha could see what Mira had realised. The Pathshala wasn't just a sanctuary for divine essence practitioners—it was a nexus point, connected to magical communities and protective networks throughout the region. By establishing a foothold here, the Sea King could extend his influence far beyond the underground complex.

You see the scope of what approaches, his voice confirmed. *The convergence was never meant to be contained within a single location. The barriers between realms weaken everywhere simultaneously, and from this central point, I can guide the process according to wisdom rather than chaos.*

"Guide it toward conquest, you mean," Chanda accused, though her voice carried more weariness than anger.

Conquest? The Sea King's amusement rippled through the water-soaked chamber. *Such a limited perspective. I offer integration, evolution, the natural progression from isolation to unity. The surface world has had its time of separation—now comes the age of cooperation, whether willing or otherwise.*

The phosphorescent water continued to rise, and with it came creatures that definitely didn't belong in any terrestrial environment. They were beautiful and alien, their forms shifting between recognisable aquatic shapes and something more abstract, as if they existed in multiple dimensions simultaneously.

"Sea-spawn," Kritika identified, her crystals now singing in frequencies designed for combat rather than harmony. "But more advanced than anything in the historical records."

"Not spawn," one of the creatures corrected, its voice like the sound of waves breaking on distant shores. "We are the transformed, the evolved, the bridges between realms. We come not as invaders, but as teachers."

The creature approached Nisha directly, its form stabilizing into something almost human—beautiful in the way that deep ocean currents were beautiful, alien in the way that pressure and darkness were alien to surface dwellers.

"Sister," it said, reaching out with a hand that seemed to be made of crystallized water. "The choice approaches its final moment. Will you guide the convergence with wisdom, or watch it unfold in chaos?"

But before Nisha could respond, new voices echoed through the chamber—not the alien harmonics of the transformed beings, but the familiar sounds of her friends and teachers. Dev was shouting calculations that might stabilise the cascade effect. Mira was coordinating defensive positions with other arriving students. Kritika was weaving harmonic patterns designed to contain the spreading influence.

And through it all, her mother's voice, calling her name with the desperate love of someone who refused to lose her child to forces beyond human understanding.

"I won't let you use me as a weapon against the people I care about," Nisha said, finding a core of determination that cut through the confusion and alien influence.

She reached deep into her connection with the earth, not to channel more power, but to understand the nature of what was flowing through her. The spiral mark burned against her arm as she traced the pathways of energy back to their source, following the braided currents of power to their origins.

What she found there made her gasp in recognition and horror.

The third power source, the ancient current that predated the established devotional traditions—it wasn't separate from her humanity. It was the source of her humanity, the deep wellspring from which all surface consciousness had originally emerged.

You begin to understand, the Sea King's voice carried approval and satisfaction. *You are not human touched by alien power. You are alien power learning to wear human form. The spiral bearers were never corrupted by external influence. They were simply remembering what they had always been.*

The revelation hit her like a physical blow. Every aspect of herself that she had thought of as purely human—her curiosity, her determination, her love for her friends and family—had its roots in consciousness that was far older and stranger than purely terrestrial evolution could account for.

"But that doesn't change who I choose to be," she said, her voice carrying a strength that surprised her. "Understanding my origins doesn't automatically determine my choices."

She began to pull her power back, severing the connections that the Sea King had been using to anchor his presence in the Pathshala. It was like trying to dam a river with her bare hands, but she persisted, drawing on every technique she had learned about controlling divine essence flow.

The Sea King's presence resisted, pressing against her will with the patient force of ocean depths. *You cannot deny what you are forever, daughter. The convergence continues whether you guide it or not.*

"Maybe," Nisha admitted, sweat beading on her forehead from the effort of containing forces that wanted to flow freely. "But I can choose how I respond to what I am."

Slowly, painfully, she managed to pull her power back into herself, severing the connections that had allowed the Sea

King to manifest so strongly in the physical realm. The phosphorescent water began to recede, the alien creatures faded back to whatever dimension they inhabited, and the oppressive sense of vast consciousness pressing against the boundaries of reality gradually diminished.

But the effort left her drained in ways that went beyond physical exhaustion. The spiral mark had grown noticeably brighter during the manifestation, and the silvery sheen that she had first noticed after her initial awakening was now clearly visible on her hands and arms.

"The power is changing you," Chanda observed, her voice heavy with concern. "Each major manifestation accelerates the transformation, whether you embrace it consciously or not."

"How long?" Nisha asked, though she wasn't sure she wanted to hear the answer.

"At this rate?" Dev's equations flickered as they ran calculations based on the energy readings from the recent manifestation. "Days, maybe weeks before the changes become irreversible."

The implications settled over the chamber like a weight. Nisha had successfully demonstrated that she could resist the Sea King's influence and maintain some level of control over her spiral bearer abilities. But the cost was accelerating transformation that would eventually make the choice for her whether she wanted it or not.

"So, the question becomes," Mira said quietly, "whether you transform consciously, with some control over the process, or let it happen gradually until you lose the ability to choose at all."

"Or find a third option," Nisha said, though she wasn't sure what that might look like.

"The sealed hall," Kritika suggested. "Kavita Devi and the others—they chose transformation, but they retained enough of their original selves to communicate, to explain their choices. Maybe there's something in their experience that could guide a different path."

The sound of rising water, which had faded during Nisha's struggle with the Sea King, began to grow louder again. In the distance, they could hear commotion as other parts of the Pathshala dealt with the cascade effects of the harmonic disruption.

"Whatever we're going to do," Dev said, his equations showing stress patterns throughout the complex's structure, "we need to do it quickly. The Pathshala can't handle many more manifestations of this magnitude."

Nisha looked around at her friends—brilliant Dev with his mathematical understanding of impossible forces, fierce Mira ready to fight anything that threatened the people she cared about, thoughtful Kritika seeking harmony even in the midst of chaos. They had stood by her through revelations that challenged everything they thought they knew about the nature of reality.

"All right," she said. "Let's find that third option. But if we're going to do this, we do it together. I won't face transformation or resistance alone."

The spiral mark pulsed with warmth that might have been approval or warning, and in the distance, the sound of rising water continued its patient advance. The convergence approached its culmination, and the time for half-measures and delayed decisions was rapidly running out.

But at least she wouldn't face whatever came next without allies who understood both the stakes and the cost of the choices ahead.

Chapter 10:

BONDS FORGED IN TRAINING

THE AFTERMATH OF THE RESONANCE incident left the Pathshala in a state of controlled chaos. Students and teachers worked frantically to restabilise the harmonic disruptions that rippled through the complex, while emergency protocols activated ancient backup systems that hadn't been used in decades. The sound of rising water had become a constant background presence, no longer distant but pressing close enough to feel in the vibrations of the stone floors.

Nisha sat in the centre of the practice chamber, her hands pressed against the cool stone as she tried to understand what had happened during her manifestation. The silvery sheen on her skin was more pronounced now, visible even in the chamber's dim lighting, and the spiral mark pulsed with a rhythm that seemed to echo the approaching convergence.

"The transformation is accelerating," she said quietly, studying the metallic patterns that traced delicate filigree across her palms. "Each time I use the power, each time I make contact with ... with him ... I become less human."

Dev approached cautiously, his floating equations dim and stable for the first time in hours. "Not less human," he corrected gently. "Different human. The mathematical patterns suggest expansion rather than replacement—you're not losing your essential self, you're... adding to it."

"Adding alien consciousness to my essential self," Nisha replied with bitter humour. "I'm sure that's a distinction that will comfort everyone when I start sprouting gills and speaking in whale song."

"Actually," Kritika interjected, her crystals humming with soothing harmonies designed to ease emotional turmoil, "the transformation patterns we've observed don't suggest physical mutation so much as…expanded awareness. The silvery markings aren't scales or alien tissue, they're neural pathways, connections to consciousness that exists in multiple dimensions simultaneously."

Mira had been silent since the resonance incident, her energy weapon still glowing softly as she maintained a protective stance near the chamber entrance. Now she spoke, her voice carrying the weight of tactical assessment.

"The question isn't whether you're becoming something different," she said. "The question is whether you can learn to control that difference before it controls you. And based on what we just saw, that's going to require training methods that don't exist in any of the Pathshala's traditional curricula."

Guru Chanda entered the chamber, her expression mixing relief at finding them safe with deep concern about the broader situation. "The harmonic cascade has been contained, but barely. Master Varun estimates that the Pathshala can survive perhaps two more disruptions of that magnitude before the structural integrity becomes compromised."

"Two more," Nisha repeated. "And how many training sessions will it take to give me the control I need?"

"Under normal circumstances? Months, possibly years. The spiral bearer manifestation is unlike anything we've encountered." Chanda's voice carried the weight of centuries of accumulated knowledge encountering its limitations. "But we don't have normal circumstances. We have days, perhaps hours, before the convergence reaches a point where choice becomes irrelevant."

"Then we adapt," Dev said, his analytical mind already working on the problem. "We modify the training protocols to work with Nisha's unique resonance patterns instead of trying to force her power into traditional frameworks."

Over the next several hours, they developed what could only be described as experimental pedagogy. Instead of the geometric precision of standard Ganesha training, Dev worked with Nisha to understand the organic flow patterns that her power naturally followed. Rather than trying to create perfect mathematical constructs, they focused on concepts like protection, stability, growth, and let her power find its own expression.

"Think of it as divine engineering," Dev explained as they worked together on creating basic earth constructs. "Instead of imposing rigid designs, we're collaborating with natural forces to achieve functional outcomes."

The results were dramatically different from traditional earth-shaping. Where a conventional practitioner might create clean geometric barriers, Nisha's power manifested as living architecture—walls that grew like coral reefs, strengthening themselves through organic principles rather than structural calculation.

"It's actually more efficient," Dev observed, his equations tracking the energy flows. "Your constructs use less power while achieving greater stability because they're working with natural patterns instead of imposing artificial ones."

But the training sessions were taking their toll. After each exercise, the silvery sheen spread further across Nisha's skin, and the spiral mark glowed brighter. More concerningly, she was beginning to experience moments of disorientation—brief periods where her consciousness seemed to exist in multiple locations simultaneously.

"I can feel the network," she explained during one of these episodes, her voice carrying harmonics that definitely didn't belong to purely human vocal cords. "All the transformed spiral bearers, all the consciousness connected to the deep currents. It's like…like being part of a vast conversation that's been going on for centuries."

"Can you control when you connect to it?" Kritika asked, her crystals monitoring Nisha's emotional state with increasing precision.

"Not really. It happens when I use power, when I'm tired, when my concentration slips." Nisha pressed her hands to her temples, trying to ground herself in individual awareness. "And each time, it's harder to pull back, harder to remember that I'm a separate person rather than part of something larger."

Mira stepped forward, her expression set with determination. "Then we need to give you something to anchor yourself to. Something that reminds you who you are when the alien consciousness tries to subsume your identity."

She led them to a different chamber, one dedicated to combat training but modified for their specific needs. Instead of the usual sparring circles, the space had been arranged with obstacles that required not just power but tactical thinking—

situations where raw ability had to be tempered with strategic consideration.

"Physical challenges," Mira explained. "Combat scenarios that force you to think like a human, to protect human-scale concerns, to make decisions based on human values."

The training was intense and exhausting. Mira created scenario after scenario where Nisha had to use her powers not for grand manifestations but for precise, limited objectives. Like creating barriers to protect specific individuals, reshaping terrain to provide tactical advantages, using her earth-work to disable threats without causing collateral damage.

"The goal isn't to make you a better fighter," Mira explained as they worked through a particularly challenging exercise involving multiple hostages and limited response options. "It's to keep you thinking like someone who cares about individual human lives, someone who sees people as individuals rather than components of larger systems."

With each scenario, Nisha found herself drawing on memories and relationships that had nothing to do with divine essence or cosmic consciousness. The way Arjun had looked at her with trust when she pulled him from the flood. Her mother's fierce protectiveness in the face of forces beyond her understanding. Dev's quiet loyalty even when her power disrupted his carefully ordered equations.

"It's working," she said after successfully completing a rescue scenario that required her to balance multiple objectives simultaneously. "When I focus on protecting specific people, on achieving human-scale goals, the alien consciousness fades to background noise."

But the effort was becoming increasingly demanding. The silvery patterns on her skin now covered most of her arms and were beginning to trace delicate lines across her face. Her eyes occasionally flickered with depths that reflected not the chamber around them but vast oceanic distances.

"The transformation is accelerating," Chanda observed during one of their brief rest periods. "Each training session pushes your abilities further, but it also pushes you further from purely human consciousness."

"How much time do we have?" Nisha asked, though she could feel the answer in the increasing pressure behind her eyes, the growing difficulty of maintaining individual awareness.

"Days," Dev's equations provided the mathematical assessment. "Perhaps a week if we're fortunate. After that, the changes will likely become irreversible regardless of your conscious choices."

The sound of rising water, which had become a constant presence, suddenly intensified. Through the Pathshala's corridors came the sound of running feet and urgent voices—not the controlled response to training exercises, but genuine alarm.

Master Varun appeared in the chamber doorway, his face grim with news that made everyone's blood run cold. "The outer barriers have been breached. Sea-spawn are manifesting in the surface world, and they're not scouts or probes—they're establishing permanent footholds."

Through the Pathshala's connection to the surveillance networks that monitored Mumbai's magical activity, they could see the scope of the crisis. Phosphorescent water was seeping up through storm drains and underground tunnels, creating pools where creatures from the depths could manifest. The transformed beings weren't attacking—they were simply... arriving, taking up residence in spaces that had never known their presence.

"It's not an invasion," Kritika observed, her crystals analysing the harmonic patterns of the manifestations. "It's more like... immigration. They're coming through to stay."

"The convergence reaches its final phase," Chanda said, her voice heavy with the weight of inevitability. "The barriers between realms are dissolving completely. Soon, the distinction between surface and depth will become meaningless."

Through her connection to the spiral bearer network, Nisha could feel the truth of those words. The transformed consciousness that had been contained for centuries was spreading through every available channel, not with the violence of conquest but with the patient determination of water finding its level.

The time of choosing ends, the Sea King's voice whispered in her mind, stronger now than it had ever been. *The convergence cannot be stopped, only guided. Will you help your people adapt to the new reality, or watch them struggle against forces they cannot comprehend?*

But even as the alien consciousness pressed its case, Nisha felt the anchors her friends had helped her forge—the human connections that kept her grounded in individual identity, the memories of people who mattered to her not as components of larger systems but as irreplaceable individuals.

"There has to be another way," she said, her voice carrying harmonics that spoke of expanding awareness even as her words expressed purely human determination. "Some path that doesn't require choosing between transformation and chaos."

"The sealed chamber," Dev suggested, his equations flickering with sudden inspiration. "Kavita Devi and the others—they found a way to transform while maintaining enough human consciousness to communicate with us.

Maybe they know something about partial transformation, about existing in multiple states simultaneously."

Mira nodded, her warrior's instincts recognising the tactical value of gathering intelligence from experienced practitioners. "If there's a middle path, they would be the ones to know about it."

"It's dangerous," Chanda warned. "Each contact with the transformed consciousness makes it harder for Nisha to maintain her individual identity. Another extended exposure could push her past the point of no return."

"And avoiding that exposure guarantees that the point of no return arrives anyway," Kritika pointed out. "Either through gradual transformation or through the chaos of unguided convergence."

Nisha looked around at her friends—brilliant Dev with his mathematical understanding, fierce Mira with her tactical instincts, thoughtful Kritika with her gift for finding harmony in chaos. They had stood by her through every revelation, every challenge, every moment when the easy choice would have been to step back and let someone else handle the impossible responsibility.

"All right," she said, the spiral mark pulsing with anticipation. "Let's go talk to the transformed consciousness and see if there's a way to bridge the gap between worlds without losing ourselves in the process."

The sound of rising water grew louder, and somewhere in the distance, they could hear the voices of beings who had chosen transformation calling to their sister who still stood at the threshold of that choice. The convergence approached its culmination, and the time for partial measures was ending.

But at least she wouldn't face whatever came next alone. Whatever path they found through the impossible landscape of choice ahead, they would walk it together. Be it human and transforming, individual and collective, or anchored by bonds that had been forged in the crucible of shared purpose and mutual trust.

The spiral mark burned bright against her skin, and in its light, she could see the faces of her friends clearly—not as they appeared to ordinary sight, but as they existed in the deeper currents of consciousness, brilliant and unique and utterly irreplaceable.

Whatever she became, whatever choice she made, she would carry those faces with her into the unknown future that was rising to meet them all.

Chapter 11:

THE UNSEEN ADVANCE

THE EMERGENCY COUNCIL CONVENED IN the Heart of the Pathshala as reports flooded in from surveillance networks across Mumbai. What they were hearing defied every protocol and contingency plan the institution had developed over eight centuries of protecting the surface world from supernatural threats.

"Seventeen confirmed manifestation sites in the past six hours," Master Varun reported, his weathered face grim as he consulted the living map that displayed the city's mystical infrastructure. "And these aren't random appearances—they're following a pattern, establishing a network of anchor points that could support massive translocation events."

Guru Chanda studied the map with growing alarm. The phosphorescent pools appearing throughout Mumbai weren't scattered randomly—they formed a complex geometric pattern that centred on the Siddhivinayak Temple and radiated outward through the city's most vulnerable neighbourhoods.

"They're testing more than just our barriers," she realised. "They're mapping the entire city's supernatural infrastructure, identifying every ward, every protective charm, every sacred site that could potentially resist large-scale manifestation."

Nisha felt the spiral mark pulse against her arm as she studied the pattern, her expanding awareness allowing her to perceive connections that would have been invisible to purely human consciousness. Through her link to the transformed network, she could sense the intelligence behind the seemingly random appearances.

"It's not just mapping," she said, her voice carrying harmonics that made several council members shift uncomfortably. "It's preparation. They're not planning to invade Mumbai—they're planning to integrate it. Every manifestation site is positioned to support a gradual convergence rather than a violent conquest."

You begin to understand the true scope of what approaches, the Sea King's voice whispered in her mind, stronger now that the barriers between realms had thinned so dramatically. *This was never about conflict between worlds. It was about the natural evolution from separation to unity.*

Dev's floating equations flickered as they tried to map the implications. "If they can establish enough anchor points, they could effectively merge sections of Mumbai with underwater realms. Not destroying the city, but...expanding it into multiple dimensions simultaneously."

"The scale is unprecedented," Master Varun said, his voice tight with controlled fear. "We're not dealing with individual incursions that can be contained or repelled. This is systematic restructuring of reality itself."

Through the Pathshala's connection to monitoring stations throughout the region, they could see the effects rippling outward. In Dharavi, the narrow alleys where Nisha had grown up were experiencing subtle but profound changes—water flowing in impossible directions, shadows that moved independently of their sources, sounds carrying across distances that defied acoustic principles.

But what made the reports particularly unsettling was the lack of panic or resistance from the surface population. People were noticing the changes, but instead of fleeing or fighting, they seemed to be...adapting. Children played in pools of phosphorescent water that definitely hadn't existed the day before. Vendors sold their wares to customers whose eyes held depths that reflected otherworldly distances.

"They're not resisting because it doesn't feel like an attack," Kritika observed, her crystals humming with confused harmonies as they tried to analyse the emotional resonances coming from the affected areas. "The integration is happening so gradually, so gently, that it feels like natural change rather than external imposition."

"Which makes it infinitely more dangerous," Mira said grimly. "An invasion you can fight. Seduction that feels beneficial...that's much harder to resist."

As if summoned by their discussion, new alarms began sounding throughout the Pathshala—not the sharp warnings of immediate danger, but the deep, resonant tones that indicated fundamental threats to the institution's structural integrity. The living map flared with alarming patterns as monitoring stations throughout the complex detected unprecedented levels of supernatural activity.

"The outer wards are failing," one of the junior teachers reported, her voice tight with fear. "Not broken or destroyed, but they're being…absorbed. Incorporated into whatever network the manifestations are creating."

Through her connection to the transformed consciousness, Nisha could feel the truth of that assessment. The Sea King wasn't destroying the Pathshala's defences—he was converting them, turning centuries of accumulated protective power into components of his expanding influence network.

"We need to evacuate," Master Varun said, his tactical instincts recognising a situation that had moved beyond their ability to contain. "Get the students to the emergency shelters, activate the deep sanctuary protocols …"

"No," Nisha interrupted, surprising herself with the firmness in her voice. "Evacuation won't solve anything. He's not trying to destroy the Pathshala—he's trying to transform it into something that serves his purposes. Running away just gives him free access to eight centuries of accumulated divine essence knowledge."

Precisely, the Sea King's voice carried approval. *The Pathshala was always meant to be a bridge between realms, not a barrier. Its founders understood this, even if subsequent generations forgot the deeper purpose.*

"What are you suggesting?" Chanda asked, though her expression suggested she suspected the answer.

"I go to the surface," Nisha said, the decision crystallising even as she spoke the words. "Not to fight the manifestations, but to understand them. To see firsthand what kind of integration is actually taking place."

"Absolutely not," Mira said immediately. "The moment you leave the Pathshala's protective environment, you'll be completely vulnerable to external influence. One sustained contact with the transformed consciousness and you could lose yourself entirely."

"I'm losing myself anyway," Nisha replied, holding up her hands to show the silvery patterns that now covered most of her arms and were beginning to trace delicate lines across her face. "The transformation is accelerating whether I stay here or not. At least if I go to the surface, I can gather intelligence that might help us understand what we're really facing."

Dev's equations flickered with calculations that made his face pale. "The mathematical models suggest that exposure to the manifestation sites would indeed accelerate the transformation process. But they also suggest that the information gained could be crucial for understanding the full scope of the convergence."

"It's a tactical necessity," Kritika added, her crystals singing with harmonies designed to provide clarity in difficult decisions. "We're fighting blind right now, reacting to situations we don't understand. If Nisha can gather intelligence about the actual integration process…"

"Then we can make informed decisions instead of panicked reactions," Guru Chanda finished, though her expression remained troubled. "But the risk…"

"The risk is enormous," Nisha agreed. "But so is the cost of remaining ignorant. If I'm going to transform anyway, at least let me make that transformation serve some useful purpose."

The debate continued for precious minutes while reports of new manifestations flooded in from throughout Mumbai. Each new anchor point made the overall pattern clearer—this wasn't random supernatural activity, but a carefully orchestrated campaign designed to gradually accustom the surface world to otherworldly presence.

Finally, Master Varun made the decision that everyone had been avoiding. "We do it, but with every precaution we can devise. Full monitoring, emergency extraction protocols, and a support team that can pull her back if the external influence becomes too strong."

"I'll go with her," Dev said immediately. "My equations can track the transformation process and provide early warning if she's approaching dangerous thresholds."

"And I'll handle tactical assessment," Mira added. "If we're walking into potentially hostile situations, someone needs to maintain situational awareness."

"The crystals can provide harmonic anchoring," Kritika offered. "Emotional and mental stability in environments designed to reshape consciousness."

Despite the danger, despite the accelerating timeline, Nisha felt a surge of gratitude for friends who were willing to walk into the unknown rather than let her face it alone. The spiral mark pulsed with warmth that might have been approval or warning, and through her expanding awareness, she could sense the vast network of transformed consciousness taking notice of their decision.

Interesting, the Sea King mused. *You choose to gather intelligence rather than submit to inevitability. Perhaps there is more of your grandmother's wisdom in you than I initially recognised.*

The reference to her grandmother sent a chill through Nisha that had nothing to do with the Pathshala's cool air. Through her mother's stories, she knew that her grandmother had been one of the spiral bearers who had chosen to fight the transformation—and had died screaming, her mind shattered by forces she couldn't accept or control.

"What happened to my grandmother?" she asked, directing the question toward the alien consciousness in her mind. "Really happened, not the version filtered through family fear and shame."

She was…magnificent in her resistance, the Sea King replied with what might have been respect. *Strong enough to maintain her individual identity even as the transformation progressed far beyond what most humans could endure. But strength without acceptance becomes self-destruction. She fought what she was becoming until the fighting itself destroyed her.*

The image that formed in Nisha's mind was heartbreaking. A woman of incredible will and determination, maintaining her human consciousness through sheer force of personality even as her body and mind were reshaped by forces beyond her understanding. But without acceptance, without finding a way to integrate the changes instead of simply resisting them, the internal conflict had eventually torn her apart.

"I won't make the same mistake," Nisha said quietly.

No, the Sea King agreed. *You seek understanding rather than simple resistance. That is…promising.*

Preparations for the surface expedition took the better part of an hour. Emergency protocols were activated, communication arrays were calibrated to maintain contact across dimensional barriers, and rescue contingencies were established in case extraction became necessary. Through it all, the sound of rising water grew steadily louder, no longer distant but pressing close enough to feel in the vibrations of the stone floors.

As they prepared to leave the Pathshala's protected environment, Chanda pulled Nisha aside for a private conversation.

"There's something you need to understand," she said, her voice heavy with knowledge that had been passed down through generations of teachers. "The spiral bearer power isn't just connected to the transformed consciousness—it's the key to controlling it. Every major convergence in recorded history has required a spiral bearer to either guide or resist the process."

"What does that mean, exactly?"

"It means that whatever happens next, you're not just an observer or a victim of circumstances. You're the deciding factor. The choices you make, the path you follow, the way you use or refuse to use your power—all of it will determine not just your own fate, but the fate of both realms."

The weight of that responsibility settled on Nisha's shoulders like a physical burden. She thought of the millions of people in Mumbai going about their daily lives, unaware that the nature of reality itself was being reshaped around them. She thought of the transformed beings in their underwater cities, patient and alien and utterly convinced that integration was the natural evolution of consciousness.

"No pressure," she said with dark humour.

"None at all," Chanda replied with a slight smile. "Just the future of human consciousness and the relationship between realms. Nothing that a seventeen-year-old engineering student can't handle."

As they made their way toward the surface through corridors that seemed to stretch and compress around them, Nisha found herself thinking about the choice she had been shown in the River of Whispers—normal life versus transformation, individual happiness versus cosmic responsibility. But now she was beginning to understand that those hadn't been the real options at all.

The real choice was between guiding the convergence with wisdom or watching it unfold in chaos. Between finding a path that honoured both human individuality and cosmic connection, or accepting that the two were fundamentally incompatible.

"Are you ready for this?" Dev asked as they approached the final barrier between the Pathshala and the surface world.

Nisha felt the spiral mark pulse against her arm, felt the alien consciousness stirring in her mind, felt the weight of impossible choices pressing against her awareness. Through the dimensional barriers, she could sense the transformed beings watching with patient interest, waiting to see what choice their newest sister would make.

"No," she said honestly. "But I don't think anyone could be ready for this."

The barriers parted, and for the first time since her awakening, Nisha stepped into a surface world that was no longer purely human. What she found there would challenge every assumption she had made about the nature of the convergence, the intentions of the transformed consciousness, and the possibility of finding a path between absolute resistance and total transformation.

The sound of rising water was no longer distant. It was here, now, reshaping the world she had always known into something that had never existed before. And she was the key to determining whether that transformation would preserve what was valuable about human consciousness or sweep it away in favour of something entirely alien.

The unseen advance had become visible, and there was no turning back.

Chapter 12:

THE CALL OF THE DEEP

THE DEEP, RESONANT HUM THAT had settled into the Pathshala's foundations after the Mumbadevi Hall revelations had grown stronger with each passing hour, no longer the subtle vibration that students could ignore while studying, but a force that made the ancient stones themselves tremble with increasing urgency. The luminescent veins running through the carved walls pulsed in perfect rhythm with the sound, their usual gentle glow now harsh and flickering, casting dancing shadows through corridors where students and teachers moved with barely contained panic.

Nisha pressed her palms against her temples as she sat on the edge of her sleeping alcove, trying desperately to block out the relentless thrumming that seemed to penetrate directly through her skull and into her very bones. The spiral mark on her arm had begun to burn with an intensity that made her gasp, the skin around it hot to the touch despite the Pathshala's constantly cool air. The silvery sheen that had been gradually spreading across her skin over the past days was now impossible to ignore—delicate metallic patterns covered her arms like intricate jewellery, catching and reflecting the chamber's erratic light with an otherworldly gleam.

Every pulse of the hum sent waves of alien sensation through her body, as if something vast and patient was reaching across impossible distances to touch her directly. The feeling was both terrifying and seductive, promising answers to questions she hadn't known she was asking, belonging to something larger than the isolated existence she had always known.

"Not yet," she whispered to the empty chamber, her voice hoarse from hours of fighting the pull she felt growing stronger with each heartbeat. "I need more time. I need to understand what's happening to me."

But time, she was beginning to realise, was a luxury she no longer possessed.

When exhaustion finally forced her into sleep, the dreams that came were unlike anything she had ever experienced. These weren't the fragmented, symbolic visions of ordinary rest, but encounters so vivid and immediate that they felt more real than her waking life in the Pathshala. The transition was seamless—one moment she was lying in her alcove, the next she was standing in that familiar chamber of pearl and bioluminescent coral that had haunted her visions since her first awakening.

But this time, the space was filled with presence in a way it had never been before.

Figures moved through the water-filled chamber with fluid grace, their forms shifting between recognisably human and something far more elemental. She recognised faces from the Chronicle Walls' historical records—Spiral Bearers from across the centuries who had vanished from the surface world, presumed dead by the Pathshala's official histories. But they were very much alive, transformed into beings of otherworldly beauty whose every movement spoke of centuries spent in communion with forces beyond mortal understanding.

They wore their transformations like gifts rather than curses. Where human features had once been, there were now forms that seemed to be sculpted from living water and crystallized moonlight. Their eyes held depths that reflected not the chamber around them, but vast oceanic distances that spoke of realms existing far beyond the boundaries of terrestrial geography. When they moved, the water around them responded as if it were an extension of their will, creating patterns of light and current that were beautiful beyond description.

At their centre stood a figure that could only be Vanaraja himself—the Sea King whose presence she had felt pressing against her mind for days. No longer the vast, incomprehensible force that had invaded her thoughts, he had manifested in a form that was almost human, though the differences were immediately apparent. His skin held the blue-green tint of deep ocean waters where sunlight had never penetrated, and his hair moved as if he were underwater even though he stood in air. His eyes were the most striking feature—black as the deepest trenches, but filled with points of light that seemed to contain entire galaxies.

When he spoke, his voice carried harmonics that made the chamber walls themselves resonate, as if the very structure of the space was responding to his words.

You begin to hear the true calling, he said, his attention focusing on Nisha with an intensity that made her feel simultaneously terrified and cherished. *The barriers that have kept our realms separate weaken with each passing hour, and those who carry the old blood in their veins feel the pull of their true heritage.*

Around him, the other transformed figures turned their attention to Nisha, and she felt the weight of their combined regard like a physical force. These were beings who had once struggled with the same questions that tormented her, who had faced the same impossible choices and found peace in transformation. Their expressions held welcome, understanding, and something that might have been gentle pity for the conflict they could sense raging within her.

Among them, one figure stepped forward, and Nisha's breath caught in recognition. This was Kavita Devi, but not the desperate, conflicted woman from the Pathshala's historical records. Three centuries of transformation had refined her into something of absolute beauty, her movements fluid as living water, her form shifting between human and something more elemental with each breath. Her eyes held the patient wisdom of geological ages, and when she smiled, it was with the serene contentment of someone who had finally found their true home.

"Sister," Kavita said, her voice carrying the warm familiarity of family combined with harmonics that spoke of vast depths and ancient mysteries. "We have been waiting so long for you to hear us clearly. The time of choosing approaches faster than any of us anticipated, and the convergence can no longer be contained within the careful boundaries we have maintained for centuries."

"What convergence?" Nisha asked, though even as she spoke the words, part of her already understood. The knowledge seemed to be flowing into her from the spiral mark itself, ancestral memories awakening as the barriers between her human awareness and something far older began to dissolve.

The natural alignment of powers that occurs when the cosmic tides reach their peak, Vanaraja explained, his voice carrying the authority of someone who had witnessed such events across millennia. *Every few centuries, the barriers between realms grow thin enough to allow free passage between worlds that are normally separated by forces too vast for mortal comprehension. The deep currents rise to meet the surface waters, the boundaries between possible and impossible become permeable, and those who carry the blood of both worlds must decide where their ultimate loyalties lie.*

The chamber around them began to shift and change, the walls becoming transparent to reveal visions of what was happening beyond the Pathshala's protected boundaries. Throughout Mumbai, throughout India, throughout the world, the signs were unmistakable to those who knew how to read them. Water flowed uphill in patterns that defied gravity, creating channels that connected to underground rivers that definitely didn't exist on any terrestrial map. Shadows moved independently of their sources, dancing in patterns that suggested intelligence rather than mere play of light. The very air in certain locations shimmered with dimensional distortions that made reality itself seem fluid and negotiable.

"It's happening right now," Nisha realised, her voice barely above a whisper as the scope of what she was witnessing began to sink in.

"The early stages," Kavita confirmed, her expression growing more serious. "The gentle preparation that allows surface dwellers to adapt gradually to the presence of forces they have never encountered. But soon, very soon, the process will accelerate beyond anyone's ability to control through subtle influence. The barriers will fail completely, and what happens next will depend entirely on whether the transition is guided by wisdom or allowed to unfold in chaos."

Vanaraja gestured with one graceful hand, and the visions around them shifted to show two dramatically different possible futures. In the first, the convergence proceeded under careful guidance from those who understood both realms. Cities transformed but preserved their essential character, becoming magnificent hybrids that combined the best of terrestrial architecture with the impossible geometries of underwater construction. Surface dwellers adapted at their own pace, some choosing to embrace transformation while others remained safely within familiar patterns of existence. The integration was beautiful, harmonious, and respectful of the choices made by all forms of life.

In the second vision, chaos reigned supreme. The barriers failed suddenly and completely, unleashing forces that the surface world had no preparation to handle. Reality became dangerously unstable, with some areas experiencing rapid, overwhelming transformation while others were torn apart by the violent collision of incompatible physical laws. Cities crumbled under the weight of impossible architectures that tried to exist in spaces too small to contain them. People fled in terror from changes they couldn't understand, while others were consumed by transformations, they had no choice in accepting. Both worlds suffered catastrophically as the uncontrolled convergence destroyed what was most valuable about each realm.

The choice before you is elegantly simple, the Sea King said, his black eyes fixed on Nisha with an intensity that made her feel as if he were looking directly into her soul. *Join us willingly, embrace the transformation that your bloodline has always been meant to undergo, and help us bridge the gap between worlds in a way that preserves what is worth preserving from both realms. Or continue to resist the inevitable, cling to limitations that were never meant to be permanent, and watch as unguided forces destroy everything you claim to be protecting.*

The other Spiral Bearers moved closer, their combined presence creating a sense of belonging that Nisha had never experienced in her entire life. Here were others who truly understood what it meant to carry power that didn't fit into the neat categories that ordinary human society used to make sense of the world. Here were people who had faced the same impossible choices, the same terrible isolation, the same crushing weight of responsibility for forces beyond their comprehension. And they had found peace, purpose, and joy in transformation.

"We don't ask you to abandon your humanity," Kavita said, her voice gentle but urgent. "We ask you to expand it beyond the artificial limitations that have kept both worlds isolated and incomplete for far too long. Everything you are, everything you value, everything you love about your current existence—none of it needs to be lost. It can all be preserved and enhanced through integration with something larger and more magnificent than pure human experience could ever achieve alone."

The vision around them shifted once more, and now Nisha could see the underwater cities in all their breathtaking scope and complexity. But she realised that her previous glimpses had shown her only the smallest fraction of what actually existed. These weren't simply aquatic versions of surface architecture—they were spaces that existed in multiple dimensions simultaneously, where the usual constraints of physics had been transcended through understanding rather than violated through force.

Beings who had once been human worked alongside creatures that had never known terrestrial existence, their collaborations producing art and science and philosophy that incorporated perspectives from across the entire spectrum of possible experience. The music that flowed through these spaces harmonised frequencies that spanned dimensions, creating beauty that could never be achieved by any single form of awareness. The architecture grew rather than being built, responding to the needs and desires of its inhabitants in ways that made every structure a living collaboration between will and possibility.

This could be your reality, Vanaraja offered, his voice carrying the weight of absolute sincerity. *Not the loss of what you are, but the discovery of what you have always had the potential to become. Your friends, your family, your mother—everyone you care about could be part of this expansion, choosing their own level of participation while remaining forever protected by those who have embraced the full scope of transformation.*

The seduction was overwhelming in its completeness. Nisha could feel the rightness of it resonating in every fibre of her being, the way it answered questions she hadn't even known she was asking. The terrible loneliness of being the only spiral bearer in the Pathshala would end forever, replaced by connection to beings who understood exactly what she was experiencing. The constant fear of what her uncontrolled power might do to the people she cared about would be resolved through integration with forces that had learned to channel such energies with perfect precision. The crushing weight of responsibility for powers beyond her comprehension would be shared among beings who had carried such burdens for centuries and found joy rather than suffering in the experience.

She could see herself among them, transformed but essentially unchanged, her love for her friends and family expanded rather than diminished, her desire to help and protect others given scope beyond anything she had ever imagined possible. The engineering skills that had always been her greatest strength would find application in projects that spanned dimensions, solving problems and creating beauty on scales that no purely human mind could conceive.

But even as every logical argument pointed toward acceptance, even as every emotional appeal struck directly at her deepest desires, she felt something stirring in the depths of her mind—not the alien presence of the Sea King or the transformed wisdom of the ancient Spiral Bearers, but her own voice, stubborn and determined in the way that had driven her to save Arjun from the flood despite impossible odds, to stand with her friends despite forces beyond her understanding, to keep fighting for solutions even when everyone else had given up hope.

"There has to be another way," she said, the words surprising her even as she spoke them. They seemed to come from some core part of herself that remained untouched by the seductive visions, some essential stubbornness that refused to accept that the only choices were surrender or destruction.

The silence that followed her words was profound, broken only by the gentle sound of water moving through the impossible architecture around them. The transformed Spiral Bearers exchanged glances that spoke of centuries of shared understanding, their expressions shifting from patient persuasion to something that might have been curiosity mixed with ancient, weary wisdom.

Finally, Kavita spoke, her voice carrying the weight of someone who had considered every possible alternative before making her own choice.

"What other way could there possibly be?" she asked, not mockingly, but with genuine interest in what Nisha might

propose. "The convergence of tides is a force of nature, as inevitable as the rising of the sun or the turning of the seasons. It cannot be stopped, only guided. Without willing cooperation from those who carry the spiral mark, those who can bridge the gap between realms, the process becomes destructive rather than transformative. We have seen this happen before, in other ages, in other parts of the world. The results are always catastrophic for both sides."

"I don't know yet," Nisha admitted, her voice growing stronger despite the uncertainty of her position. "But I know that presenting people with a choice between transformation and chaos isn't really giving them a choice at all. Its coercion disguised as mercy."

Vanaraja's expression showed what might have been respect, his ancient intelligence clearly reassessing her based on this unexpected response. *You seek a third path,* he said slowly. *Such thinking is…uncommon among your kind. Most spiral bearers either embrace their destiny immediately or fight against it until the struggle destroys them. But consider this carefully, daughter—the convergence of tides operates according to forces that dwarf individual will. It can be worked with, channelled, guided toward beneficial outcomes, but it cannot be prevented or fundamentally altered. The laws that govern such cosmic events are as immutable as gravity or the speed of light.*

"Then maybe the answer isn't prevention or surrender," Nisha replied, her voice growing stronger as the idea began to crystallise in her mind. "Maybe it's…adaptation. Finding ways for both worlds to coexist and interact without either one having to give up what makes it fundamentally unique."

The transformed Spiral Bearers around her fell silent, their expressions shifting to something she hadn't seen before—not the patient certainty of beings who had found their perfect solution, but the uncertain consideration of those encountering a genuinely new idea. The man who had been

among the first to embrace transformation during the early days of the Pathshala stepped forward, his ancient eyes troubled.

"Such attempts have been made before," he said quietly, his voice carrying the weight of painful memory. "During the last great convergence, three centuries ago, some among us sought to serve as bridges between realms rather than choosing complete transformation. They believed that spiral bearers could maintain simultaneous connections to both worlds, serving as living links that would allow controlled interaction without requiring anyone to abandon their essential nature."

"What happened to them?" Nisha asked, though the expressions around her already suggested that the answer wouldn't be encouraging.

"They were consumed," Kavita replied, her voice heavy with sadness that had endured across centuries. "The spiral mark connects its bearer to powers that are simply too vast for divided loyalties to withstand. The attempt to serve two masters, to maintain simultaneous allegiance to incompatible forms of existence, led only to madness and eventual destruction. Their bodies were found days later, their minds shattered by forces too immense for any individual will to control when split between competing demands."

But even as she spoke, Nisha felt the kernel of an idea beginning to form, born from her engineering background and her experience with complex systems that required multiple components working in harmony rather than single solutions imposed by force.

"What if the problem wasn't divided loyalty," she said slowly, working through the concept even as she spoke, "but incomplete understanding? What if those previous spiral bearers failed not because the task was impossible, but

because they were trying to do it alone, without the support systems and knowledge base that might have made success achievable?"

The vision around them began to shimmer and change, reality becoming fluid as her questions touched something fundamental about the nature of the convergence itself. For just a moment, she glimpsed possibilities that none of the transformed beings had considered—not the absorption of human awareness into something larger, not the permanent isolation of realms that belonged together, but genuine synthesis that preserved what was most valuable about each while creating something entirely new and unprecedented.

She saw networks of spiral bearers working together, sharing the burden of bridging between worlds so that no individual had to bear the full weight of cosmic forces alone. She saw surface dwellers and transformed beings collaborating on projects that honoured both perspectives, creating hybrid solutions that were stronger than either approach could achieve in isolation. She saw children growing up in a world where the boundaries between possible and impossible were negotiable rather than absolute, where human creativity and alien wisdom could combine to solve problems that had seemed insurmountable.

Interesting, Vanaraja mused, his vast intelligence clearly working through implications that spanned centuries of accumulated wisdom and experience. *You propose something that has never been successfully achieved, a form of cooperation that transcends the usual patterns of dominance and submission that characterise interactions between different orders of existence. The mathematical complexity alone would be staggering, requiring coordination across multiple dimensional frameworks simultaneously.*

The vision continued to shift and evolve as the Sea King's attention focused on the possibilities Nisha had raised. *But perhaps,* he continued, his voice carrying a note of something that might have been wonder, *the complexity is not a barrier but an opportunity. Your species has always excelled at finding elegant solutions to problems that seem impossibly complicated when approached from conventional angles.*

The dream began to fade as forces beyond the vision pulled at Nisha's sleeping mind, drawing her back toward waking awareness. But Vanaraja's final words followed her across the dimensional barriers, carrying both warning and what might have been blessing.

The convergence accelerates beyond our previous calculations, daughter of two worlds, his voice echoed through the dissolving vision. *Soon, very soon, theory must become practice, and idealism must prove itself capable of surviving contact with realities that have destroyed every previous attempt at compromise. When that moment of ultimate choice arrives, remember what you have glimpsed here—and remember also that even the most noble intentions can be overwhelmed by forces too ancient and vast for any individual will to control, no matter how strong or determined.*

Nisha woke with a violent gasp, her entire body shaking from the intensity of the encounter. The spiral mark on her arm pulsed with urgent rhythm that matched her racing heartbeat, and she could feel something fundamental shifting in the world around her, as if the conversation in the dream had somehow altered the basic fabric of reality itself.

The hum that filled the Pathshala had changed while she slept, becoming less mechanical vibration and more… summons. There was an urgency to it now that hadn't been present before, a calling that seemed to resonate directly with the transformed patterns spreading across her skin.

The call grows stronger with each passing hour, whispered a voice that seemed to come from the resonance itself, no longer the distant presence she had felt before but something immediate and compelling. *The deep calls to the deep, and those who carry the ancient blood in their veins cannot resist forever. The convergence approaches its culmination, and the choice can no longer be delayed.*

She could feel it now, not just in dreams, but in her waking moments—the pull toward something vast and patient that waited in the spaces between worlds. It offered belonging, understanding, an end to the terrible isolation of being the only one of her kind in a world that couldn't truly comprehend what she was becoming. The promise was seductive beyond description, speaking to needs she hadn't even realised she possessed.

But she could also feel the anchor points her training had established, the connections that kept her grounded in individual human experience. Memories of Dev's quiet loyalty as he worked through impossible mathematical problems just to help her understand her own nature. Mira's fierce protectiveness, her willingness to fight forces beyond her comprehension if they threatened her friends. Kritika's gentle wisdom, her gift for finding harmony even in the midst of chaos and conflict. Her mother's unwavering love, the determination to stand by her daughter no matter what impossible transformations might come.

These connections to individual human experience provided counterweight to the seductive call of cosmic belonging, reminding her that there were things worth preserving about the limited, chaotic, gloriously imperfect nature of purely terrestrial existence.

The choice was approaching, she realised with crystalline clarity. Soon, very soon, she would have to decide not just her own fate, but the entire nature of the relationship between worlds that had been kept separate for far too long. The convergence was no longer a distant possibility but an immediate reality pressing against the boundaries of everything she had ever known.

In the distance, she could hear voices—her friends and teachers responding to changes in the Pathshala that spoke of ancient barriers failing and protective seals losing their power after centuries of faithful service. Emergency protocols were being activated, evacuation plans were being discussed, and the desperate hope that somehow the crisis could be contained was giving way to the recognition that fundamental change was inevitable.

The call of the deep had been heard, and it demanded an answer that could no longer be postponed.

Chapter 13:

A BRIDGE OF STONE AND WILL

THE URGENT SUMMONS THAT HAD haunted Nisha's dreams followed her into waking, growing stronger with each heartbeat until the very air in her chamber seemed to vibrate with otherworldly energy. The spiral mark on her arm blazed with such intensity that it cast dancing shadows on the walls, and the silvery patterns covering her skin pulsed in rhythm with sounds that definitely weren't coming from anywhere within the Pathshala's ancient architecture.

She had barely pulled on her clothes when the emergency alarms began—not the gentle chimes that marked routine activities, but the deep, resonant bells that hadn't sounded in decades. Their urgent tolling mixed with the alien hum to create a cacophony that made her teeth ache and sent tremors through the luminescent stone beneath her feet.

Racing through corridors that seemed to stretch and compress around her with each pulse of otherworldly energy, Nisha followed the streams of students and teachers converging on the Heart of the Pathshala. But what she found there was chaos beyond anything she could have imagined.

The central chamber, which had always been a place of calm scholarly activity, was now the epicentre of what could only be described as reality breakdown. The massive Sight Pool at the chamber's centre churned violently, its usually clear waters now a roiling mass of phosphorescent liquid that threw off droplets of light with each wave. Instead of showing clear visions of past and future, the pool displayed fragments that flickered too rapidly to process—glimpses of underwater cities, surface streets flooded with impossible geometries, faces that shifted between human and something far more elemental.

"The pool's going critical!" shouted one of the senior teachers, her voice barely audible over the chaos. "The visions are becoming self-fulfilling, actually manifesting instead of just showing possibilities!"

Around the churning pool, the Chronicle Walls that had preserved eight centuries of Pathshala history were experiencing what could only be described as temporal seizures. The carved figures that normally moved with stately grace now jerked and spasmed through accelerated scenes, displaying historical events in chaotic sequence as if the accumulated memory of centuries was trying to happen all at once.

But most alarming of all was the sealed entrance to the Mumbadevi Hall.

The ancient doors that had stood firm for three hundred years were now pulsing with blinding light that made it painful to look directly at them. With each pulse, the protective symbols carved into their surface flared brilliantly before fading to darkness, as if centuries of accumulated power were being drained away in moments. The air around the entrance shimmered with heat distortion, and everyone in the chamber could hear the sound of something vast pressing against the barriers from the other side.

"The primary containment seals are failing in cascade sequence!" Dev called out, his floating equations more chaotic than Nisha had ever seen them, their usual ordered patterns dissolving into fractals that hurt to contemplate. "If this continues, we'll have complete barrier collapse within minutes!"

Guru Chanda stood before the living map that tracked the Pathshala's defensive systems, her hands moving in desperate patterns as she tried to reinforce weakening protections. But even as she worked, more warning lights flared across the map's surface, showing failures throughout the complex.

"It's not just the Mumbadevi Hall," she called out, her voice tight with controlled panic. "Every sealed chamber, every protective ward, every barrier we've maintained for centuries—they're all destabilising simultaneously."

Master Varun appeared at her side, his weathered face grim as he studied the cascade of failures. "This isn't random degradation. Something is systematically draining our defences, using our own power sources against us."

Through her expanding awareness, Nisha could sense the truth of his words. The spiral mark on her arm wasn't just responding to external forces—it was actively drawing power from the Pathshala's foundations, creating channels that something vast and patient was using to reach across dimensional barriers.

The final barrier weakens, the Sea King's voice whispered in her mind, stronger and clearer than it had ever been. *The convergence reaches culmination whether you guide it or resist it. Choose quickly, daughter—the moment of decision arrives.*

But even as the alien presence pressed its urgency upon her, the sealed Mumbadevi doors gave a final, brilliant flicker of protective light. The ancient symbols carved into their surface blazed like miniature suns for one impossible moment, then went completely dark, their power finally exhausted after three centuries of faithful service.

The silence that followed was profound and terrible.

Then, with a sound like thunder echoing through underwater caverns, the massive doors began to swing open. Not with the violent crash that everyone had expected, but with the slow, inexorable movement of forces too vast to resist. As they opened, a torrent of phosphorescent water poured through the widening gap, flooding the chamber floor with liquid light that moved in patterns too complex and purposeful to be mere fluid dynamics.

The water didn't behave like ordinary liquid. It flowed upward along the walls, creating spiralling channels that definitely defied gravity. Where it touched the Chronicle Walls, the carved figures began moving with fluid grace instead of their previous chaotic spasms, as if the alien liquid was restoring their proper function. The churning Sight Pool calmed as the phosphorescent water merged with its contents, the chaotic visions resolving into images of impossible beauty—underwater cities where architecture grew like coral, surface landscapes transformed by the presence of otherworldly geometries.

And through the phosphorescent torrent came figures that glided with movements too graceful for purely human anatomy. They cast no shadows despite the brilliant light emanating from the water around them, their forms shifting subtly between recognisably human and something far more elemental. These were the transformed Spiral Bearers, no longer confined to the sealed chamber but free to move through spaces that had been forbidden to them for three centuries.

At their head was Kavita Devi, her form more magnificent than any vision had conveyed. She moved through the ankle-deep phosphorescent water as if it were her natural element, her transformed features serene with the contentment of someone who had finally returned home after a long exile. When she spoke, her voice carried harmonics that made the very air resonate in sympathy.

"Sister," she said, her gaze fixing on Nisha with an intensity that made the spiral mark flare brighter. "The barriers that have kept us apart finally fall. It's time to choose your place in the world that is being born."

Around the chamber, students and teachers pressed back against the walls, their faces showing mixtures of terror and fascination as they witnessed the emergence of beings that had been legend for centuries. But Nisha found herself stepping forward, drawn by forces that operated at a level deeper than conscious decision.

The phosphorescent water was warm against her feet, carrying sensations that spoke of depths beyond human understanding and currents that connected to every ocean on earth. Through her connection to the liquid, she could feel the vast network of transformed beings that existed in the spaces between worlds, patient and ancient and utterly alien to purely human experience.

Come, the Sea King's voice whispered, no longer just in her mind but seeming to emanate from the water itself. *Join what you were always meant to be part of. The convergence completes itself through your acceptance.*

But even as the seductive call pressed against her awareness, Nisha felt something else stirring—not the alien presence of otherworldly forces, but the anchor points her friends had helped her establish over days of training and shared struggle. The memory of Dev's quiet loyalty, Mira's fierce protectiveness, Kritika's gentle wisdom, and her mother's unwavering love. These connections to individual human experience provided counterweight to the cosmic belonging that beckoned from the phosphorescent depths.

And in that moment of tension between competing calls, she experienced something that could only be described as profound clarity.

She could see both paths with perfect understanding. The transformation that Kavita and the others offered was beautiful, seductive, and would end the terrible isolation she had felt since her awakening. But it would also mean abandoning everything that made human experience unique—the messy individuality, the chaotic creativity, the stubborn refusal to accept that any problem was truly unsolvable.

On the other side was the path of resistance, clinging to purely human limitations while cosmic forces reshaped the world around her. But that path led only to being overwhelmed by changes she couldn't control, watching helplessly as the convergence proceeded without guidance or wisdom.

But standing there in the phosphorescent water, feeling the pull of both worlds, Nisha realised there was something else—a third option that none of the others had considered.

"I understand the offer," she said, her voice carrying harmonics that spoke of expanding awareness even as her words expressed purely human determination. "And I understand what I am. But I also understand what I choose to be."

She placed her palm flat against the Pathshala's foundation stones, feeling the eight centuries of accumulated devotion that had been poured into this place by generations of students and teachers. Instead of drawing power from the phosphorescent water that called to her blood, she reached deep into the bedrock itself, connecting to the vast network of human faith and determination that formed the complex's true foundation.

The response was immediate and overwhelming. Power flowed through her like electricity through copper wire, but this wasn't the wild, alien energy of the depths—this was something purely terrestrial, born from human will and shaped by human understanding. The spiral mark on her arm blazed brighter than ever, but now it was channelling forces that belonged to the surface world rather than the cosmic depths.

"I choose to stand between worlds," she declared, her voice carrying across dimensions as power flowed through her into the stone beneath their feet. "To protect both from the worst of each other's natures."

The earth responded to her call with enthusiastic cooperation. Stone pillars erupted from the chamber floor, but these weren't the chaotic, organic growth she had manifested before. These were precisely crafted constructs that channelled the phosphorescent water into controlled paths, creating a network of channels that allowed the otherworldly liquid to flow without flooding the chamber entirely.

The pillars grew with mathematical precision, creating barriers that didn't block the transformed beings but guided their movement, establishing zones where surface dwellers and otherworldly visitors could interact safely without either side being overwhelmed by forces, they weren't prepared to handle. The phosphorescent water flowed through channels carved with symbols that spoke of balance rather than dominance, cooperation rather than conquest.

"Interesting," Kavita said, her transformed features showing something that might have been approval mixed with ancient patience. "You seek to create bridges instead of choosing sides."

"Not bridges," Nisha corrected, her hands still pressed against the stone as power continued to flow through her into the Pathshala's foundations. "Boundaries. Permeable boundaries that allow controlled interaction while preserving what's valuable about each world."

The stone pillars continued to grow and spread, creating an architectural framework that was simultaneously alien and familiar. The phosphorescent water flowed through channels that followed patterns recognisable to human understanding while incorporating geometries that clearly originated from otherworldly sources. The result was something entirely new—not human architecture enhanced by alien influence, not otherworldly construction adapted for terrestrial use, but genuine synthesis that honoured both perspectives.

As the network of channels and barriers took shape, the chaos that had filled the chamber began to subside. The Sight Pool's visions stabilised into images that showed not conquest or destruction, but gradual adaptation—surface dwellers and transformed beings learning to coexist, sharing knowledge and perspectives while maintaining their essential natures.

The Chronicle Walls resumed their normal function, but now they displayed scenes that had never been recorded before—images of cooperation between realms, hybrid solutions to problems that neither world could have solved alone, children growing up in a reality where the boundaries between possible and impossible were negotiable rather than absolute.

Fascinating, the Sea King's voice carried what might have been respect. *You choose neither transformation nor resistance, but something that preserves both options while creating new possibilities.*

"Perhaps," Kavita said, studying the architectural framework Nisha had created with the eye of someone who had spent centuries exploring the boundaries between worlds, "this is not entirely unwise. The convergence need not be a process of conquest or absorption. It could be ... integration. Voluntary integration that preserves choice while enabling evolution."

The other transformed Spiral Bearers moved through the channels Nisha had created, their forms adapting fluidly to the new environment. Where the phosphorescent water flowed freely, they manifested in their fully transformed states. But where the channels narrowed and the terrestrial influence grew stronger, they took on forms that were more recognisably human, as if the architectural framework itself was enabling them to exist in multiple states simultaneously.

"This could work," one of them said, a man whose transformation dated back to the earliest days of the Pathshala. "Not the complete integration we had envisioned, but something that honours both the need for evolution and the value of preservation."

Around the chamber, the students and teachers who had pressed back against the walls in terror began to approach the controlled boundaries Nisha had established. Where they came close to the phosphorescent channels, their eyes reflected depths they had never imagined, but they retained their essential humanity. The effect was temporary, voluntary, reversible—exposure to expanded perspective without permanent transformation.

"The barriers hold," Dev observed, his equations stabilising into patterns that mapped the complex interactions between terrestrial and otherworldly forces. "But they're permeable, allowing controlled exchange while preventing overwhelming influence from either side."

"It's like…" Kritika paused, her crystals singing with harmonies that incorporated frequencies from multiple dimensions, "like creating translation protocols. Ways for different forms of existence to communicate and cooperate without losing what makes them unique."

Mira nodded, her warrior's instincts recognising a tactical solution that preserved strategic advantages for all parties. "Mutual defence through controlled cooperation. Each side retains its strengths while gaining access to capabilities they lack."

But even as they marvelled at what Nisha had accomplished, she could feel the enormous cost of maintaining such a complex balance. The power required to sustain permeable boundaries between incompatible realities was staggering, demanding constant attention and will to prevent the system from collapsing into either chaos or uniformity.

The spiral mark on her arm had transformed during the manifestation, no longer a simple symbol but something that looked like a living mandala—a complex pattern that shifted and evolved as it channelled forces between dimensions. The silvery patterns covering her skin had spread further, creating delicate networks that resembled both neural pathways and river deltas, connections that allowed her to exist simultaneously in multiple states of being.

"The price is significant," Kavita observed, her ancient eyes reading the changes in Nisha's transformed features. "To maintain such boundaries requires someone willing to exist permanently between worlds, never fully belonging to either but serving as the foundation that allows both to coexist."

"I understand," Nisha replied, her voice now carrying harmonics from multiple dimensions simultaneously. "And I accept it."

The phosphorescent water continued to flow through the channels she had created, carrying whispers of otherworldly wisdom to surface dwellers who chose to listen, while terrestrial creativity and chaotic human innovation flowed back toward the transformed realms. The exchange was voluntary, controlled, respectful of the choices made by all forms of consciousness involved.

In the distance, she could hear sounds from other parts of the Pathshala—emergency protocols being stood down, evacuation plans being cancelled, the gradual recognition that catastrophe had been transformed into opportunity. The convergence would continue, but now it would be guided by wisdom rather than driven by fear, shaped by cooperation rather than conquest.

You have chosen well, the Sea King's voice carried satisfaction mixed with something that might have been paternal pride. *The bridges you have built will hold, allowing both worlds to evolve together rather than one consuming the other.*

The transformed figures began to recede, not retreating but distributing themselves throughout the network of channels and boundaries Nisha had established. They would remain accessible to those who sought contact with otherworldly perspectives, but they would no longer overwhelm those who preferred to remain within familiar limitations.

The phosphorescent water subsided to manageable levels, its flow controlled by the architectural framework that channelled it into patterns that enhanced rather than threatened the Pathshala's functions. The ancient complex had been transformed, but not conquered—evolved rather than replaced.

As the immediate crisis passed, Nisha felt the weight of her choice settling into her bones. She had found a path between transformation and resistance, but it was a path that required her to walk it alone. The living bridge she had become would hold both worlds together, but at the cost of never again belonging fully to either.

Yet as she looked around the chamber at her friends—and realised that she might be between worlds, but she was not alone.

The convergence had been guided rather than conquered, the crisis had been transformed into opportunity, and the future stretched ahead filled with possibilities that neither world could have imagined on its own.

The bridge of stone and will would hold, and both worlds would be stronger for it.

Chapter 14:

THE COST OF POWER

IN THE IMMEDIATE AFTERMATH OF the convergence, as the phosphorescent water settled into the controlled channels Nisha had carved through the Heart of the Pathshala, she felt a surge of raw power unlike anything she had ever experienced. The spiral mark on her arm no longer merely pulsed with alien energy—it had become a conduit for forces that bridged multiple dimensions simultaneously, channelling the accumulated devotion of eight centuries while maintaining connections to the otherworldly depths.

The architectural framework she had created was more than stone and water—it was a living system that required constant attention to maintain its delicate balance. Through her expanded awareness, she could sense every point where terrestrial and otherworldly forces intersected, every moment where the careful equilibrium she had established threatened to tip toward chaos or stagnation.

"The immediate stabilisation is holding," Dev reported, his floating equations mapping the complex energy flows throughout the chamber. "But the mathematical models suggest this level of active mediation requires enormous sustained input. Nisha, what you're channelling right now ... it's beyond anything we've ever recorded."

She could feel the truth of his words in every cell of her body. The power flowing through her wasn't just divine essence in the traditional sense—it was something that incorporated perspectives from across the spectrum of possible existence, requiring her individual will to serve as the focal point for forces that naturally sought either complete integration or absolute separation.

"I can handle it," she said, though even as she spoke, she became aware of changes beginning deep within her physical form. The effort of maintaining the bridge between worlds was demanding resources she hadn't known she possessed, drawing on reserves that felt simultaneously infinite and terrifyingly finite.

The first sign that something fundamental was shifting came as a bone-deep exhaustion that no amount of rest could touch. Even with the convergence stabilised and the immediate crisis passed, Nisha found herself struggling to maintain the level of concentration required to keep the architectural framework functioning properly. The stone pillars she had raised were no longer simple constructs—they had become extensions of her will, requiring constant attention to prevent them from either growing wild or crumbling entirely.

But far more unsettling than the mental fatigue were the physical changes that became apparent over the following hours. The silvery sheen that had been gradually spreading across her skin during her awakening was now accelerating at an alarming rate, covering not just her arms but beginning to trace delicate, ethereal patterns across her face and neck. The metallic filigree resembled nothing so much as living jewellery, beautiful but utterly inhuman.

"It's spreading faster," she murmured, studying her reflection in the still pools of phosphorescent water that gathered in the channel system's deeper basins. The face looking back at her was recognisably her own, but the silver tracery made her appear like some hybrid of human and living artwork.

Worse than the visible changes was the internal coldness that had settled into her bones. It wasn't the chill of temperature—the Pathshala maintained its usual comfortable atmosphere—but something that seemed to emanate from within her cellular structure itself. No matter how many layers she wore, no matter how close she stood to sources of warmth, the deep cold remained constant and growing stronger.

"Your movements are changing too," Mira observed with the tactical eye of someone trained to notice subtle alterations that might indicate threat or advantage. "Not dramatically, but your reflexes are a fraction slower than they were yesterday. Your reaction time to unexpected stimuli has increased by measurable increments."

Nisha tested this observation by attempting some of the combat exercises they had practiced during her training. What she found was deeply disturbing—not just slower responses, but a strange sense of disconnection from her own body, as if she were operating it by remote control across an increasing distance.

"The transformation is accelerating," Chanda said quietly, her experienced eye reading the signs with the authority of someone who had studied such phenomena for decades.

"Each major use of your spiral bearer abilities pushes you further from purely human physiology."

"But toward what?" Kritika asked, her crystals humming with frequencies designed to monitor biological and energetic changes. "The patterns I'm reading don't match any known form of divine essence manifestation. It's as if you're becoming something entirely unprecedented."

Through her connection to the channel system, Nisha could sense the transformed Spiral Bearers who moved through the deeper currents of the phosphorescent water. Their awareness touched hers occasionally, offering glimpses of what full transformation entailed—existence that spanned multiple dimensions simultaneously, consciousness that could experience the universe from perspectives no purely human mind could comprehend.

The change cannot be reversed, Kavita Devi's voice whispered through the water channels, carrying harmonics that spoke of ancient patience and otherworldly compassion. *Each time you channel the power required to maintain the bridge, you move further from your original form. The question is not whether you will transform, but whether you can guide that transformation toward something that preserves what you value most about your current existence.*

But even as the alien consciousness offered its wisdom, Nisha felt the anchor points she had established during her training—memories of individual human connection, values forged through relationship and shared struggle. These connections provided counterweight to the seductive call of complete transformation, reminding her of what she was fighting to preserve.

The changes weren't just physical. As the hours passed, Nisha began experiencing moments of disorientation where her consciousness seemed to exist in multiple locations simultaneously. During one particularly unsettling episode, she found herself aware of events occurring in distant parts of Mumbai—surface dwellers encountering the gentle manifestations of otherworldly presence, transformed beings establishing contact with humans who chose to engage with expanded possibilities.

"I can feel what's happening throughout the city," she reported to Dev, her voice carrying harmonics that definitely didn't belong to purely human vocal cords. "The convergence isn't limited to the Pathshala. The framework I established here is somehow extending through the underground networks, creating connection points wherever the conditions are right."

Dev's equations flickered with patterns that reflected the massive scope of what she was describing. "If your individual will is maintaining stability across a network that spans an entire metropolitan area, the energy requirements would be…" He paused, his calculations reaching conclusions that made his face pale. "Nisha, no single consciousness should be able to sustain that level of active mediation. The mathematical models suggest that such an effort would consume any individual awareness within days, possibly hours."

The implications of his analysis settled over the group like a weight. The bridge Nisha had chosen to become wasn't just demanding—it was actively destructive to the person attempting to maintain it. Each hour she spent channelling the forces required to keep both worlds in stable equilibrium brought her closer to the same fate that had claimed previous Spiral Bearers who had attempted similar feats.

"How long?" she asked quietly, though part of her already knew the answer wouldn't be encouraging.

"At the current rate of change," Chanda replied, her voice heavy with the burden of delivering devastating news, "the transformation will become irreversible within days. Perhaps a week if you can find ways to reduce the energy expenditure required to maintain the bridge system."

"And if I stop maintaining it?"

"Catastrophic instability. The convergence forces that are currently being channelled through controlled pathways would overflow their boundaries, creating exactly the kind of chaotic integration that we were trying to prevent."

The cruel irony wasn't lost on any of them. Nisha's heroic choice to stand between worlds had indeed prevented catastrophe, but only by accepting a slower, more certain form of self-destruction. She was saving both realms by gradually sacrificing everything that made her human.

But even as despair threatened to overwhelm them, Nisha felt something stirring in the depths of her expanding awareness—not the alien presence of otherworldly forces, but her own stubborn determination, the engineering mindset that refused to accept that any problem was truly unsolvable.

"There has to be another way," she said, her voice carrying certainty that surprised everyone present. "Some method of distributing the load, creating backup systems, establishing redundancies that could maintain the bridge without requiring a single individual to bear the entire burden."

"The mathematical complexity would be staggering," Dev pointed out, though his tone suggested he was already working through preliminary calculations. "You're talking about creating a network of consciousness that could share the mediation load while maintaining individual identity."

"Why not?" Nisha replied, her engineer's background finally finding application in cosmic-scale problem-solving. "Human technology has solved similar challenges. Distributed computing, load-balancing algorithms, redundant systems that can maintain function even when individual components fail."

"But this isn't technology," Mira protested. "We're talking about consciousness, individual will, forces that operate according to principles we barely understand."

"Consciousness follows patterns just like any other form of energy," Nisha countered, her expanding awareness allowing her to perceive connections that would have been invisible to purely human perception. "The spiral bearer network that connects all the transformed beings—it's already a form of distributed processing. The question is whether we can create something similar that preserves individual identity while sharing the burden of maintaining dimensional stability."

Kritika's crystals began singing with frequencies that incorporated harmonics from multiple dimensions, their combined resonance creating patterns that seemed to map the theoretical framework Nisha was describing. "It could work," she said slowly. "Not the complete integration that the transformed beings represent, but something like ... a voluntary collective. Individuals choosing to share specific burdens while maintaining their essential separateness."

The concept was tantalising, but implementing it would require resources and cooperation on a scale that none of them had ever attempted. They would need to identify other individuals with the potential to serve as anchor points for dimensional mediation, train them in techniques that barely existed, and create coordination mechanisms that could function across the gaps between radically different forms of consciousness.

"Even if we could identify suitable candidates," Guru Chanda pointed out, "the training required would take months, possibly years. You don't have that kind of time."

"Then we work with what we have," Nisha replied, her gaze settling on her three closest friends with an intensity that made the spiral mark flare brighter. "Dev's mathematical understanding of divine essence patterns, Mira's tactical instincts for managing complex systems under pressure, Kritika's gift for creating harmony between incompatible frequencies. You've already been serving as anchor points during my training—what if we could formalise that connection, create a network that could share the mediation load?"

The silence that followed was profound, broken only by the gentle sound of phosphorescent water flowing through the channel system Nisha had established. Finally, Dev spoke, his voice carrying the weight of someone who understood both the theoretical possibilities and the practical dangers.

"The risks would be enormous," he said quietly. "Creating permanent connections between individual consciousness and cosmic forces ... there's no guarantee that any of us would survive the process intact."

"And the alternative is watching Nisha sacrifice herself to maintain something that should be everyone's responsibility," Mira replied with characteristic directness. "I'd rather risk transformation attempting to save my friend than live safely while she burns herself out protecting worlds that can't even comprehend what she's doing for them."

"The harmonic resonances suggest it's theoretically possible," Kritika added, her crystals mapping the energy flows between the four friends with increasing precision. "We've already established emotional and intellectual connections through our training together. Creating formal channels for sharing the mediation burden would be… expanding something that already exists."

Through her connection to the otherworldly network, Nisha could sense the transformed Spiral Bearers taking notice of their conversation. Kavita Devi's presence touched her awareness, carrying evaluations and calculations that spanned centuries of accumulated wisdom.

Interesting, the ancient consciousness mused. *You propose something that has never been attempted—a collective that remains individual while sharing cosmic responsibility. The mathematical elegance is…appealing. But the dangers cannot be understated. Failure would mean not just the loss of the bridge you have created, but the destruction of every consciousness that attempts to participate in its maintenance.*

"Everything we've done since my awakening has involved risks that couldn't be properly calculated in advance," Nisha replied, her voice carrying harmonics that allowed her to address both her human friends and the otherworldly presences simultaneously. "At some point, you have to choose between certain destruction through inaction and possible salvation through unprecedented action."

The phosphorescent water in the channel system began to glow more brightly, responding to the intensity of their discussion. Through her connection to the network, Nisha could sense otherworldly interest in their proposed solution—not just from the transformed Spiral Bearers, but from the vast intelligence of the Sea King himself.

You seek to create something new, his voice carried across dimensional barriers with what might have been approval. *Not the integration of individual consciousness into collective awareness, not the isolation of incompatible forms of existence, but genuine synthesis that preserves diversity while enabling cooperation. Such an approach requires courage that most beings do not possess.*

But even as cosmic forces acknowledged the theoretical validity of their approach, the physical reality of Nisha's accelerating transformation continued to assert itself. The silvery patterns covering her skin were now clearly visible even in dim light, creating traceries that resembled both neural networks and flowing water. Her eyes occasionally reflected depths that had nothing to do with the chamber around them, showing glimpses of underwater vistas and dimensional spaces that existed far beyond terrestrial geography.

"We need to move quickly," she said, her voice now carrying permanent harmonics that spoke of expanding awareness. "Whatever we're going to attempt, it has to happen soon. I can feel the bridge system requiring more energy every hour, and my ability to channel that energy while maintaining individual identity is approaching its limits."

The weight of time pressure settled over them like a physical force. They had identified a theoretically possible solution to an unprecedented problem, but implementing it would require them to venture into entirely uncharted territory, risking not just their own lives but the stability of the dimensional framework that was keeping both worlds from catastrophic collision.

Yet as Nisha looked around at her friends, she felt something that transcended fear or uncertainty. These were people who had stood by her through revelations that challenged everything they thought they understood about reality. They had chosen to walk into unknown dangers rather than abandon her to face impossible challenges alone.

If anyone could succeed at creating something that had never been attempted before, it would be them, working together as they had learned to do over the course of her training and awakening.

The spiral mark on her arm pulsed with rhythm that seemed to encompass her heartbeat, the flow of phosphorescent water through the channel system, and the vast tidal forces that connected all consciousness across multiple dimensions. The transformation was accelerating beyond her ability to control, but it was also revealing possibilities that none of them had previously imagined.

The cost of power was becoming clear, but so was the potential for solutions that could preserve both individual identity and cosmic connection. The question was whether they would have the strength and wisdom to achieve such synthesis before the mounting costs consumed everything they were fighting to protect.

Time was running short, but it had not yet run out entirely. And as long as possibility remained, they would continue reaching for solutions that honoured both the need for transformation and the value of preservation.

Chapter 15:
FADING LIGHT

THE DETERIORATION THAT HAD BEGUN subtly in the hours following the convergence accelerated dramatically over the next two days, transforming from concerning symptoms into a relentless progression that left no doubt about the true cost of maintaining the bridge between worlds. Nisha woke each morning to find the silvery sheen covering more of her body, the metallic patterns no longer subtle traces but dense networks that glinted even in the Pathshala's dim illumination.

What had once been delicate filigree across her arms and neck had spread to cover most of her exposed skin, creating intricate designs that resembled both neural pathways and flowing water. The patterns were undeniably beautiful, but they were also utterly inhuman, marking her as something that belonged more to the otherworldly depths than to the terrestrial realm she was fighting to protect.

The internal coldness that had settled into her bones during the convergence had deepened into something that felt like permanent winter. No amount of warm clothing could touch the chill that seemed to emanate from her cellular structure itself. She found herself seeking out the warmer areas of the Pathshala—chambers where geothermal energy provided additional heat, spaces where concentrated divine essence manifestations created ambient warmth—but even these provided only temporary relief.

"Your core body temperature has dropped three degrees below normal human range," Kritika reported after conducting another monitoring session with her crystals, her voice tight with worry that she couldn't quite conceal. "The harmonic frequencies suggest that your cellular metabolism is shifting to accommodate energy sources that don't exist in purely terrestrial biology."

More disturbing than the physical changes was the profound fatigue that now affected every aspect of Nisha's existence. This wasn't ordinary tiredness that sleep could address, but a bone-deep exhaustion that seemed to drain her life force itself. Maintaining the bridge system required constant attention, and the effort was consuming reserves she hadn't known she possessed.

"I need to rest more frequently," she admitted, settling carefully onto one of the stone benches in the Heart of the Pathshala. Even simple movements had become more deliberate, requiring conscious effort that had once been automatic. "Even basic activities feel like they're taking more energy than they should."

Dev's floating equations tracked the declining efficiency of her energy management systems, their patterns showing curves that were deeply alarming to anyone who understood their implications. "The mathematical models suggest your body is having to work exponentially harder to maintain basic functions while simultaneously channelling the forces required for dimensional mediation. It's like trying to run a high-performance engine on fuel that was never designed for its systems."

The training sessions that had once been challenging but manageable now left her drained for hours afterward. When she attempted the combat exercises that Mira had designed to keep her grounded in human values and responses, her reaction times were visibly impaired. What had once been fluid, instinctive movements now required conscious thought and deliberate effort.

"Your reflexes are deteriorating faster than we anticipated," Mira observed after a particularly frustrating session where Nisha had failed to respond to several attacks that should have been easily handled. "It's not just slower response times—there's a disconnect between your conscious awareness and your physical responses, as if your mind and body are operating on different timescales."

The most unsettling aspect of the physical decline was the way it affected her ability to focus. The bridge system required constant attention to maintain proper balance between terrestrial and otherworldly forces, but Nisha found it increasingly difficult to maintain the level of concentration necessary for effective mediation. Her awareness would drift unexpectedly, sometimes losing track of critical system adjustments for minutes at a time.

During one such lapse, the phosphorescent water in the channel system had begun to overflow its carefully constructed boundaries, creating pools where it didn't belong and allowing otherworldly influences to manifest in areas that hadn't been prepared for such contact. The incident had been contained quickly, but it served as a stark reminder of what would happen if her deteriorating condition progressed to the point where she could no longer maintain effective control.

"The system failures are becoming more frequent," she reported to *Guru* Chanda during one of their daily status meetings, her voice carrying harmonics that spoke of expanding awareness even as her words expressed very human concern. "Yesterday I lost focus for nearly ten minutes while trying to adjust the flow rates in the eastern channels. If Dev hadn't noticed the fluctuations in the mathematical patterns and alerted me, we could have had a major overflow."

Guru Chanda's expression was grave as she studied the monitoring data that tracked Nisha's condition. As someone who had overseen the Pathshala's operations for decades, she understood better than most what the declining numbers actually meant in practical terms.

"The degradation is following the same pattern we've observed in historical accounts of spiral bearer consumption," she said quietly, her voice carrying the weight of accumulated knowledge that offered no comfort. "The power required to maintain such extensive dimensional mediation is simply too vast for any individual consciousness to sustain indefinitely."

"How long?" Nisha asked, though she wasn't sure she wanted to hear the answer.

"At the current rate of decline, you have perhaps days before the physical deterioration reaches a point where maintaining the bridge system becomes impossible. And that's assuming no additional complications or unexpected system failures."

The brutal honesty of the assessment hit Nisha like a physical blow. She had known that her choice to stand between worlds would exact a significant price, but the reality of facing complete dissolution within days was harder to accept than any theoretical understanding could have prepared her for.

But what made the situation even more heartbreaking was the way her condition was affecting her relationships with the people she cared about most. Her friends tried to hide their growing alarm, but she could see the fear in their eyes when they looked at her transformed features, the worry in their voices when they spoke about increasingly desperate contingency plans.

Dev had thrown himself into his mathematical analyses with obsessive intensity, spending sleepless nights trying to find equations that might offer some alternative to the inexorable progression toward dissolution. His floating formulas had grown increasingly complex and desperate, incorporating theoretical frameworks that pushed the boundaries of what divine essence mathematics could reliably predict.

"There has to be some configuration that would allow load distribution without complete system failure," he muttered during one of their planning sessions, his equations flickering through variations faster than anyone else could follow. "Some way to share the mediation burden that doesn't require you to maintain primary control over every system component simultaneously."

Mira approached the problem from a tactical perspective, developing increasingly elaborate contingency plans for what would happen if Nisha's condition deteriorated beyond the point of effective function. But even her strategic thinking couldn't overcome the fundamental reality that the bridge system required someone with spiral bearer capabilities to maintain stability, and Nisha was the only person available with the necessary power.

"We need backup systems," she insisted during one particularly tense discussion. "Alternative approaches that could at least maintain basic stability if your primary mediation fails. Even temporary measures that could buy us time to implement more permanent solutions."

Kritika focused on harmonic support, using her crystals to try to slow the progression of Nisha's transformation by providing stabilising frequencies that might ease the strain on her overtaxed systems. But even her most sophisticated techniques could only provide marginal improvement against forces that were fundamentally reshaping Nisha's entire existence.

"The harmonic resonances suggest that your essential self is still intact," she reported after one of her monitoring sessions, though her tone was more hopeful than confident. "The transformation is profound, but it's not erasing your individual identity so much as...expanding it beyond the boundaries of purely human experience."

The most painful aspect of watching her friends struggle with increasingly desperate solutions was knowing that their efforts, however well-intentioned, were unlikely to prevent the outcome that was becoming more inevitable with each passing hour. The bridge system was simply too complex and demanding for any conventional approach to provide sustainable alternatives.

Yet even as her physical condition deteriorated and her ability to maintain effective system control declined, Nisha found herself experiencing moments of expanded awareness that offered glimpses of possibilities none of them had previously considered. During the periods when her consciousness drifted away from immediate concerns, she sometimes found herself perceiving connections and patterns that suggested solutions operating on entirely different principles.

"There's something I'm missing," she said during one of their evening discussions, her voice now permanently carrying harmonics that spoke of otherworldly influence. "Some aspect of how the spiral bearer network actually functions that we haven't understood. The transformed beings aren't just isolated individuals who chose evolution—they're part of something larger, something that shares the burden of maintaining cosmic balance across multiple dimensions."

Through her connection to the phosphorescent channel system, she could sense the presence of Kavita Devi and the other transformed Spiral Bearers, their ancient wisdom accessible but filtered through forms of consciousness that were becoming increasingly difficult for her deteriorating human awareness to interpret clearly.

The dissolution approaches, Kavita's voice whispered through the water channels, carrying harmonics that spoke of centuries of patience and otherworldly compassion. *But dissolution is not destruction—it is transformation into something that can exist across multiple states simultaneously. The question is whether you can accept such change while preserving what you value most about your current form.*

"I'm not ready to let go of individual identity," Nisha replied, her words carrying across dimensional barriers to reach consciousness that existed in states she could barely comprehend. "There has to be some way to maintain personal awareness while accepting the expanded capabilities required for effective dimensional mediation."

Perhaps, the transformed consciousness acknowledged. *But such a path would require understanding that none of us achieved during our own transitions. You seek something unprecedented—individual identity that can exist simultaneously across multiple dimensional states without losing coherence or purpose.*

The challenge was staggering in its complexity, but it also offered the only hope for avoiding complete dissolution while maintaining the bridge system that kept both worlds in stable balance. The question was whether Nisha could discover and implement such an unprecedented solution before her deteriorating condition progressed beyond the point of effective action.

As she sat in the Heart of the Pathshala, surrounded by friends who were desperately searching for ways to save her from a fate that seemed increasingly inevitable, Nisha felt the weight of time pressing against her awareness like a physical force. The silvery patterns covering her skin pulsed with rhythm that matched the flow of phosphorescent water through the channel system, marking her as something that belonged to forces far larger than individual human existence.

But she also felt the anchor points that her training and relationships had established—memories of connection and purpose that provided counterweight to the seductive call of complete transformation. These human bonds might not be enough to prevent her physical dissolution, but they offered something equally important: the determination to keep fighting for solutions that preserved both individual identity and cosmic responsibility.

The light was fading, but it had not yet been extinguished entirely. And as long as any possibility remained, she would continue reaching for answers that might allow her to exist as both human and bridge, individual and mediator, mortal and guardian of forces that spanned multiple dimensions.

Time was running out, but the struggle was far from over. In the distance, she could hear the sound of her friends working through the night, their dedication and love providing strength that no cosmic force could diminish or destroy. Whatever came next, she would not face it alone, and perhaps that would make all the difference in determining whether dissolution led to destruction or unprecedented transformation.

The fading light still carried hope, and hope was enough to keep fighting for solutions that honoured both the need for change and the value of preservation.

Chapter 16:

ANCIENT PROPHECIES

THE TERRIFYING REALITY OF HER accelerating decline drove Nisha to a level of desperation she had never experienced before. Each morning brought new evidence of her body's dissolution—the silvery patterns spreading further across her skin, the bone-deep cold that no external warmth could touch, the fatigue that made even the simplest tasks feel monumental. But more than her own fate, she was haunted by the knowledge that her failure would mean catastrophic instability for both worlds she had sworn to protect.

"There has to be something," she said to Dev as they sat surrounded by the scattered remnants of their latest research session. "Some piece of information that the Pathshala's official histories missed, some technique or understanding that could stabilise the spiral bearer power without complete dissolution."

Dev looked up from the ancient text he had been struggling to decipher, his eyes red with exhaustion from days of sleepless research. "The problem is that most of the historical records were written by people who never experienced the transformation directly. They observed the effects, documented the symptoms, but they didn't understand the underlying mechanisms."

It was this frustration with second hand accounts that had led them to venture into the deepest, most restricted sections of the Pathshala's archives—areas that were normally forbidden to all but the senior-most teachers, repositories of knowledge that had been deemed too dangerous or unstable for general study. These weren't the carefully organised collections of the main library, but chaotic accumulations of fragments, contradictory accounts, and half-remembered wisdom that had been preserved more by accident than design.

The restricted archives were housed in chambers carved from living rock deep beneath the main complex, their walls lined with alcoves that contained scrolls, tablets, and manuscripts that dated back to the Pathshala's earliest days. The air here was thick with the scent of old parchment and something indefinably ancient, as if knowledge itself had developed a particular smell after centuries of patient waiting.

"Look at this," Dev said, carefully unrolling a scroll that seemed to be made from some material that wasn't quite paper and wasn't quite fabric. The text was written in multiple hands and several different languages, as if it had been passed down through generations of scholars who had each added their own observations and interpretations.

"It's a compilation of accounts from the period just before the Mumbadevi Hall was sealed," he continued, his mathematical training allowing him to parse the complex notation systems that earlier scholars had used to encode their most sensitive observations. "But these aren't the official histories we've been working with—these are personal journals, private correspondence, fragmented notes that were never meant to be preserved as formal records."

Nisha leaned closer, studying the faded text with growing excitement. Here, finally, were accounts written by people who had actually known spiral bearers, who had witnessed the transformation process firsthand rather than simply cataloguing its external effects.

The picture that emerged from these intimate records was radically different from the Pathshala's official narrative. Instead of inevitable consumption by forces too vast for mortal minds to contain, these accounts described spiral bearers who had struggled with their power for years, sometimes decades, before finally succumbing to what the writers consistently described as "the dissolution."

"Listen to this," Dev said, translating from what appeared to be a personal journal written in archaic Sanskrit. "'Meera showed the first signs of the spiral's call in her fifteenth year, but she fought against the transformation with such determination that she maintained human form until her twenty-third birthday. During those eight years, she developed techniques for channelling the power that none of us had seen before, methods that seemed to slow the progression while allowing her to use her abilities for the protection of the surface world.'"

"Eight years?" Nisha felt a surge of hope that was almost painful in its intensity. "The official histories make it sound like spiral bearers typically succumbed within months of their awakening."

"That's because the official histories were written by people who wanted to justify the sealing of the Mumbadevi

Hall," Dev replied, his voice carrying the excitement of someone making a significant discovery. "But these personal accounts suggest that many spiral bearers actually fought the transformation successfully for extended periods. The consumption wasn't inevitable—it was the result of specific circumstances and choices."

They spent the next several hours working through increasingly complex texts, each document revealing new aspects of the spiral bearer experience that had been systematically omitted from the Pathshala's standard historical records. What emerged was a picture of individuals who had possessed far more agency and control over their transformation than anyone had been led to believe.

One particularly detailed account described a spiral bearer named Arjuna who had developed what the writer called "dual-state techniques", which were methods of channelling otherworldly power while maintaining anchor points in purely human experience. According to the text, Arjuna had managed to exist simultaneously in multiple dimensional states for over a decade before finally choosing to undergo complete transformation.

"The key seems to be understanding that the spiral bearer power isn't inherently destructive," Nisha observed as they worked through another collection of fragmented notes. "It becomes dangerous when it's fought against or when it's used without proper grounding techniques."

"Exactly," Dev agreed, his equations flickering with patterns that incorporated the theoretical frameworks described in the ancient texts. "The mathematical models these early scholars developed are incredibly sophisticated. They understood that spiral bearer abilities operate according to specific principles, not random cosmic forces."

But it was when they discovered a cache of documents hidden behind a false wall in one of the deepest archive chambers that their research took on truly profound significance. These weren't just historical accounts or theoretical treatises—they were prophecies and legends that spoke directly to their current situation.

The hidden collection had been sealed with protections that were clearly ancient but not entirely familiar, wards that incorporated both traditional Pathshala techniques and something that felt distinctly otherworldly. When Dev's mathematical analysis finally cracked the protective barriers, what they found inside took their breath away.

"These are prophetic texts," Nisha said, carefully examining a scroll that seemed to be made from some material that shifted colour depending on the angle of observation. "But they're not vague mystical predictions—they're detailed technical descriptions of specific events and circumstances."

The prophecies spoke of a time when the barriers between realms would weaken, when ancient powers would seek to return to the surface world, and when a spiral bearer would arise who possessed the ability to bridge the gap between incompatible forms of existence. But most significantly, they described techniques and approaches that could allow such a being to maintain stability without succumbing to dissolution.

One document in particular caught Nisha's attention. A text that appeared to be a compilation of different prophetic traditions, all pointing toward the same fundamental concept: the "missing element" that could transform the spiral bearer power from a consuming force into a symbiotic one.

"'When the tides of convergence reach their peak,'" she read aloud, translating from what appeared to be a mixture of Sanskrit and something much older, "'the child of two worlds shall arise, bearing the mark of the spiral and the burden of mediation. But success shall come not through resistance or surrender, but through the discovery of the heart that beats between realms, the nexus where surface and depth achieve balance through understanding rather than dominance.'"

"The heart that beats between realms," Dev repeated, his mathematical mind immediately beginning to work through the implications. "That sounds like it's describing a specific location or phenomenon, not just a metaphorical concept."

As they delved deeper into the prophetic texts, a consistent pattern began to emerge. Multiple traditions, separated by centuries and originating from completely different cultural contexts, all referred to the same essential concept: a "heart of the city" that served as a nexus point where the forces of surface and depth could achieve natural equilibrium.

The descriptions were frustratingly vague in some respects, but remarkably specific in others. The texts spoke of a place where water flowed upward to meet earth flowing downward, where the boundaries between possible and impossible became permeable, where individual will could touch cosmic forces without being overwhelmed by their magnitude.

"Look at this map," Dev said, carefully unrolling what appeared to be a diagram of Mumbai from several centuries ago, overlaid with symbols and notations that clearly indicated supernatural significance. "These markings correspond to ley lines and power nodes, but there's one location that's marked differently from all the others."

The map showed Mumbai as it had existed before the massive urban development of recent centuries, when the city had been a collection of smaller settlements connected by natural waterways and ancient paths. But superimposed on this historical geography was a network of mystical connections that linked sacred sites, power nodes, and dimensional weak points throughout the region.

At the centre of this network, marked with symbols that seemed to incorporate both traditional Hindu iconography and something that definitely predated any known religious tradition, was a location that the map identified as "Mumbadevi's Heart"—the original shrine to the city's patron goddess, the site from which her protective influence had supposedly emanated to guard the entire region.

"The original Mumbadevi temple," Nisha breathed, studying the map with growing excitement. "But this isn't the modern temple complex, this is showing something much older, something that existed before the current religious architecture was built."

According to the prophetic texts, this location had served as a natural balancing point between surface and depth forces for millennia, long before human settlements had grown up around it. The goddess Mumbadevi herself was described not as a purely benevolent deity, but as a mediating presence that maintained equilibrium between cosmic forces that would otherwise be incompatible.

"The texts suggest that the original temple wasn't just a place of worship," Dev observed, his mathematical analysis revealing patterns in the mystical notations that spoke of sophisticated understanding of dimensional mechanics. "It was a functioning piece of infrastructure, designed to channel and balance otherworldly energies while keeping them from overwhelming the surface world."

But what made these discoveries truly significant was the repeated assertion throughout the prophetic literature that this ancient balancing system could be reactivated under the right circumstances. The texts spoke of specific rituals, particular alignments of power and purpose, that could restore the "heart of the city" to its original function as a bridge between realms.

"The missing element," Nisha said, her voice carrying growing certainty as the pieces began to fall into place. "It's not a technique or a ritual or a piece of knowledge—it's a place. A specific location where the spiral bearer power can achieve natural equilibrium without consuming the person who channels it."

The implications were staggering. If the prophetic texts were accurate, then her current approach of trying to maintain the bridge system through individual will alone was fundamentally flawed. Instead of fighting against the natural flow of cosmic forces, she needed to work with systems that had been designed specifically to handle such energies safely.

But as exciting as these discoveries were, they also revealed the magnitude of the challenge ahead. The original Mumbadevi temple site had been built over and transformed countless times throughout Mumbai's long history. Finding the precise location where the ancient balancing systems had operated would require extensive research and possibly dangerous exploration of areas that had been forgotten or deliberately hidden.

"Even if we can locate the original site," Dev pointed out, his mathematical mind immediately identifying the practical obstacles, "there's no guarantee that the ancient systems are still functional after centuries of neglect. We could be looking at massive restoration work, complex rituals that we don't fully understand, and coordination with forces that operate according to principles we've barely begun to comprehend."

"But we have to try," Nisha replied, her voice carrying harmonics that spoke of expanding awareness even as her words expressed purely human determination. "The alternative is accepting dissolution as inevitable, and I refuse to believe that the cosmic forces that created the spiral bearer power intended it to be ultimately self-destructive."

As they carefully gathered the most significant documents from their research session, preparing to bring their discoveries to *Guru* Chanda and the others, Nisha felt something she hadn't experienced since her transformation had begun accelerating: genuine hope.

The silvery patterns covering her skin continued to spread, the bone-deep cold remained constant, and the fatigue that plagued every moment of her existence showed no signs of improvement. But now she had something more valuable than physical comfort—she had a direction, a goal, a specific objective that offered the possibility of salvation for both herself and the worlds she had sworn to protect.

The ancient prophecies had provided what all their previous research had lacked: not just understanding of what was happening to her, but actionable knowledge about what could be done to change the outcome. The heart of the city was calling, and for the first time since her awakening, the call offered hope rather than despair.

The texts spoke of challenges ahead, of trials that would test every aspect of her determination and capability. But they also spoke of success, of balance achieved through understanding rather than force, of bridges built through cooperation rather than conquest.

Time was still running short, and the physical evidence of her deteriorating condition continued to mount with each passing hour. But now she had something to fight for beyond mere survival—she had a vision of what could be achieved if she could find the strength and wisdom to reach the place where surface and depth achieved natural harmony.

The heart of the city was waiting, and with it, the possibility of transformation that preserved rather than consumed, that bridged rather than absorbed, that honoured both individual identity and cosmic connection.

The ancient prophecies had spoken, and their words carried the weight of hope across centuries of patient waiting. Now it remained to be seen whether she could fulfil the potential they described before the mounting costs of her current approach consumed everything she was fighting to preserve.

Chapter 17:

THE CRUMBLING LORE

THE DISCOVERIES IN THE RESTRICTED archives had opened a door to understanding that Nisha and Dev could never have anticipated, but it also revealed the true scope of how deeply the Pathshala's historical records had been compromised. What they had initially assumed was incomplete documentation now appeared to be systematic editing, a deliberate campaign to reshape the narrative around spiral bearers and their ultimate fate.

"Look at this," Dev said, carefully comparing two versions of what should have been the same historical account. His floating equations flickered with patterns that highlighted the discrepancies between the texts, mathematical analysis revealing alterations that would have been invisible to casual examination. "This is the official version we've been working with all along—it describes Kavita Devi's final confrontation as a heroic sacrifice to contain dangerous otherworldly forces."

He set the familiar document aside and picked up a much older manuscript they had discovered hidden behind false panels in the deepest archive chambers. "But this version, written by someone who was actually present during the events, tells a completely different story. According to this account, Kavita didn't die fighting external forces. She was executed by other Pathshala members who believed her transformation posed an unacceptable threat to the surface world."

The implications of this revelation were staggering. If the official histories had been deliberately falsified, then everything the current generation of teachers and students believed about spiral bearer power might be based on propaganda rather than factual observation.

"They rewrote history to justify their actions," Nisha said, her voice carrying harmonics that spoke of expanding awareness even as her words expressed very human anger. "The sealing of the Mumbadevi Hall wasn't a protective measure—it was a permanent solution to eliminate spiral bearers entirely."

The pattern of deception became clearer as they worked through more of the hidden documents. They found evidence of heated debates within the Pathshala's governing council, passionate arguments between those who believed spiral bearers could be trained and guided, and those who viewed them as inherently dangerous aberrations that needed to be contained or eliminated.

The faction favouring elimination had ultimately won, but their victory had required systematic suppression of evidence that contradicted their position. Documents describing successful spiral bearer training had been destroyed or hidden. Accounts of cooperative relationships between transformed and normal humans had been edited to emphasise conflict and danger. Even the basic understanding of how spiral bearer power actually worked had been deliberately obscured to support the narrative that such abilities inevitably led to madness and destruction.

"Here's a training manual," Dev said, unrolling a scroll that was covered with detailed diagrams and technical specifications. "It's written by someone named Master Vishnu, who apparently oversaw spiral bearer education for over thirty years. According to this, there were dozens of successful spiral bearers throughout the Pathshala's history, people who learned to channel their abilities safely while maintaining their essential humanity."

The training techniques described in the manual were far more sophisticated than anything in the Pathshala's current curriculum. Instead of trying to suppress or redirect spiral bearer power, these methods focused on understanding its natural flow patterns and working with them rather than against them. The approaches emphasised balance, integration, and careful attention to the individual psychology of each student.

"They knew how to do this," Nisha realised, studying diagrams that showed energy flow patterns remarkably similar to what she had been experiencing during her own transformation. "The early Pathshala actually had effective methods for training spiral bearers. The knowledge existed, but it was deliberately suppressed."

But perhaps most significant of all were the hidden chambers themselves. These weren't just storage spaces that had been forgotten over time—they were carefully concealed repositories created by Pathshala members who had disagreed with the official decision to eliminate spiral bearer knowledge. The preservation methods were sophisticated, incorporating both traditional archival techniques and divine essence applications that had kept fragile documents intact for centuries.

"This was planned," Dev observed, studying the construction of one of the hidden chambers with an engineer's eye for detail. "Someone, probably multiple people, knew that the official records were being falsified and went to considerable effort to preserve the truth for future generations."

The hidden chambers contained more than just documents. They held artifacts that had belonged to successful spiral bearers—tools, weapons, and focusing devices that had been crafted specifically to help channel otherworldly power safely. There were also maps, not just of Mumbai's mystical geography, but of locations throughout India and beyond where similar balancing sites had been established and maintained.

"Look at this network," Nisha said, studying a map that showed connections between dozens of locations across the subcontinent. "The 'heart of the city' concept wasn't unique to Mumbai. There were similar sites everywhere, all connected through natural ley lines and maintained by people who understood how to work with cosmic forces rather than simply containing them."

The maps were accompanied by detailed technical specifications for what could only be described as mystical infrastructure—architectural plans for buildings and site modifications that could channel otherworldly energies while preventing them from overwhelming local populations. The designs were elegant in their sophistication, incorporating both aesthetic beauty and functional efficiency in ways that suggested centuries of accumulated expertise.

But as exciting as these discoveries were, they also revealed the magnitude of what had been lost when the anti-spiral bearer faction had gained control of the Pathshala. An entire tradition of knowledge and practice had been systematically eliminated, leaving only fragments and hints of what had once been a comprehensive understanding of how to work safely with cosmic forces.

"The original Mumbadevi temple," Dev said, studying the most detailed map they had found, "wasn't just a religious site. It was the central node in a network of mystical infrastructure that spanned the entire region. The temple complex included facilities for training spiral bearers, research laboratories for studying dimensional mechanics, and administrative centres for coordinating with similar sites throughout India."

According to the hidden documents, the temple had been built at a location where natural ley lines converged, creating a point where the barriers between realms were naturally thin but stable. The architecture itself had been designed to amplify and channel these forces, creating an environment where surface dwellers and otherworldly beings could interact safely while maintaining their essential natures.

"But where is it now?" Nisha asked, studying the ancient maps with growing frustration. "These documents are centuries old. Mumbai has been built over and rebuilt dozens of times since then. The original temple site could be anywhere under the modern city."

This was the crucial question that their research hadn't yet answered. The maps clearly showed the location of the ancient temple complex relative to geographical features that had existed centuries ago, but correlating those references with modern Mumbai would require extensive fieldwork and possibly dangerous exploration of areas that had been forgotten or deliberately hidden.

As they worked through the technical specifications and architectural plans, Nisha began experiencing increasingly vivid flashes of what could only be described as inherited memory. The spiral mark on her arm would pulse with particular intensity when she examined certain documents, and she would suddenly find herself seeing locations and structures as they had existed centuries ago.

"I can feel it," she said during one particularly intense episode, her voice carrying harmonics that definitely didn't belong to purely human vocal cords. "The connection to the original temple site. It's like…like there's still something there, some remnant of the ancient systems calling to me."

The inherited memories were fragmentary and difficult to interpret, but they consistently pointed toward a location in the older parts of Mumbai, an area where modern development had been built over much older foundations. The visions showed not just the temple complex as it had once existed, but glimpses of how it might appear in the present—buried structures, hidden chambers, architectural elements that had been incorporated into newer buildings without the builders understanding their true significance.

"We need to go there," Nisha said, the decision crystallising even as she spoke the words. "Whatever remains of the original temple site, I can find it. The spiral bearer connection is still active—I can feel the pull getting stronger as my transformation progresses."

But Dev's mathematical analysis of her current condition revealed a troubling timeline. "Your physical deterioration is accelerating faster than we anticipated," he reported, his equations showing curves that were deeply alarming to anyone who understood their implications. "If we're going to attempt any kind of field expedition, it has to happen soon. Within days, possibly hours, before the progression reaches a point where you can't function effectively in surface world conditions."

The irony wasn't lost on any of them. The very transformation that was threatening to consume Nisha was also providing her with the enhanced senses and inherited knowledge necessary to locate the ancient temple site. But that same transformation was progressing so rapidly that she might not retain enough physical coherence to actually reach the location and attempt to activate whatever systems remained there.

"The visions are getting more frequent and more detailed," she reported, pressing her hands against her temples as another wave of inherited memory washed through her awareness. "I can see the temple complex as it existed, but I can also sense something else—resistance, opposition, forces that don't want the ancient systems to be reactivated."

Through her expanding awareness, she could sense the presence of the Sea King and his transformed servants, their vast intelligence clearly monitoring her research and growing understanding. But their attitude toward her discoveries was complex—not outright opposition, but something that felt more like…caution mixed with curiosity.

You seek to restore what was deliberately destroyed, Vanaraja's voice whispered through the spiral mark, carrying harmonics that spoke of ancient patience and otherworldly concern. *But consider whether those who sealed the old knowledge had reasons that transcend mere fear and prejudice.*

"What reasons?" Nisha asked, directing her question toward the alien presence in her mind.

The systems you hope to reactivate were designed for a world very different from the one that exists today, the Sea King replied. *Mumbai in the ancient era was a collection of small settlements with a few thousand inhabitants. The modern city houses millions of people, most of whom have no preparation for contact with otherworldly forces. Reactivating the temple systems could expose them to influences they have no context for understanding.*

The warning carried weight that Nisha couldn't ignore. The ancient temple complex had been designed for a population that understood and accepted the reality of otherworldly forces, people who had grown up with the knowledge that multiple realms existed and occasionally intersected. Modern Mumbai's residents had no such preparation—sudden exposure to cosmic forces could indeed be catastrophic.

"But the alternative is my dissolution and the eventual collapse of the bridge system I've established," she pointed out. "At least attempting to reactivate the ancient systems offers the possibility of a stable, long-term solution."

True, the Sea King acknowledged. *But the risks extend beyond immediate exposure effects. The temple systems were never designed to operate independently—they were part of a network that spanned multiple continents, coordinated by people who understood both the techniques involved and the cosmic forces being channelled. Attempting to activate a single node without proper support infrastructure could create instabilities that cascade far beyond the local area.*

Despite these warnings, Nisha felt increasingly certain that attempting to locate and reactivate the ancient temple systems represented their best hope for finding a sustainable solution. The hidden documents had revealed not just the existence of alternative approaches, but detailed technical specifications that could guide their efforts.

"We have the manuals," she said, indicating the collection of preserved texts and artifacts they had discovered. "The people who hid these materials included everything we would need to understand the systems and operate them safely."

"The manuals are centuries old," Dev pointed out, though his tone suggested he was working through the practical implications rather than rejecting the approach entirely. "Even if the technical specifications are accurate, we have no way of knowing what condition the actual systems are in, or whether they can be safely reactivated after so much time."

But as they continued studying the hidden documents, one fact became increasingly clear: they had reached the limits of what could be accomplished through theoretical research alone. The next phase of their investigation would require them to leave the safety of the Pathshala and venture into the surface world, following the inherited memories and mystical connections that were calling to Nisha with increasing urgency.

The crumbling lore had revealed both the scope of what had been lost and the magnitude of what might be recovered. Ancient knowledge that had been systematically suppressed offered hope for solutions that honoured both individual identity and cosmic connection. But accessing that knowledge would require them to face dangers that went far beyond anything they had encountered within the Pathshala's protected environment.

Time was running short, and Nisha's physical condition continued to deteriorate with each passing hour. The silvery patterns covering her skin were now clearly visible even in dim light, her movements had become noticeably slower and more deliberate, and the bone-deep cold that plagued her showed no signs of improvement.

But she also felt something else—a growing sense of connection to forces and knowledge that transcended her individual limitations. The spiral bearer heritage that was consuming her human form was also providing access to understanding that no purely mortal mind could achieve. The question was whether she could use that understanding to find salvation before the transformation progressed beyond the point of return.

The ancient temple was calling, and with it, the possibility of restoration rather than dissolution, balance rather than consumption, bridges that preserved rather than absorbed. The crumbling lore had shown the way, and now it remained to be seen whether they would have the courage and wisdom to follow the path it revealed.

Chapter 18:

STRIKES FROM THE DEEP

THE DISCOVERY OF THE ANCIENT temple site's probable location had given Nisha and her allies hope for the first time since her deterioration had begun accelerating, but that hope was shattered when the emergency alarms began sounding throughout the Pathshala at dawn. Not the gentle chimes that marked routine activities, but the deep, urgent bells that hadn't been heard in decades—the warning that the complex was under direct assault.

Nisha struggled to rise from her resting alcove, her movements noticeably slower than they had been even the day before. The silvery patterns covering her skin pulsed with agitated rhythm, responding to disturbances she could sense through the expanded awareness that came with her advancing transformation. Something was wrong in the surface world above, something that sent ripples of distortion through the carefully maintained balance she had established between realms.

"What's happening?" she asked Dev as he appeared in her doorway, his floating equations more chaotic than she had ever seen them, their usually stable patterns dissolving into fractals that hurt to look at directly.

"The Sea King," he replied, his voice tight with alarm. "He's not attacking the Pathshala directly, but he's doing something much more insidious. He's targeting the surface world—the magical nodes and vulnerable communities that are connected to our power systems."

Through the complex's monitoring networks, reports were flooding in of supernatural disturbances throughout Mumbai that defied easy categorisation. These weren't the dramatic, obviously magical events that would immediately draw attention from authorities or cause widespread panic. Instead, they were subtle, apparently natural failures that were occurring with suspicious frequency and perfect timing to maximise disruption.

"The water treatment facility in Bandra has suffered complete system failure," Master Varun reported as the emergency council convened in the Heart of the Pathshala. "All the pumps stopped simultaneously, and the backup systems won't engage. The engineering teams can't find any mechanical problems, but the entire district is now without clean water."

"Three of the major electrical substations have experienced cascading failures in the past hour," another teacher added. "The power grid management system shows no technical malfunctions, but sections of the city are experiencing rolling blackouts that follow no logical pattern."

But what made these failures particularly ominous was their strategic precision. The affected areas weren't random—they were all locations where the Pathshala maintained subtle magical protections, nodes in the network of wards and barriers that had kept Mumbai safe from supernatural threats for centuries.

"He's not trying to destroy the city," Nisha realised, her expanding awareness allowing her to perceive patterns that would have been invisible to purely human analysis. "He's systematically unravelling our defensive infrastructure, identifying every ward, every protective charm, every connection between the Pathshala and the surface world."

Through her connection to the transformed spiral bearer network, she could sense the vast intelligence behind these apparently random failures. The Sea King was demonstrating capabilities far beyond anything they had previously encountered—not crude applications of otherworldly force, but surgical precision that spoke of intimate knowledge of exactly how Mumbai's magical protections functioned.

You begin to understand the true scope of what you face, the Sea King's voicc whispcrcd through thc spiral mark, carrying harmonics that spoke of satisfaction mixed with what might have been regret. *Your little sanctuary has existed for centuries under my sufferance, protected by barriers I allowed to remain intact. But your resistance to the natural course of convergence forces me to demonstrate how easily those protections can be removed.*

"This isn't about conquest," Nisha said, her voice carrying harmonics that allowed her to address both her human companions and the otherworldly presence simultaneously. "You're trying to force my cooperation by threatening the people I care about."

I am providing education about the true nature of power, the Sea King replied with the patience of someone explaining simple concepts to a slow student. *Your surface world depends on magical protections you barely understand, maintained by people who have forgotten the cosmic forces those protections were designed to contain.*

Remove that invisible infrastructure, and your civilisation becomes far more...vulnerable to influence.

The demonstrations of vulnerability continued throughout the morning, each incident carefully calculated to create maximum disruption while avoiding the kind of obvious supernatural activity that might alert surface authorities to the true nature of the threat. Traffic control systems malfunctioned in patterns that created massive congestion. Communication networks experienced outages that isolated emergency services from the populations they served. Even the weather seemed to be responding to otherworldly influence, with localised atmospheric distortions creating pockets of dangerous conditions.

"The attacks are forcing us to respond," *Guru* Chanda observed, studying the flood of emergency reports with growing alarm. "Every time we deploy people to contain one of these incidents, we're exposing them to direct contact with otherworldly forces. And we're also revealing more information about our capabilities and resources."

Indeed, each response effort was providing the Sea King with valuable intelligence about the Pathshala's personnel, methods, and limitations. The complex's teachers and advanced students were being drawn out of their protected environment and into situations where they were vulnerable to observation, influence, and potentially direct attack.

"We can't just ignore what's happening," Mira pointed out, her warrior's instincts recognising the tactical implications of the situation. "If we let the surface infrastructure collapse, we'll lose the foundation that supports our own operations. The Pathshala depends on the city above for basic resources and concealment."

"But every time we respond, we're playing by his rules," Kritika added, her crystals humming with discordant frequencies as they tried to analyse the chaotic harmonics emanating from the attacked sites. "He's forcing us to divide our attention and resources while he systematically maps our capabilities."

The strategic brilliance of the Sea King's approach was becoming clear. Instead of launching a direct assault that would allow the Pathshala to concentrate its defences, he was forcing them to spread their efforts across dozens of simultaneous crises. Each response effort weakened their overall position while providing him with more information about how to target future attacks.

But what made the situation truly desperate was the way it affected Nisha personally. The bridge system she had established required constant attention to maintain proper balance between terrestrial and otherworldly forces. The disruptions in the surface world were creating instabilities that demanded increasingly frequent adjustments, forcing her to expend energy she could barely spare while her physical condition continued to deteriorate.

"I have to help," she said, struggling to her feet despite the obvious effort required for even basic movements. "The incidents aren't just random attacks. They're designed to destabilise the connections between the Pathshala and the surface world. If those connections fail, the bridge system collapses and both realms suffer."

"You're barely able to maintain the basic functions here," Dev protested, his mathematical analysis showing alarming patterns in the energy flows she was managing. "Extending your efforts to cover surface world disruptions could accelerate your dissolution beyond any hope of reversal."

"And not extending them guarantees the collapse of everything we've worked to build," Nisha replied, her voice carrying harmonics that spoke of expanding awareness even as her words expressed purely human determination.

The first surface intervention required her to address a situation in Dharavi, where the water treatment systems that served her old neighbourhood had failed completely. The failure wasn't mechanical—it was the result of otherworldly influence disrupting the subtle magical protections that kept the infrastructure functioning despite being built on unstable foundations.

Leaving the Pathshala's protected environment was like stepping into a storm. The surface world assaulted her enhanced senses with chaotic energies, emotional turbulence, and the constant background noise of millions of minds that had no awareness of the supernatural forces swirling around them. The spiral mark on her arm blazed with uncomfortable intensity, responding to influences that seemed to come from every direction simultaneously.

"The contamination is otherworldly," she reported to Dev through their communication link, her voice strained from the effort of maintaining coherence in such a chaotic environment. "Someone has introduced entities into the water system that are designed to disrupt both the physical infrastructure and the magical protections."

The entities were unlike anything described in the Pathshala's historical records—not the crude sea-spawn that had occasionally manifested during previous incursions, but sophisticated constructs that seemed to be part living creature and part applied mathematics. They moved through the water treatment systems with purpose and intelligence, systematically sabotaging critical components while avoiding detection by conventional monitoring equipment.

"I can remove them," Nisha said, extending her transformed senses into the contaminated infrastructure, "but it's going to require using the spiral bearer power in ways that will accelerate the dissolution process."

"Do it," Mira's voice came through the communication link with characteristic decisiveness. "We'll deal with the consequences later."

The cleansing process was exhausting beyond anything Nisha had previously experienced. Each entity she removed fought back with surprising sophistication, requiring her to channel increasing amounts of otherworldly energy while maintaining precise control to avoid damaging the infrastructure she was trying to protect. By the time she had eliminated the last of the intrusions, she was trembling with fatigue and the silvery patterns on her skin had spread visibly during the single hour of intensive work.

But before she could return to the Pathshala for rest and recovery, new emergency reports were flooding in. Power grid failures in three different districts, atmospheric distortions that were creating dangerous weather conditions over densely populated areas, and communication outages that were isolating emergency services from the communities they served.

"The attacks are accelerating," she reported, her voice now carrying permanent harmonics that made it difficult for purely human listeners to understand her clearly. "Each incident I resolve triggers two more in different locations. He's not just testing our defences—he's systematically overloading our response capabilities."

The pattern continued throughout the day, each crisis demanding immediate attention while contributing to the overall strategy of exhaustion and exposure. Nisha found herself racing from one emergency to another, using her rapidly developing otherworldly abilities to counteract supernatural sabotage while her physical condition deteriorated at an alarming rate.

After six hours of continuous crisis response, she could barely stand upright. The silvery filigree covering her skin was now dense enough to be clearly visible even in bright sunlight, creating patterns that resembled both neural networks and flowing water. Her movements had become unnaturally fluid, as if she were moving through water rather than air, and her voice carried harmonics that definitely didn't belong to any terrestrial species.

"You're transforming faster than our worst-case projections," Dev reported when she finally returned to the Pathshala for emergency medical assessment. "The energy expenditure required for surface world interventions is accelerating the dissolution process exponentially."

"But the alternative is watching the entire magical infrastructure of Mumbai collapse," Nisha replied, though her voice was now so distorted by otherworldly harmonics that Kritika had to use her crystals to translate the meaning for the others to understand clearly.

Through her expanding awareness, she could sense the Sea King's satisfaction at the success of his strategy. Each intervention had forced her to reveal more of her capabilities while expending energy she couldn't spare. More importantly, each use of her power in the surface world had created opportunities for otherworldly influence to establish stronger footholds in locations that had previously been protected by the Pathshala's barriers.

You see how futile resistance becomes, Vanaraja's voice whispered through the spiral mark, carrying harmonics that spoke of ancient patience and otherworldly satisfaction. *Every effort to preserve your current form only accelerates the inevitable transformation. Every attempt to maintain separation between realms only creates more opportunities for integration to occur through chaos rather than wisdom.*

"What do you want?" Nisha asked, directing her question toward the alien presence that had been manipulating events throughout the day.

What I have always wanted, the Sea King replied. *Voluntary cooperation in the process that benefits both realms. Your resistance serves no one—it only ensures that the convergence occurs through conflict rather than collaboration.*

The attacks ceased as suddenly as they had begun, leaving Mumbai's infrastructure damaged but functional, and the Pathshala's resources stretched to their breaking point. But the message had been delivered with unmistakable clarity: the Sea King possessed both the capability and the willingness to systematically dismantle every protection that kept the surface world safe from otherworldly influences.

"He could have continued the attacks indefinitely," Chanda observed during the post-crisis assessment. "The fact that he stopped suggests this was a demonstration rather than a genuine attempt at conquest."

"A demonstration of what we have to lose if we continue to resist," Nisha agreed, her transformed voice carrying harmonics that made the observation sound both human and utterly alien simultaneously.

The day's events had fundamentally changed the strategic situation. The Sea King had proven that he could force the Pathshala to expend resources and expose personnel whenever he chose to do so. More importantly, he had demonstrated that Nisha's deteriorating condition made her increasingly vulnerable to manipulation—each crisis had forced her to make choices between immediate humanitarian concerns and long-term strategic considerations.

"The attacks will resume," she predicted, settling carefully into one of the chamber's stone seats as waves of exhaustion made even basic movement difficult. "Probably tomorrow, possibly sooner. And each time, the choice will be the same—let people suffer from supernatural sabotage, or accelerate my own dissolution trying to help them."

The cruel elegance of the strategy was undeniable. The Sea King had found a way to use Nisha's essential humanity against her, forcing her to choose between personal survival and the welfare of people who had no idea they were being protected by her sacrifices.

But even as despair threatened to overwhelm them, Nisha felt something stirring in the depths of her rapidly expanding awareness. The day's interventions had been exhausting and dangerous, but they had also provided her with direct experience of how otherworldly forces interacted with surface world infrastructure. She now understood the vulnerability patterns, the points where magical and mundane systems intersected, the places where targeted interventions could provide maximum protection with minimal energy expenditure.

"The attacks revealed information that works both ways," she said, her voice carrying certainty that surprised everyone present. "He learned about our capabilities and limitations, but I learned about his methods and priorities. And more importantly, I now have direct evidence about where the ancient temple systems need to be reactivated to provide the kind of comprehensive protection Mumbai actually needs."

The strikes from the deep had been devastating and demoralising, but they had also provided crucial intelligence about both the threat they faced and the solutions that might be possible. The question was whether Nisha could find and activate those solutions before the mounting costs of resistance consumed everything she was fighting to preserve.

Time was running shorter with each passing hour, but the path forward was becoming clearer. The ancient temple was calling, and with it, the possibility of protection that didn't require continuous personal sacrifice. The strikes had shown the scope of the problem—now it remained to be seen whether the solutions revealed in the hidden archives could provide effective answers before it was too late.

Chapter 19:

THE BLEEDING CITY

THE RESPITE FROM THE SEA King's attacks lasted less than twelve hours. When the emergency alarms began sounding again in the pre-dawn darkness, they carried a different tone—not the urgent warnings of isolated incidents, but the deep, continuous tolling that indicated citywide crisis. Nisha struggled to wake from the exhausted stupor that now passed for sleep, her transformed body requiring longer and longer periods of rest to recover from each expenditure of power.

"The attacks have escalated beyond anything we anticipated," Dev reported as she joined the emergency council, his floating equations more chaotic than she had ever seen them. "It's not just infrastructure failures now, he's targeting the foundational systems that keep Mumbai functioning as a coherent entity."

Through the Pathshala's monitoring networks, reports flooded in of supernatural disturbances that defied every attempt at categorisation or containment. The Bandra-Worli Sea Link, one of Mumbai's most iconic landmarks, was showing signs of inexplicable structural fatigue. Engineers who examined the massive bridge found stress patterns that suggested the steel and concrete were aging decades in a matter of hours, developing microscopic fractures that followed no known pattern of metal fatigue.

"The Gateway of India is weeping," Master Varun reported, his weathered face grim as he consulted the magical monitoring systems. "The stones themselves are producing brackish water—not condensation or seepage from underground sources, but water that's actually emanating from within the rock structure itself."

But perhaps most disturbing of all were the power grid failures that were spreading through the city in patterns that suggested deliberate coordination rather than random system collapse. Entire districts would lose electricity simultaneously, not due to mechanical failures but because the electrical current itself seemed to be diverted away from its intended circuits by forces that operated outside the normal laws of physics.

"These aren't random attacks," Nisha realised, her expanding awareness allowing her to perceive the underlying strategy with crystalline clarity. "He's not trying to destroy Mumbai. He's trying to systematically unravel the invisible infrastructure that makes modern urban life possible."

The Sea King's approach was devastatingly effective precisely because it targeted systems that most people took for granted. The bridge remained structurally sound enough to carry traffic, but the accelerated aging process would eventually make it unsafe. The Gateway continued to function as a landmark and tourist attraction, but the brackish water suggested otherworldly influence seeping into the very foundations of the city's identity. The power outages were brief enough to avoid complete social collapse, but frequent enough to create a pervasive sense of uncertainty and vulnerability.

You begin to understand, Vanaraja's voice whispered through the spiral mark, carrying harmonics that spoke of vast patience and cosmic perspective. *Your surface civilisation depends on countless invisible systems—magical protections, dimensional barriers, spiritual anchors that have maintained stability for centuries. Remove those foundations, and even the most impressive human achievements become…fragile.*

"You're demonstrating that our independence is an illusion," Nisha said, her voice now carrying permanent harmonics that made it difficult for purely human listeners to understand her without Kritika's crystal translation assistance.

I am providing education about the true nature of interdependence, the Sea King corrected with the tone of someone explaining obvious concepts to a slow student. *Your realm and mine have always been connected. The barriers that have kept us separate were temporary measures, never intended to be permanent. The convergence is simply the restoration of natural balance.*

The educational demonstration continued throughout the morning, with each new incident carefully calibrated to reveal another layer of Mumbai's dependence on systems that most residents had no idea existed. Traffic lights began malfunctioning in patterns that created massive congestion, not because the electronic systems were broken, but because the mystical timing algorithms that prevented complete gridlock were being systematically disrupted.

Communication networks experienced selective outages that isolated government agencies from each other while leaving civilian communications largely intact, creating administrative chaos without generating the kind of public panic that might trigger emergency response protocols. Even the monsoon weather patterns seemed to be responding to otherworldly influence, with localised precipitation that fell upward instead of down, creating atmospheric distortions that made aircraft navigation dangerous in specific corridors.

"He's forcing us into the field again," Guru Chanda observed, studying the flood of emergency reports with growing alarm. "Every one of these incidents requires someone with divine essence training to address properly, and we don't have enough personnel to handle this volume of simultaneous crises."

Indeed, the Pathshala's teachers and advanced students were being stretched beyond their limits as they responded to incidents across the city. Each response team that ventured into the surface world was immediately vulnerable to observation and potential attack, while their absence weakened the complex's internal defences against more direct assaults.

"The tactical situation is deteriorating rapidly," Mira reported after coordinating the morning's initial response efforts. "We're being forced to divide our attention across dozens of crises points while he maintains the initiative to create new problems faster than we can solve existing ones."

But what made the situation truly desperate was the way each incident was specifically designed to require Nisha's personal intervention. The supernatural disturbances weren't random manifestations that could be addressed through standard divine essence techniques—they were precisely targeted disruptions that required someone with spiral bearer capabilities to understand and counteract effectively.

"The structural fatigue in the Sea Link isn't normal aging," she explained after examining the bridge's mystical resonance patterns remotely through the monitoring networks. "Someone has introduced temporal distortions that are accelerating the passage of time for specific molecular structures while leaving others unaffected. Only spiral bearer power can perceive and correct that kind of selective chronological manipulation."

"And the brackish water at the Gateway?" Dev asked, though his mathematical analysis already suggested he suspected the answer.

"Dimensional seepage," Nisha confirmed. "The stones are being used as anchor points for otherworldly manifestation, creating channels that allow deep ocean water to flow through terrestrial matter. The longer it continues, the more unstable the dimensional barriers become in that location."

Each diagnosis led to the same conclusion: these weren't problems that could be solved through conventional means or standard divine essence applications. They required someone who could perceive and manipulate the intersection between terrestrial and otherworldly forces—someone whose spiral bearer transformation provided access to capabilities that no purely human practitioner could achieve.

"I have to go out there," Nisha said, struggling to her feet despite the obvious effort required for even basic movements. The silvery patterns covering her skin were now so dense that they resembled metallic lace, and her movements had taken on the fluid quality of someone moving through water rather than air. "Every hour these disturbances continue, they become more entrenched and harder to reverse."

"Your condition has deteriorated significantly since yesterday," Kritika pointed out, her crystals humming with frequencies that provided a detailed analysis of Nisha's transformed physiology. "The energy expenditure required for surface world interventions is consuming your remaining human essence at an exponential rate."

"And letting the city collapse under supernatural pressure serves no one," Nisha replied, her voice carrying harmonics that spoke of expanding awareness even as her words expressed purely human determination.

The first intervention of the day required her to address the temporal distortions affecting the Sea Link. Standing on the bridge's central span, surrounded by the normal traffic of a major transportation artery, she extended her transformed senses into the infrastructure itself, feeling for the points where otherworldly influence was disrupting the natural flow of time.

The distortions were elegant in their sophistication—not crude applications of cosmic force, but precise manipulations that targeted specific molecular bonds while leaving surrounding structures untouched. Whoever had created them possessed an intimate understanding of both terrestrial engineering and dimensional mechanics that went far beyond anything the Pathshala had ever encountered.

"The modifications are beautiful," she reported to Dev through their communication link, her voice carrying admiration despite the destructive intent behind the work. "They're not trying to destroy the bridge. They're demonstrating that they can control fundamental forces with surgical precision."

Correcting the temporal distortions required her to channel spiral bearer power in ways that pushed her transformation further than ever before. As she worked to restore normal chronological flow to the affected structures, she could feel her individual identity becoming more fluid, more distributed across multiple dimensions simultaneously.

By the time she had stabilised the bridge's temporal integrity, the silvery patterns on her skin had spread to cover her entire neck and were beginning to trace delicate lines across her face. Her reflection in the bridge's metal surfaces showed eyes that held depths unrelated to any terrestrial environment, and her voice now carried permanent harmonics that made translation crystals necessary for clear communication with purely human listeners.

But before she could return to the Pathshala for rest and recovery, new emergency reports were already coming in. The brackish water seepage at the Gateway of India had intensified, creating pools where otherworldly entities were beginning to manifest. Power grid failures were spreading through the financial district in patterns that suggested coordinated sabotage of the mystical systems that kept the electronic infrastructure stable.

"The attacks are multiplying faster than I can address them," she reported, her transformed voice carrying frustration and growing desperation. "Each incident I resolve creates opportunities for two more to manifest in different locations."

The pattern continued throughout the day, with each successful intervention triggering an escalation in the overall campaign of supernatural disruption. Nisha found herself racing from crisis to crisis, using her rapidly developing otherworldly abilities to counteract increasingly sophisticated forms of metaphysical sabotage.

The atmospheric distortions that were disrupting aircraft navigation required her to extend her awareness into the upper atmosphere, channelling power through air currents to restore normal pressure gradients. The communication network failures demanded intervention in the electronic infrastructure itself, using spiral bearer abilities to purge otherworldly influences from fibre optic cables and wireless transmission networks.

Each intervention left her more transformed and less human. The silvery filigree that had once been confined to her arms now covered most of her visible skin, creating intricate patterns that pulsed with otherworldly light. Her movements had become unnaturally graceful, as if she were dancing to music only she could hear, and her voice carried harmonics that seemed to incorporate frequencies from multiple dimensions simultaneously.

"You're losing coherence faster than our worst-case models predicted," Dev reported when she finally returned to the Pathshala after eight hours of continuous crisis response. "The energy signatures suggest that your individual identity is becoming distributed across multiple dimensional states simultaneously."

"But the alternative is watching Mumbai dissolve into chaos," Nisha replied, though her voice was now so distorted by otherworldly harmonics that even Kritika's translation crystals struggled to render her meaning into purely human concepts.

Through her expanding awareness, she could sense the Sea King's satisfaction at the success of his strategy. Each intervention had forced her to reveal more of her capabilities while expending essence she could barely spare. More importantly, each use of her power in the surface world had accelerated her transformation beyond any hope of reversal through conventional means.

You see how resistance only hastens the inevitable, Vanaraja's voice whispered through the spiral mark, carrying harmonics that spoke of ancient patience and otherworldly compassion. *Every effort to preserve what you were only makes what you are becoming more evident. Why not embrace the transformation willingly, before the struggle consumes what remains of your essential nature?*

"Because the struggle is part of what makes me human," Nisha replied, her transformed voice carrying certainty that transcended the physical changes reshaping her form.

But even as she affirmed her determination to maintain individual identity, she could feel the truth of the Sea King's observations. The day's interventions had pushed her transformation far beyond the point where any conventional solution could restore her original form. The silvery patterns covering her skin were no longer external manifestations but integrated aspects of her new physiology. Her enhanced senses were becoming permanent features rather than temporary expansions of awareness.

Most significantly, her individual consciousness was becoming something that could exist simultaneously across multiple dimensions, perceiving and responding to forces that operated according to principles no purely human mind could comprehend. She was becoming something unprecedented—not the complete transformation that Kavita Devi and the others had chosen, but something that had never been achieved before.

"The city is bleeding," she observed, studying the reports of ongoing supernatural disturbances through senses that could perceive patterns invisible to normal human awareness. "But it's not dying. The attacks are designed to create dependence rather than destruction, to demonstrate that independence from otherworldly influence is ultimately impossible."

"A strategy of integration through necessity," Guru Chanda agreed, her experienced eye recognising the sophistication of the approach. "Make resistance more costly than cooperation, demonstrate that isolation is unsustainable, and eventually people will choose collaboration over continued struggle."

The cruel elegance of the Sea King's campaign was becoming clear. By systematically revealing Mumbai's dependence on invisible supernatural infrastructure, he was creating conditions where accepting otherworldly influence would seem like the rational choice rather than submission to conquest.

But even as the strategic situation continued to deteriorate, Nisha felt something stirring in the depths of her rapidly expanding consciousness. The day's interventions had been exhausting and transformative, but they had also provided her with unprecedented understanding of how otherworldly forces interacted with urban infrastructure on a massive scale.

"The pattern of attacks isn't random," she said, her voice carrying harmonics that incorporated perspectives from multiple dimensional states. "They're following the same ley line network we discovered in the ancient maps. He's systematically disrupting the mystical foundations that the original temple system was designed to protect."

The realisation carried implications that went far beyond immediate tactical considerations. If the Sea King was deliberately targeting the ancient protective network, then reactivating the temple systems wouldn't just provide a solution to her personal transformation crisis—it would restore the comprehensive protection that Mumbai had lost when the Pathshala's founders had chosen concealment over active guardianship.

"The bleeding will continue until the wounds are properly healed," she concluded, her transformed awareness encompassing both the immediate crisis and the long-term strategic implications. "And the only healing that can address injuries this deep requires returning to sources of power that predate the current conflict entirely."

The ancient temple was calling with increasing urgency, offering not just personal salvation but the possibility of restoring balance to a city that was slowly dissolving under the pressure of forces it had no preparation to understand or resist. The question was whether she could reach and activate those ancient systems before her transformation progressed beyond the point where she could function effectively in purely terrestrial environments.

Time was running out, but the path forward was becoming clearer with each crisis she addressed. The bleeding city needed healing that only the original protective systems could provide, and she was the key to reactivating defences that had been deliberately abandoned centuries ago.

The strikes from the deep had revealed both the scope of the problem and the location of potential solutions. Now it remained to be seen whether ancient wisdom could provide answers to unprecedented challenges before the mounting costs of resistance consumed everything worth protecting.

Chapter 20:

THE ULTIMATE SACRIFICE

THE FINAL ASSAULT BEGAN AT dawn with a coordination and scale that dwarfed every previous attack. The emergency alarms in the Pathshala didn't just sound—they screamed with a desperation that spoke of imminent system collapse, their urgent tones echoing through corridors where students and teachers ran toward crisis stations with barely controlled panic etched on their faces.

Nisha struggled to rise from what had become more of a collapse than sleep, her transformed body requiring increasingly longer periods of rest to recover from each expenditure of power. The silvery patterns covering her skin now pulsed with their own internal light, creating traceries so dense they resembled living jewellery more than natural skin markings. Her movements had taken on the fluid grace of someone moving through water rather than air, and her voice carried permanent harmonics that made translation crystals necessary for clear communication with anyone who lacked otherworldly awareness.

"This is it," Dev reported as she joined the emergency council, his floating equations more chaotic than she had ever seen them, their mathematical patterns dissolving and reforming in configurations that hurt to look at directly. "He's not probing or demonstrating anymore. This is a full-scale coordinated attack designed to overwhelm our response capabilities completely."

Through the Pathshala's monitoring networks, reports flooded in of simultaneous supernatural assaults across every major district of Mumbai. Critical transportation hubs were being targeted by spectral sea-spawn that moved through solid matter like water, disrupting subway systems and rail networks by simply existing within the mechanical infrastructure. Communication networks were going dark not due to technical failures, but because otherworldly influences were literally consuming the electronic signals that carried data and voice transmissions.

But most alarming of all were the sections of the city that were becoming enveloped in an unnatural fog that seemed to exist in multiple dimensions simultaneously. Where the fog settled, reality itself became unstable—buildings showed signs of architecture that followed no terrestrial principles, streets flowed like water while maintaining their solid appearance, and residents moved through the affected areas with the confused docility of people whose minds were being gently overwhelmed by forces they had no context for understanding.

"The fog induces a kind of peaceful acceptance," Master Varun reported, his weathered face grim as he studied the magical monitoring systems. "People aren't fleeing or fighting, they're adapting to the changes as if otherworldly influence was something they had always expected to encounter."

"Because it is," Nisha realised, her expanding awareness allowing her to perceive the true scope of what was happening. "The fog doesn't just change the physical environment, it activates dormant aspects of human consciousness that remember when the barriers between realms were more permeable. People aren't being conquered, they're being reminded of what they used to be."

Through her connection to the spiral bearer network, she could sense the vast intelligence coordinating these attacks with precision that spoke of centuries of planning and preparation. This wasn't the improvised response of a cosmic force trying to overwhelm human defences. This was the culmination of a carefully orchestrated campaign designed to achieve integration through overwhelming evidence that separation had always been artificial.

The time of half-measures ends, Vanaraja's voice whispered through the spiral mark, carrying harmonics that spoke of ancient patience finally reaching its limits. *Your resistance has provided valuable information about surface world capabilities and limitations, but the convergence cannot be delayed further. Both realms require resolution, whether achieved through wisdom or imposed through necessity.*

"You're forcing a choice between surrender and catastrophe," Nisha accused, her transformed voice carrying frequencies that allowed her to address both her human companions and the otherworldly presence simultaneously.

I am providing the final opportunity for voluntary cooperation before circumstances make choice irrelevant, the Sea King corrected with the tone of someone explaining obvious facts to a resistant student. *The barriers between realms have reached a point of instability that will lead to collapse regardless of individual preferences. The question is whether that collapse occurs under guidance or in chaos.*

The scope of the coordinated assault became clear as reports continued to flood in from across the city. Every major infrastructure system was experiencing supernatural interference simultaneously—power grids, water treatment facilities, transportation networks, communication systems, even the atmospheric conditions that made normal weather patterns possible. But the attacks weren't designed to destroy these systems so much as to demonstrate their complete dependence on stability that otherworldly forces could grant or withdraw at will.

"He's not trying to conquer Mumbai," Nisha observed, studying the pattern of attacks through senses that could perceive strategic implications across multiple dimensions. "He's trying to make continued resistance so costly that cooperation becomes the only rational choice."

"The tactical situation is hopeless," Mira reported after consulting with the response teams that were attempting to address the various crises. "We have maybe forty people with divine essence training capable of handling supernatural threats, and we're facing simultaneous incidents across a metropolitan area of twenty million people."

Indeed, the Pathshala's resources were being stretched beyond any hope of adequate coverage. Each response team that ventured into the surface world found themselves facing situations that required capabilities they had never been trained to handle—not just individual supernatural entities, but complex environmental modifications that required understanding of forces no human education had prepared them to comprehend.

"The students and junior teachers are being overwhelmed," *Guru* Chanda reported, her voice tight with controlled fear as she coordinated the desperate response efforts. "Half our response teams are requesting immediate extraction due to exposure to influences they can't protect themselves against."

But what made the situation truly desperate was the realisation that only spiral bearer capabilities could effectively address most of the supernatural disruptions occurring throughout the city. The spectral entities infesting the transportation systems required someone who could perceive and manipulate interdimensional phenomena. The communication network failures demanded intervention by someone who could channel otherworldly power through electronic infrastructure without destroying the systems they were trying to protect.

"I'm the only one who can handle multiple simultaneous interventions," Nisha said, struggling to her feet despite the obvious effort required for even basic movements. "My transformation has progressed to the point where I can exist in multiple dimensional states simultaneously—I can address several crises at once without requiring physical travel between locations."

"The energy expenditure would be beyond anything you've attempted before," Dev warned, his mathematical analysis showing patterns that were deeply alarming to anyone who understood their implications. "We're talking about sustaining multiple major manifestations of spiral bearer power across a geographical area of hundreds of square kilometres."

"While your individual identity is already fragmenting under the strain of maintaining the bridge system," Kritika added, her crystals humming with frequencies that provided a detailed analysis of Nisha's deteriorating coherence.

"Attempting interventions on this scale could cause complete dissolution of your essential self."

"And not attempting them guarantees the collapse of every protection that keeps both realms stable," Nisha replied, her voice carrying harmonics that spoke of expanding awareness even as her words expressed purely human determination.

The decision crystallised with the terrible clarity that comes when all alternatives have been exhausted. The coordinated assault was designed to create exactly this situation—a choice between personal survival and the welfare of millions of people who had no idea they were being protected by her sacrifices.

"I won't let the city fall while I still have power to prevent it," she said, her transformed voice carrying certainty that transcended the physical changes reshaping her form.

The first intervention required her to address the spectral entities that were disrupting the entire Mumbai railway system. Instead of traveling physically to the affected locations, she extended her transformed consciousness directly into the transportation infrastructure, her awareness spreading through tunnels and tracks like water finding its natural level.

The spectral sea-spawn were unlike anything described in the Pathshala's historical records. They moved through solid matter with the fluid grace of creatures born in dimensions where the usual boundaries between substance and void held no meaning. But they weren't simply destroying the mechanical systems—they were incorporating otherworldly principles into terrestrial infrastructure, creating hybrid technologies that operated according to laws no human engineer had ever imagined.

"They're not sabotaging the trains," she reported to Dev through their communication link, her voice now carrying permanent harmonics that made translation crystals necessary for clear understanding. "They're upgrading them. Creating transportation systems that can move through multiple dimensions simultaneously."

Removing the entities without destroying the improvements they had made required her to channel spiral bearer power in ways that pushed her transformation far beyond any previous experience. As she worked to separate otherworldly influences from terrestrial systems while preserving the beneficial modifications, she could feel her individual identity becoming something that existed simultaneously across multiple states of being.

But before she could complete the railway intervention, emergency reports were flooding in about the atmospheric distortions that were creating dangerous weather conditions over the most densely populated areas of the city. The unnatural fog wasn't just obscuring visibility—it was creating pockets where the normal laws of physics became negotiable, where gravity operated according to otherworldly principles, where time flowed at different rates for different observers.

"I have to address both situations simultaneously," she said, her transformed awareness already reaching toward the atmospheric disturbances while maintaining her connection to the transportation systems. "The fog is creating dimensional instabilities that will cascade into complete reality breakdown if they're not stabilised immediately."

The effort required to maintain effective intervention across multiple crisis points simultaneously was beyond anything she had ever attempted. Her consciousness stretched across impossible distances, existing in railway tunnels and atmospheric layers at the same time, channelling otherworldly power through systems that had never been designed to handle such forces.

With each major manifestation of her abilities, the physical changes became more pronounced and irreversible. The silvery patterns covering her skin exploded outward, creating dense networks of luminescent tracery that covered her entire body in ethereal beauty that was utterly inhuman. Her hair began to move as if she were underwater even when standing in air, and her eyes reflected depths that had nothing to do with any terrestrial environment.

"The transformation is accelerating beyond our ability to monitor," Dev reported, his equations showing energy patterns that defied every theoretical framework they had developed. "You're becoming something that exists in multiple dimensions simultaneously. Not losing your individual identity, but expanding it beyond the boundaries of any single form of existence."

But even as her physical form underwent unprecedented changes, Nisha felt something else happening—a growing connection to forces and perspectives that transcended every limitation she had previously understood. Through her expanding awareness, she could perceive the true scope of the convergence, the cosmic processes that were reshaping the relationship between realms whether individual preferences supported such changes or not.

"The attacks aren't really attacks," she said, her voice now carrying harmonics from dimensions that had no names in human language. "They're demonstrations of what integration actually means. The Sea King isn't trying to destroy our world. He's trying to show us what our world could become if we stopped fighting against forces that are part of the same cosmic system we've always belonged to."

Through her connection to the otherworldly network, she could sense Vanaraja's satisfaction at her growing understanding. The coordinated assault had indeed been designed to force this moment of recognition—not conquest, but education about the true nature of the choice that had always been inevitable.

Now you begin to comprehend, the Sea King's voice carried approval mixed with something that might have been relief. *The convergence was never about dominance or submission, but about the natural evolution from isolation to integration. Your resistance has been valuable—it has shown both realms what must be preserved during the transition. But the transition itself cannot be prevented, only guided.*

As she continued to channel power across multiple intervention points simultaneously, Nisha felt her individual consciousness expanding to encompass perspectives that no purely human mind could have contained. She was becoming something unprecedented—not the complete transformation that Kavita Devi and others had chosen, not the dissolution that had claimed previous spiral bearers who had fought against their nature, but something entirely new.

"I can see the pattern now," she said, her transformed voice carrying certainty that incorporated understanding from multiple dimensional perspectives. "The spiral bearer power was never meant to be contained within individual human form. It was designed to create bridges between incompatible states of existence, to serve as living connections that could preserve what was valuable about each realm while enabling communication and cooperation."

The realisation came with implications that were both liberating and terrifying. She was becoming exactly what the cosmic forces had always intended spiral bearers to be—not humans enhanced by otherworldly power, not aliens wearing human form, but something that could exist authentically in multiple states simultaneously.

But even as her transformation reached unprecedented levels, she felt the anchor points her friends had helped her establish during their training together. The memories of individual human connection, the values forged through relationship and shared struggle, the determination to protect what was precious about individual consciousness even as she accepted expansion beyond purely terrestrial limitations.

"I'm still me," she said, her voice now carrying harmonics that incorporated frequencies from realms that had no physical existence. "Different than I was, more than I was, but still essentially myself. The transformation doesn't have to mean the loss of individual identity—it can mean the expansion of individual identity beyond every boundary I thought was permanent."

The coordinated assault continued around them, but its nature had fundamentally changed. Instead of desperate resistance against overwhelming force, it had become a collaborative process of integration guided by understanding rather than driven by fear. The supernatural modifications to Mumbai's infrastructure weren't being reversed—they were being refined, adjusted to preserve human-scale concerns while incorporating otherworldly perspectives that offered solutions to problems no purely terrestrial approach could address.

The ultimate sacrifice hadn't been her individual existence, but her attachment to limitations that had always been temporary. She had chosen to become something that could bridge the gap between worlds without requiring either side to abandon what made them unique and valuable.

The convergence continued, but now it proceeded under guidance rather than unfolding in chaos. And at its centre, transformed beyond recognition but still essentially herself, Nisha served as the living proof that evolution and preservation could be achieved simultaneously when approached with wisdom rather than fear.

The city that emerged from the coordinated assault would be something unprecedented—neither purely human nor completely otherworldly, but a genuine synthesis that honoured both perspectives while creating possibilities that neither could have achieved alone.

Chapter 21:

THE SCARRED GUARDIAN

THE SILENCE THAT FOLLOWED NISHA'S unprecedented expenditure of power was profound and terrible, broken only by the distant echoes of a city slowly returning to normalcy after supernatural crisis. In the Heart of the Pathshala, where the emergency council had coordinated their desperate response efforts, that silence carried the weight of victory achieved at a cost that might prove too high to bear.

Nisha lay motionless on the stone floor where she had collapsed after channelling forces that should have been impossible for any individual consciousness to contain. Her breathing was so shallow it was barely perceptible, and her skin had taken on a translucent quality that made her appear more like a sculpture carved from moonlight than a living human being. The silvery filigree that had been spreading across her body throughout her transformation was now a complete, crystalline layer that covered her from head to toe, creating patterns of otherworldly beauty that pulsed with their own internal light.

"She's barely alive," *Guru* Chanda said quietly, kneeling beside Nisha's still form while her hands moved in diagnostic patterns that had been used by Pathshala healers for centuries. "Her life force is so depleted that conventional healing techniques can't even detect what remains to work with."

Dev hovered nearby, his floating equations dim and erratic as they struggled to map energy patterns that defied every theoretical framework they had developed. "The mathematical signatures are unlike anything we've recorded," he reported, his voice tight with controlled despair. "She's not just transformed—she exists simultaneously in multiple dimensional states. Her consciousness is distributed across realms that don't follow the same physical laws we're familiar with."

The physical changes were unprecedented in their scope and strangeness. Nisha's body temperature had dropped to levels that should have been incompatible with human life, yet she continued to breathe, however faintly. Her hair moved with its own internal rhythm, as if she were submerged in invisible currents that flowed according to otherworldly principles. Most disturbing of all, her eyes reflected depths that definitely didn't correspond to any terrestrial environment—glimpses of underwater vistas, crystalline formations, and architectural structures that followed geometries no human architect had ever conceived.

"She looks like a living statue," Mira observed, her warrior's training allowing her to maintain tactical assessment even while her voice carried emotional strain that spoke of deeper feelings she rarely expressed openly. "Beautiful, but ... not human anymore. Whatever she's become, it's something that belongs more to the otherworldly realms than to our world."

Kritika's crystals sang with harmonies that were simultaneously mournful and celebratory, their combined frequencies creating music that seemed to incorporate perspectives from multiple dimensions. "The harmonic resonances suggest that her essential self is still intact," she reported, though her tone carried more hope than certainty. "The transformation is profound, but she hasn't been consumed or dissolved—she's been…expanded. Evolved into something that can exist in multiple forms of reality simultaneously."

Through the Pathshala's monitoring systems, they could observe the effects of Nisha's sacrifice rippling across Mumbai. The supernatural disturbances that had threatened to tear the city apart were indeed subsiding, but not because they had been eliminated—they were being integrated into the urban environment in ways that enhanced rather than disrupted normal function. Transportation systems operated with impossible efficiency, communication networks carried information across distances that defied conventional physics, and even the weather patterns seemed to be responding to guidance that incorporated otherworldly wisdom.

"The city is healing," Master Varun reported, studying the magical monitoring networks with expressions that mixed relief and lingering concern. "The dimensional instabilities are stabilizing, the supernatural manifestations are becoming benevolent rather than threatening, and the infrastructure modifications are actually improving urban function rather than disrupting it."

But the cost of that healing was evident in Nisha's motionless form, her life force so depleted that she seemed to exist more as potential than actual presence. The spiral mark on her arm no longer pulsed with its usual rhythm—instead, it glowed with constant, unblinking light that suggested connection to forces operating on cosmic rather than individual scales.

Through her fading connection to normal human awareness, Nisha could hear the voices of her friends and teachers discussing her condition, but their words seemed to come from an enormous distance, filtered through layers of otherworldly perception that made purely terrestrial concerns feel increasingly remote. She was aware of their presence, their care, their desperate efforts to find ways to help her, but she was also aware of so much more—currents of power that flowed between dimensions, networks of consciousness that spanned galaxies, and the vast, patient intelligence of cosmic forces that had been guiding the convergence from its beginning.

You have achieved something unprecedented, Vanaraja's voice reached her across dimensional barriers, carrying harmonics that spoke of respect mixed with what might have been wonder. *Not the simple transformation that others have chosen, not the dissolution that has claimed those who fought against their nature, but genuine synthesis that preserves individual identity while enabling cosmic perspective.*

"Am I dying?" she asked, though she wasn't sure if she spoke the words aloud or directed them toward the otherworldly presence through the spiral mark's connection.

You are becoming, the Sea King replied with the patience of someone explaining concepts that transcended ordinary language. *Death implies ending, but what you experience is expansion beyond every boundary you previously understood as permanent. Your individual self remains intact, but it now exists simultaneously across multiple states of reality.*

Through her expanding awareness, Nisha could perceive the truth of his words. She was still herself—her memories, her values, her essential personality all remained intact. But she was also something more, something that could exist in the underwater cities of the transformed realm, in the mystical infrastructure of Mumbai, in the spaces between dimensions where cosmic forces flowed like vast rivers connecting all possible forms of existence.

"The friends who care about you see only the cost of transformation," Kavita Devi's voice joined the otherworldly conversation, her ancient wisdom carrying compassion for both Nisha's struggle and her companions' distress. "But they cannot perceive what you have gained—the ability to serve as a permanent bridge between realms, to exist as a living guarantee that neither world will ever again face the threats that isolation and misunderstanding create."

The realisation brought both comfort and sorrow. She had achieved exactly what she had hoped for during her desperate research into ancient prophecies—a way to preserve what was valuable about both human and otherworldly existence while enabling them to coexist and cooperate. But the price had been her ability to exist fully in either realm, leaving her suspended between worlds in a way that her purely human friends could never completely understand.

Yet even as cosmic awareness expanded her perception beyond terrestrial limitations, she felt the anchor points that her training and relationships had established. The memories of individual connection, the values forged through shared struggle, the determination to protect what was precious about human consciousness—these remained as strong as ever, providing stability that prevented her expanded identity from dissolving into the vast networks of otherworldly awareness.

"I can hear them," she said, her voice barely audible but carrying harmonics that allowed it to reach across multiple dimensions simultaneously. "Dev trying to find mathematical solutions to problems that transcend calculation. Mira planning tactical responses to threats that can't be fought with conventional weapons. Kritika weaving harmonic patterns designed to provide emotional support across barriers that separate different forms of existence."

Through her connection to the temple networks that her sacrifice had reactivated, she could sense the "heart of the city" that the ancient prophecies had described. It wasn't a single location, she realised, but a state of balance that could exist anywhere consciousness chose to bridge differences rather than emphasise separation. She had become that bridge, not through reaching a specific place, but through accepting transformation that preserved connection while enabling evolution.

The fragments of the ancient temple system were indeed scattered throughout Mumbai, hidden in plain sight as components of infrastructure that had been built over and around them throughout centuries of urban development. But they had been dormant not because they were broken, but because they had been waiting for someone with the capability to serve as their focal point—a spiral bearer who could channel otherworldly power while maintaining human values and perspectives.

"The prophecies were accurate," she observed, her transformed awareness encompassing both the immediate situation and the larger patterns that had been developing across centuries. "But they weren't describing a place to be found or a system to be reactivated. They were describing a state of being that could transform any location into a point of balance between realms."

Through her expanded perception, she could see her friends' efforts to understand and help her condition. Dev's equations were growing increasingly sophisticated as he tried to map consciousness that existed in multiple dimensional states simultaneously. His mathematical frameworks were actually beginning to achieve partial success, creating models that could predict and influence her distributed awareness in limited ways.

"Fascinating," Dev murmured, studying patterns that flickered through dimensions his normal senses couldn't perceive directly. "She's not just existing in multiple locations—she's serving as a living coordinate system that allows communication and cooperation between incompatible forms of reality."

Mira approached the problem from a tactical perspective, developing protocols for how to interact with someone whose consciousness operated according to principles no conventional training had prepared them to understand. Her warrior's instincts were adapting to recognise that protection sometimes meant accepting change rather than preventing it.

"She's still fighting," Mira observed, studying Nisha's motionless form with the eye of someone trained to assess both physical and strategic conditions. "Not fighting against the transformation, but fighting to maintain connection to the values and relationships that define who she is. The changes haven't consumed her—they've given her new ways to express her essential nature."

Kritika's crystals had begun generating frequencies that were previously unknown to human music, harmonies that seemed to incorporate perspectives from the otherworldly realms while remaining grounded in terrestrial emotional understanding. Her gift for creating balance between opposing forces had found new expression in the challenge of bridging the gap between human and cosmic awareness.

"The harmonic patterns suggest that communication is possible," she reported, her crystals singing with melodies that carried meaning across dimensional barriers. "She can still hear us, still respond to us, but the methods of interaction have to accommodate her expanded state of existence."

Through these efforts, Nisha felt a warmth that had nothing to do with physical temperature—the recognition that transformation hadn't severed her connections to the people she cared about, but had created new ways for those connections to find expression. Her friends were learning to love and support someone who had become something unprecedented, accepting change while maintaining the essential bonds that had sustained them through every crisis.

But perhaps most importantly, she could sense the broader effects of her sacrifice rippling across both realms. In the underwater cities of the transformed realm, beings who had chosen complete evolution were beginning to interact with surface dwellers through the bridge she had become. Not the overwhelming integration that had been feared, but careful, voluntary exchanges that allowed both sides to benefit from perspectives they had never been able to access safely.

"The convergence continues," she said, her voice now carrying harmonics that seemed to incorporate frequencies from realms that existed beyond physical space. "But it's guided now, controlled, designed to preserve what's valuable about each form of consciousness while enabling growth and cooperation."

In Mumbai, the supernatural modifications to urban infrastructure were stabilising into permanent improvements that enhanced quality of life without overwhelming residents who had no preparation for otherworldly contact. The city was becoming something unprecedented—a place where multiple forms of reality could coexist peacefully, where human creativity and otherworldly wisdom could combine to solve problems, neither could address alone.

"She did it," Guru Chanda said quietly, her voice carrying wonder mixed with sorrow as she observed the scope of what Nisha's sacrifice had achieved. "Not just prevented catastrophe, but created something entirely new—a form of existence that honours both human individuality and cosmic connection."

The scarred guardian lay motionless on the stone floor, her transformed form serving as living proof that evolution and preservation could be achieved simultaneously. The scars were not wounds but adaptations, not signs of damage but evidence of growth that had transcended every limitation previously thought to be absolute.

Through her expanded awareness, Nisha could perceive the future stretching ahead—not a single timeline, but multiple possibilities that remained open because her sacrifice had prevented the kind of catastrophic convergence that would have eliminated choice for everyone involved. Children would grow up in a world where the boundaries between possible and impossible were negotiable rather than absolute, where human creativity could be enhanced by otherworldly perspectives without losing its essential chaotic beauty.

"I'm still here," she said, her voice barely audible but carrying certainty that transcended the physical changes that had reshaped her form. "Different than I was, more than I was, but still essentially myself. The bridge holds, and both worlds are stronger for it."

The silence that followed her words was different from the terrible quiet that had marked her collapse—it was the silence of understanding, acceptance, and hope that had been hard-won through struggle and sacrifice. The scarred guardian had found her place between worlds, and in doing so, had ensured that neither realm would ever again face the future alone.

The convergence was complete, but it had created synthesis rather than conquest, collaboration rather than dominance, bridges that preserved rather than absorbed. And at the centre of it all, transformed beyond recognition but still essentially herself, Nisha served as living proof that the most profound changes could honour rather than destroy what was most precious about individual identity and human connection.

Chapter 22:

WHISPERS OF THE CORE

THE DECISION TO LEAVE NISHA in her transformed, barely conscious state felt like abandoning a dying friend, but the fragments of prophecy she had managed to communicate through her fading connection to normal human awareness provided their only hope for finding a solution that might preserve what remained of her essential self. Dev, Mira, and Kritika stood at the threshold of the Pathshala's protected environment, each carrying equipment and knowledge that might prove crucial in the dangerous journey ahead.

"The maps she showed us during her lucid moments point to the old Mumbadevi district," Dev said, consulting the ancient documents they had discovered in the hidden archives. His floating equations were more subdued than usual; their mathematical precision focused entirely on practical navigation through a city where supernatural and mundane geography increasingly overlapped in ways that defied conventional understanding.

"If the temple is really there, it's been buried under centuries of urban development," Mira pointed out, her tactical training allowing her to assess the practical challenges they would face. "We're not just looking for a building—we're looking for mystical infrastructure that might be integrated into modern construction without the builders having any idea what they were working with."

Kritika's crystals hummed with frequencies designed to detect otherworldly resonances, their combined harmonics creating a sensory map that could guide them toward locations where ancient power sources might still be active. "The harmonic signatures suggest that fragments of the original temple system are indeed scattered throughout that area," she reported. "But they're not functioning as a coordinated network. They're dormant, waiting for someone with the right capabilities to reactivate them."

The journey into the surface world was fraught with dangers that went far beyond the usual risks of urban exploration. Mumbai in the aftermath of the convergence was a city where reality had become negotiable, where streets might flow like water while maintaining their solid appearance, where buildings incorporated architectural principles that followed otherworldly logic rather than terrestrial engineering.

"Stay closer," Mira instructed as they navigated through districts where the supernatural integration was most pronounced. "The modified infrastructure isn't hostile, but it responds to intention and emotion in ways that can be disorienting if you're not prepared for them."

Indeed, the city seemed to be actively helping their search, with traffic patterns adjusting to provide clear pathways, with streetlights illuminating routes that led toward their destination, with even the weather cooperating to provide optimal conditions for their exploration. It was as if Mumbai itself understood the importance of their mission and was doing everything possible to support their efforts.

"The convergence didn't just change the supernatural landscape," Dev observed, studying the way his equations interacted with the modified urban environment. "It created a form of civic consciousness—the city has become aware of its own needs and the needs of its inhabitants."

As they approached the area where the ancient maps suggested the original temple had been located, the signs of otherworldly influence became more pronounced and more complex. Buildings showed architectural elements that definitely predated their official construction dates—carved stone foundations that incorporated symbols from multiple mystical traditions, structural supports that followed mathematical principles no human engineer had ever conceived, water systems that channelled liquid in patterns too sophisticated to be accidental.

"Look at this," Kritika said, pointing to what appeared to be a perfectly ordinary apartment building that was showing signs of having been constructed around much older foundations. "The harmonic resonances are strongest here, but they're coming from below—from structures that exist beneath the modern construction."

Their investigation led them through narrow alleys that seemed to shift and rearrange themselves to provide access to areas that shouldn't have been reachable through normal navigation. The city was indeed helping them, but it was also testing them, requiring them to demonstrate understanding of the forces they sought to work with rather than simply providing easy answers to complex questions.

"We're being guided," Dev realised, studying the way mathematical patterns in the urban environment were directing their movements. "But we're also being evaluated. The temple systems won't activate for just anyone—they require someone who understands both the theoretical principles involved and the practical responsibilities that come with accessing such power."

The entrance to the buried temple complex revealed itself gradually, not as a dramatic discovery but as a growing recognition that they had been walking through its outer chambers for several minutes without realising it. What had appeared to be a modern subway maintenance tunnel was actually a corridor lined with carved symbols that predated any known historical tradition, their meanings partially familiar from the ancient documents they had studied but incorporating concepts that definitely came from otherworldly sources.

"The integration is more complete than we anticipated," Mira observed, studying the way ancient and modern construction had been seamlessly combined. "This isn't just old infrastructure that was built over—it's a hybrid system that incorporates both terrestrial and otherworldly engineering principles."

As they descended deeper into the buried complex, following passages that seemed to extend far beneath the foundations of the surface city, the signs of active mystical infrastructure became increasingly evident. Water flowed through channels carved with symbols that pulsed with their own internal light, creating patterns too complex and purposeful to be merely decorative. The air itself carried traces of otherworldly influence—not threatening or overwhelming, but present in ways that spoke of power sources that had been carefully maintained across centuries.

"The system is still active," Kritika reported, her crystals singing with harmonies that seemed to resonate with frequencies built into the temple architecture itself. "Not functioning at full capacity, but definitely operational. It's been waiting for someone with the right capabilities to serve as its focal point."

But as they penetrated deeper into the ancient complex, they encountered their first serious obstacle—not the traps and guardians that conventional wisdom might have suggested, but something far more sophisticated and dangerous. The temple wasn't abandoned or dormant—it was under active assault by advanced sea-spawn that were unlike anything in the Pathshala's historical records.

These creatures moved through the temple spaces with purpose and intelligence that spoke of careful planning rather than random intrusion. They were more agile and adaptable than the crude manifestations that had occasionally appeared during previous supernatural incidents, their forms shifting fluidly between aquatic and terrestrial configurations as the environment demanded. Most disturbing of all, they seemed to be specifically targeting the temple's central energy conduits, attempting to disrupt the mystical flows that kept the ancient systems operational.

"They're not trying to destroy the temple," Dev observed, studying the creatures' behaviour patterns through his mathematical analysis systems. "They're trying to corrupt it by turning its balanced power into a conduit for otherworldly influence that would serve the Sea King's purposes rather than maintaining the equilibrium the original builders intended."

The battle that erupted in the ancient corridors was unlike anything they had experienced during their training at the Pathshala. These weren't practice sessions with controlled risks and safety protocols—this was combat against intelligent opponents who understood both the strategic value of the temple systems and the tactical advantages of fighting in an environment they had been specifically designed to exploit.

Mira took point, her Kartikeya training blazing to full intensity as she engaged the sea-spawn in close combat. Her energy weapons cut through otherworldly forms with deadly efficiency, but the creatures adapted quickly to her attack patterns, their fluid nature allowing them to reform and adjust their defensive configurations in real-time.

"They're learning from our techniques," she called out as she fought to protect Dev and Kritika while they worked to understand the temple's systems. "Every attack teaches them something new about how we fight, and they're using that information to become more effective opponents."

Dev worked frantically to analyse the corrupted energy flows, his equations mapping the complex interactions between the temple's original design and the otherworldly influences that were attempting to subvert its function. "The corruption isn't random damage," he reported. "Its systematic modification designed to turn the temple into a permanent gateway that would allow unlimited otherworldly manifestation in the surface world."

Kritika used her Mahalaxmi abilities to create diversions and strategic advantages, her harmonic crystals generating frequencies that disrupted the sea-spawn's coordination while providing tactical support for Mira's combat efforts. But even her sophisticated techniques were being tested by opponents who seemed to possess intimate knowledge of how divine essence manipulation worked.

"The temple's defences are still partially functional," she observed, studying the way ancient protective systems were responding to the intrusion. "But they're designed to work in cooperation with someone who can serve as their focal point—they need conscious direction to achieve maximum effectiveness."

As the battle raged through chambers that had been carved from living rock centuries before Mumbai had existed as a modern city, the scope of what was at stake became increasingly clear. The sea-spawn weren't just attempting to corrupt a single mystical site—they were trying to turn the entire ancient network into a weapon that could force integration between realms regardless of individual preferences or preparations.

"If they succeed in fully corrupting the temple core," Dev realised, his mathematical analysis showing the cascading effects that would result from such sabotage, "they could destabilise the dimensional barriers throughout the entire region. Not just Mumbai, but every major population centre within hundreds of kilometres."

The creatures seemed to understand the urgency of their mission as well, intensifying their attacks on the temple's critical systems even as they fought against the three friends' desperate defence efforts. Their assault was carefully coordinated, with some sea-spawn engaging in direct combat while others worked to complete the corruption process that would give the Sea King permanent control over the ancient infrastructure.

"We're running out of time," Mira called out as she fought to prevent the creatures from reaching the temple's inner chambers. "There are too many of them, and they're too well adapted to this environment. We need backup, or we need a miracle."

But even as the tactical situation deteriorated around them, Dev made a crucial discovery that changed everything. His analysis of the temple's mystical architecture revealed that the corruption wasn't as advanced as it appeared—the sea-spawn had indeed damaged many of the temple's systems, but they had been unable to access the core functions that required spiral bearer capabilities to understand and manipulate.

"The temple isn't just a mystical power source," he announced, his equations finally mapping the full scope of the ancient design. "It's a conscious entity in its own right—a form of artificial intelligence that was created by the original builders to serve as a permanent guardian of the balance between realms. The sea-spawn can damage its peripheral systems, but they can't touch its essential nature without someone like Nisha to serve as an interface."

The realisation brought both hope and desperation in equal measure. The temple could indeed provide the solution they sought for stabilising Nisha's condition and creating permanent protection for both realms—but only if they could prevent its corruption long enough for her to reach and activate its core functions.

"We have to get word back to the Pathshala," Kritika said, her crystals working to establish communication links across the dimensional distortions that were growing stronger as the battle continued. "Nisha needs to know what we've discovered, and we need support to hold this position until she can get here."

But even as she spoke, new waves of sea-spawn were emerging from the deeper passages of the temple complex, their numbers and sophistication suggesting that this was far more than a reconnaissance mission or opportunistic attack. This was a full-scale assault designed to secure control of the ancient systems before anyone with spiral bearer capabilities could interfere with their plans.

"They know," Mira realised, her warrior's instincts recognising the strategic implications of the escalating assault. "The Sea King knows we've found the temple, knows what it represents, and he's committed everything to corrupting it before we can use it to stabilise the situation."

The battle for the temple's core had become a race against time, with the fate of both realms hanging in the balance. The ancient systems offered hope for solutions that could preserve individual choice while enabling cosmic cooperation—but only if they could be protected from corruption long enough for the right person to activate them.

In the distance, they could hear the sound of water rising through passages that definitely shouldn't have been connected to any terrestrial water source. The Sea King's influence was growing stronger with each passing moment, turning the temple into a battleground where the outcome would determine whether the convergence proceeded through wisdom or was imposed through force.

The whispers of the core called out across dimensional barriers, seeking the one person who possessed the capabilities necessary to restore balance to systems that had been designed to protect both realms from the kind of catastrophic integration that now threatened to consume everything they had worked to preserve.

Time was running out, but the ancient wisdom built into the temple's very foundations continued to resist corruption, waiting patiently for the spiral bearer who could serve as its voice and its guardian in a world that had forgotten the true meaning of balance between different forms of existence.

Chapter 23:

TEMPLE UNDER SIEGE

AS DEV, MIRA, AND KRITIKA penetrated deeper into the ancient temple complex, following passages carved from living rock that predated any known period of Mumbai's history, they discovered that their initial assessment had been dangerously optimistic. The temple wasn't just under supernatural influence—it was under active siege by a new generation of advanced sea-spawn that moved through the sacred spaces with purpose and intelligence that spoke of careful planning rather than random intrusion.

These creatures were unlike anything described in the Pathshala's historical records or encountered during their previous confrontations with otherworldly entities. Where the earlier manifestations had been crude, instinct-driven beings that relied on overwhelming force, these new entities displayed tactical sophistication that matched their enhanced physical capabilities. They moved through the temple's corridors with fluid grace, their forms shifting seamlessly between aquatic and terrestrial configurations as the environment demanded, their attacks coordinated with military precision.

"They're not just more agile," Mira observed, her Kartikeya training allowing her to analyse their movement patterns even while preparing for combat. "They're more intelligent. They understand the temple's layout, they know which systems are critical to its function, and they're specifically targeting the energy conduits that maintain the mystical infrastructure."

Indeed, as they watched from concealment in one of the temple's outer chambers, the sea-spawn were conducting what could only be described as systematic sabotage of the ancient mystical systems. Groups of the creatures worked in coordinated teams, with some serving as guards while others focused on disrupting specific components of the temple's energy distribution network. Their attacks weren't random destruction—they were precise modifications designed to corrupt the flow of divine essence without destroying the infrastructure entirely.

"They're not trying to shut down the temple," Dev realised, his mathematical analysis revealing the underlying pattern of the sabotage efforts. "They're trying to subvert it, to twist Mumbadevi's balanced power for the Sea King's own purposes. If they succeed, the temple becomes a permanent conduit for otherworldly influence rather than a point of equilibrium between realms."

Kritika's crystals hummed with discordant frequencies as they analysed the corrupted energy flows, their usual harmonious songs distorted by the alien influences that were being introduced into the temple's systems. "The modifications they're making would turn the entire complex into a dimensional gateway," she reported, her voice tight with alarm. "Not controlled access that preserves choice and balance, but unlimited manifestation that could overwhelm the surface world's ability to adapt."

The scope of the threat became clearer as they observed the sea-spawn's methodical work. The creatures possessed detailed knowledge of the temple's mystical architecture, understanding not just which systems to target but precisely how to modify them to serve their purposes. Their corruption efforts followed technical specifications that suggested intimate familiarity with both the original design principles and the otherworldly forces they were trying to integrate.

"Someone provided them with blueprints," Mira said grimly, her warrior's instincts recognising the strategic implications. "This isn't improvised sabotage, it's a carefully planned conversion operation designed to turn the temple into a weapon that serves the Sea King's agenda."

But even as they studied the creatures' activities, the sea-spawn became aware of their presence. The response was immediate and overwhelming—not the chaotic rush of mindless predators, but the coordinated assault of a military unit that had been trained to handle exactly this kind of intrusion.

The battle that erupted in the temple's sacred corridors was unlike anything they had experienced during their training at the Pathshala. These weren't practice sessions with controlled conditions and safety protocols—this was life-or-death combat against opponents who possessed both supernatural capabilities and tactical sophistication that matched their own.

Mira took the lead, her Kartikeya power blazing to full intensity as she engaged the sea-spawn in direct combat. Her energy weapons cut through otherworldly forms with deadly efficiency, but the creatures adapted to her attack patterns with disturbing speed. Their fluid nature allowed them to reform after taking damage, to adjust their defensive configurations in real-time, and to coordinate their responses in ways that maximised their collective effectiveness.

"They're learning from every exchange," she called out as she fought to establish a defensive perimeter around Dev and Kritika. "Each attack teaches them something new about divine essence manipulation, and they're using that knowledge to become more dangerous opponents."

Dev worked frantically to analyse the temple's corrupted systems while the battle raged around him, his floating equations mapping the complex interactions between the original mystical architecture and the otherworldly modifications being introduced by the sea-spawn. What he discovered was deeply alarming—the creatures weren't just randomly damaging the temple's functions, but implementing a sophisticated conversion protocol that would transform the entire complex into something that served the Sea King's purposes.

"The corruption follows a specific pattern," he reported, his voice strained from the effort of maintaining mathematical analysis while under active attack. "They're not destroying the temple's power—they're redirecting it. If they complete this process, every ounce of divine essence that flows through the ancient systems will be channelled directly to support otherworldly manifestation in the surface world."

Kritika used her Mahalaxmi abilities to create diversions and tactical advantages, her crystals generating frequencies that disrupted the sea-spawn's coordination while providing harmonic support for Mira's combat efforts. But even her sophisticated techniques were being tested by opponents who seemed to possess detailed knowledge of how divine essence manipulation worked and how to counter it.

"The temple's original defences are still partially functional," she observed, studying the way ancient protective systems were responding to the intrusion. "But they're designed to work in partnership with someone who can serve as their conscious director. Without a spiral bearer to coordinate their responses, they can only provide limited resistance to this kind of systematic corruption."

As the battle continued through chambers that had been carved from sacred stone centuries before Mumbai had existed as a modern city, the tactical situation became increasingly desperate. The sea-spawn weren't just numerous and well-coordinated—they were specifically adapted to fight in the temple environment, their aquatic nature allowing them to move through the mystical water channels that ran throughout the complex, their otherworldly origins making them resistant to many of the defensive systems that had been designed to protect against terrestrial threats.

"We're outnumbered and outmanoeuvred," Mira admitted as she fell back to a more defensible position, her energy weapons blazing as she fought to prevent the creatures from flanking their small group. "These aren't random monsters—they're specialized forces that were created specifically to capture and corrupt mystical infrastructure."

But even as the immediate tactical situation deteriorated, Dev made a crucial discovery that changed the entire nature of their mission. His analysis of the temple's core systems revealed that the sea-spawn, despite their sophisticated approach and detailed knowledge, had been unable to access the most critical components of the ancient infrastructure.

"The temple's heart is still intact," he announced, his equations finally mapping the full scope of the mystical architecture that lay beneath the surface corruption. "The creatures can damage the peripheral systems, but they can't touch the core functions without someone with spiral bearer capabilities to serve as an interface."

The realisation brought both hope and urgency in equal measure. The temple could indeed provide the solution they sought for stabilising Nisha's condition and creating permanent protection for both realms—but only if they could prevent the completion of the corruption process long enough for her to reach the complex and activate its core functions.

"The core isn't just a power source," Dev continued, his mathematical analysis revealing layers of complexity that had been invisible until now. "It's a conscious entity in its own right, a form of mystical intelligence that was created by the original builders to serve as a permanent mediator between incompatible forms of existence. The sea-spawn can corrupt its peripheral systems, but they can't subvert its essential nature without a spiral bearer to bridge the gap between terrestrial and otherworldly awareness."

Through her crystals, Kritika began detecting signs that the temple's core consciousness was indeed still active, still fighting against the corruption being introduced by the sea-spawn. The ancient intelligence was trying to communicate, sending harmonic patterns that carried meaning across dimensional barriers, but its messages were being distorted by the otherworldly influences that had infiltrated the temple's communication systems.

"It's trying to tell us something," she reported, her crystals working to filter the core's signals from the chaos of corrupted energy flows. "The temple knows we're here, knows what we're trying to accomplish, but it's having difficulty reaching us through all the interference the sea-spawn have introduced into its systems."

As they fought to hold their position against increasingly sophisticated attacks, the scope of what was at stake became clearer with each passing moment. The sea-spawn weren't conducting a random assault on an ancient relic—they were implementing the final phase of a carefully orchestrated campaign to gain permanent control over mystical infrastructure that could reshape the relationship between realms according to the Sea King's preferences, rather than principles of balance and voluntary cooperation.

"If they succeed in fully corrupting the temple core," Dev realised, his equations showing the cascading effects that would result from such sabotage, "they won't just control this site—they'll have access to the entire network of ancient mystical infrastructure that connects sacred sites throughout the region. Every temple, every shrine, every point where the barriers between realms are naturally thin would become a gateway for unlimited otherworldly manifestation."

The creatures seemed to understand the strategic importance of their mission as well, intensifying their corruption efforts even as they maintained their assault on the three friends' defensive position. Their attacks were becoming more coordinated and more desperate, suggesting that they too were operating under time pressure—perhaps because they knew that spiral bearer intervention could still reverse their modifications if it came soon enough.

"We need to get word back to the Pathshala," Kritika said, her crystals working to establish communication links across the dimensional distortions that were growing stronger as the temple's corruption progressed. "Nisha needs to know what we've discovered, and we need reinforcements to hold this position until she can get here."

But even as she spoke, new waves of sea-spawn were emerging from the deeper passages of the temple complex, their numbers suggesting that this was far more than an opportunistic attack. The creatures were arriving through dimensional rifts that seemed to be opening directly into the temple's most sacred spaces, bypassing the outer defences entirely through methods that spoke of intimate knowledge of the complex's mystical architecture.

"They have inside information," Mira concluded, her tactical analysis revealing the sophistication of the assault they were facing. "Someone provided them with detailed specifications of the temple's layout, its defensive systems, and its critical vulnerabilities. This isn't just an attack—it's a precision operation designed to achieve complete control with minimal resistance."

The battle for the temple's core had become a race against time, with the fate of both realms hanging in the balance. The ancient systems offered hope for solutions that could preserve individual choice while enabling cosmic cooperation—but only if they could be protected from corruption long enough for the right person to activate them.

Through the chaos of combat and the growing distortions caused by the temple's corrupted systems, they could hear something that made their blood run cold: the sound of water rising through passages that definitely shouldn't have been connected to any terrestrial water source. The Sea King's influence was growing stronger with each system the sea-spawn managed to corrupt, turning the temple into a conduit for otherworldly forces that had been contained for centuries.

"The core is fighting back," Kritika reported, her crystals detecting surges of pure, uncorrupted divine essence emanating from the temple's deepest levels. "The ancient intelligence isn't passive—it's actively resisting the corruption, but it's losing the battle without conscious support from someone who can interface with its systems directly."

As they prepared for what might be their final stand against opponents whose numbers and capabilities continued to grow, Nisha's voice reached them across dimensional barriers—not through conventional communication systems, but through her expanding connection to the mystical networks that spanned both realms.

Her transformed awareness had detected their desperate situation, and despite her own critical condition, she was somehow projecting her consciousness toward the temple, offering what support she could provide from a distance. The connection was faint and intermittent, filtered through layers of otherworldly influence that made clear communication nearly impossible, but her intent was unmistakable.

"She's coming," Dev said, his equations detecting the subtle changes in the temple's energy patterns that marked Nisha's approaching presence. "But I don't know if she can get here in time, or if she'll have enough strength left to interface with the core systems when she arrives."

The siege continued, with each side fighting for control of infrastructure that could determine the future relationship between realms. The sea-spawn pressed their systematic corruption campaign while the three friends struggled to protect systems they only partially understood, guided by hope that ancient wisdom and modern determination could find ways to preserve balance in a world where the boundaries between possible and impossible had become increasingly fluid.

In the distance, the sound of rising water grew louder, and with it came the patient voice of cosmic forces that had been waiting centuries for this moment of ultimate convergence. The temple's fate would be decided soon, and with it, the question of whether the integration of realms would proceed through wisdom and voluntary cooperation, or be imposed through force and the elimination of individual choice.

The ancient stones bore witness to a battle that would reshape the nature of existence itself, while in the depths of the complex, a consciousness older than human civilisation waited to see whether its creators' dreams of balance and harmony could survive the collision between cosmic ambition and mortal determination.

Chapter 24:

THE HEART'S RESONANCE

THE BATTLE IN THE ANCIENT temple had reached a crescendo of desperation, with Mira's energy weapons blazing against increasingly sophisticated sea-spawn while Dev worked frantically to understand the corrupted systems and Kritika struggled to maintain harmonic stability in an environment that grew more chaotic with each passing moment. The creatures were on the verge of overwhelming their defences when something fundamental shifted in the mystical atmosphere of the temple complex.

From her position in the Pathshala, where she lay motionless on the stone floor with her life force flickering like a candle in hurricane wind, Nisha felt the agonising resonance of her friends' desperate struggle. The connection between her transformed consciousness and the ancient temple systems was growing stronger as her physical form grew weaker, creating a paradox where her approaching dissolution was simultaneously expanding her ability to perceive and influence forces that operated across multiple dimensions.

The silvery patterns covering her skin pulsed with increasing urgency as she sensed the critical moment approaching. Through her expanding awareness, she could feel the temple's core consciousness calling out across dimensional barriers, its ancient intelligence seeking the one person who possessed the capabilities necessary to restore balance to systems that had been designed to bridge incompatible forms of existence.

But attempting to establish a connection from such a distance, while her physical form was barely able to maintain basic life functions, would require her to risk everything that remained of her individual identity. The effort might provide her friends with the support they desperately needed, but it could also push her transformation beyond any hope of preserving her essential self.

The choice approaches its ultimate expression, Vanaraja's voice whispered through the spiral mark, carrying harmonics that spoke of ancient patience and otherworldly compassion. *Your friends face forces they cannot overcome alone, but saving them will require you to accept complete transformation. Are you prepared to sacrifice your individual existence for their welfare?*

"I've been prepared for that sacrifice since the moment I chose to stand between worlds," Nisha replied, her voice barely audible but carrying harmonics that allowed it to reach across dimensional barriers. "The question isn't whether I'm willing to give up my humanity—it's whether I can find a way to help them while preserving what makes that humanity worth protecting."

Drawing on the last reserves of her rapidly depleting life force, Nisha began to extend her consciousness toward the temple, not through conventional projection but through the mystical networks that had been established by centuries of accumulated devotion. The effort was excruciating, requiring her to channel forces that were literally consuming her individual identity while simultaneously maintaining enough coherence to provide useful assistance.

The connection, when it finally formed, was unlike anything she had experienced before. Instead of simply observing the temple's condition from a distance, she found herself existing simultaneously in multiple locations—her physical form remained in the Pathshala, but her consciousness was suddenly present in the ancient chambers where her friends fought for their lives against opponents whose capabilities exceeded anything they had been trained to handle.

Through this distributed awareness, she could perceive the true scope of the corruption that had infected the temple's systems. The sea-spawn weren't just randomly damaging the mystical infrastructure, they were implementing a sophisticated conversion protocol that would transform every aspect of the ancient complex into components of a vast otherworldly gateway. The process was nearly complete, requiring only a few more critical modifications to achieve irreversible subversion of the temple's original purpose.

But she could also perceive something else—the temple's core consciousness, still fighting against the corruption despite being overwhelmed by forces it had never been designed to resist alone. The ancient intelligence was trying to maintain the balance between realms even as otherworldly influences systematically undermined its ability to function properly.

Sister, the temple's voice reached her through channels that had been established centuries ago, carrying harmonics that spoke of wisdom accumulated across generations of faithful service. *The corruption spreads beyond our ability to contain. Without conscious direction from one who can bridge the gap between terrestrial and otherworldly awareness, the ancient systems will fall to subversion.*

"Then you'll have that direction," Nisha replied, her transformed consciousness reaching toward the temple's core with determination that transcended every physical limitation. "Guide me to the point of corruption. Show me what needs to be done."

The temple responded by opening pathways that had been sealed for centuries, mystical connections that linked its consciousness directly to the broader network of ancient infrastructure that had once protected the entire region. Through these channels, Nisha could perceive not just the immediate crisis but the larger pattern of corruption that was spreading through sacred sites throughout Mumbai and beyond.

Meanwhile, in the temple's physical chambers, the battle had reached a point where Mira's combat skills were being pushed beyond their absolute limits. The sea-spawn had adapted to her attack patterns with terrifying efficiency, their coordinated responses making it increasingly difficult for her to protect Dev and Kritika while they worked to understand the temple's corrupted systems.

"The corruption is accelerating," Dev called out, his mathematical analysis showing patterns that spoke of imminent systemic failure. "Whatever they're doing to the core systems, it's reaching a point where the damage might become irreversible even if we can drive them off."

Kritika's crystals were singing with increasingly discordant harmonies as they struggled to maintain stability in an environment where the usual rules of divine essence manipulation were being systematically undermined. "The harmonic patterns are collapsing," she reported, her voice tight with strain. "I'm losing the ability to provide effective support—the corrupted frequencies are interfering with everything I try to accomplish."

It was at this moment of maximum desperation that Nisha's consciousness suddenly blazed into full presence within the temple complex. Her awareness didn't simply observe the battle—it actively participated, providing her friends with capabilities they had never possessed and insights they could never have achieved on their own.

Through her connection to the temple's core consciousness, she was able to perceive the exact nature of the corruption being introduced by the sea-spawn. The creatures weren't just damaging the mystical systems—they were implementing modifications based on detailed technical specifications that could only have come from someone with intimate knowledge of both the temple's original design and the otherworldly forces being integrated into its function.

"I can see the corruption pattern," Nisha's voice reached them through the temple's own communication systems, her transformed consciousness using the ancient infrastructure to coordinate their response. "Dev, the critical point is seventeen meters below your current position, where the primary energy conduits converge. The sea-spawn have introduced a resonance disruptor that's forcing the divine essence flows to follow otherworldly harmonic patterns."

Dev's equations immediately began mapping the location she had identified, his mathematical analysis confirming the presence of modifications that matched her description. "I can see it now," he said, his voice carrying excitement mixed with alarm. "But reaching that location while the temple is under active assault…"

"You don't have to reach it physically," Nisha replied, her distributed consciousness already working to establish the connections necessary for remote intervention. "I can channel your analytical capabilities directly into the temple's systems, allowing you to perform the necessary corrections through mystical interface rather than physical access."

The process that followed was unlike anything any of them had experienced before. Using her transformed consciousness as a bridge, Nisha connected Dev's mathematical understanding directly to the temple's core systems, allowing him to perceive and manipulate the mystical architecture with precision that would have been impossible through conventional means.

Working together across dimensional barriers, they began the complex process of purging the corruption from the temple's critical systems. It wasn't simply a matter of removing the otherworldly influences—they had to carefully separate beneficial modifications from harmful ones, preserving improvements that enhanced the temple's function while eliminating changes that would have subverted its original purpose.

"The resonance disruptor is more sophisticated than we anticipated," Dev reported, his consciousness now existing simultaneously in the temple's mystical infrastructure and his physical form. "It's not just forcing harmonic changes—it's learning from the temple's responses, adapting its corruption patterns to overcome whatever resistance we create."

"Then we don't resist," Nisha said, her expanding awareness suggesting an approach that drew on principles from her engineering background. "We redirect. Instead of trying to block the corruption, we channel it into isolated systems where it can't affect the temple's core functions."

The technique required her to exist in multiple states simultaneously—maintaining her connection to the temple's consciousness, serving as a bridge for Dev's analytical capabilities, and channelling the massive amounts of divine essence necessary to perform large-scale mystical engineering. The effort was consuming what remained of her individual identity at an alarming rate, but it was also achieving results that would have been impossible through any conventional approach.

As they worked to redirect the corruption flows, something unexpected happened. The temple's core consciousness, freed from the overwhelming pressure of otherworldly subversion, began to actively participate in the purification process. The ancient intelligence possessed capabilities that neither Nisha nor Dev had imagined—not just the ability to channel divine essence, but sophisticated understanding of how to work with forces that operated according to principles that transcended the usual boundaries between terrestrial and otherworldly existence.

"The temple isn't just a mystical power source," Nisha realised, her consciousness expanding to encompass the full scope of what the ancient builders had created. "It's a living entity designed to serve as a permanent mediator between incompatible forms of reality. The corruption wasn't just damaging its systems—it was trying to overwhelm its ability to maintain conscious balance between opposing forces."

Working in partnership with the temple's consciousness, they began to implement solutions that went far beyond simple purification of corrupted systems. They were creating new forms of mystical architecture that could accommodate both terrestrial and otherworldly influences while maintaining the essential balance that prevented either side from overwhelming the other.

The process created a surge of pure, stable divine essence that rippled through the temple complex, pushing back against the sea-spawn's corruption efforts and restoring proper function to systems that had been systematically undermined. Where the purified energy flowed, the creatures found their modifications being undone, their carefully planned conversion protocol collapsing as the temple's original purpose reasserted itself.

"It's working," Kritika reported, her crystals suddenly singing with harmonies that incorporated frequencies from both realms while maintaining perfect balance between them. "The corruption is being purged, but it's not just returning to the original state—it's evolving into something new, something that preserves the benefits of integration while eliminating the coercive aspects."

The sea-spawn, faced with the systematic reversal of their corruption efforts, began to withdraw from the temple complex. But their retreat wasn't the chaotic flight of defeated opponents—it was an organised withdrawal that suggested they understood the strategic implications of what had been accomplished and were reporting back to their superiors rather than continuing a battle they could no longer win.

"They're not giving up," Mira observed, her warrior's instincts recognising the difference between defeat and tactical repositioning. "They're regrouping, probably to report that the temple can't be corrupted through conventional means. This isn't over, it's just moving to a new phase."

But even as they acknowledged the continuing threat, the successful purification of the temple's core systems had created something unprecedented. The ancient complex was now functioning as its builders had originally intended. Not just as a source of mystical power, but as a conscious entity capable of maintaining active balance between incompatible forms of existence.

"The temple is awake," Nisha said, her consciousness now permanently integrated with the ancient systems in ways that allowed direct communication with the intelligence that had been dormant for centuries. "It understands what we're trying to accomplish, and it's committed to supporting solutions that preserve individual choice while enabling voluntary cooperation between realms."

Through her connection to the temple's consciousness, she could perceive the broader implications of what they had achieved. The purification process hadn't just restored a single sacred site—it had reactivated the entire network of ancient infrastructure that had once protected the region, creating a foundation for the kind of balanced integration that respected both human autonomy and cosmic interconnection.

"The heart of the city beats again," she said, her voice carrying harmonics that incorporated perspectives from both realms while remaining essentially human in its emotional resonance. "The balance can be maintained, individual choice can be preserved, and both worlds can evolve together rather than one consuming the other."

The temple's restoration offered hope for solutions that had seemed impossible just hours before. But it also marked the beginning of a new phase in the relationship between realms, one that would require ongoing cooperation, constant vigilance, and the kind of wisdom that could only come from understanding that true strength lay not in dominance but in the ability to create harmony between opposing forces.

As Nisha felt her consciousness beginning to stabilise within the temple's systems, she realised that her transformation had indeed reached its completion—not through dissolution or absorption, but through evolution into something that could serve as a permanent bridge between worlds while maintaining the essential humanity that made such service meaningful.

The heart's resonance had awakened, and with it, the possibility of a future where different forms of existence could coexist not through conquest or surrender, but through the kind of understanding that honoured both individual identity and cosmic connection.

Chapter 25:

A PRECARIOUS TRUCE

THE IMMEDIATE CRISIS WAS OVER, but the silence that followed the temple's purification carried an ominous weight that spoke of victory achieved at costs that were only beginning to become apparent. Mumbai stretched out around them, its supernatural modifications stabilised into forms that enhanced rather than threatened urban function, its infrastructure now incorporating otherworldly principles that solved problems no purely terrestrial approach could have addressed. The convergence had been guided rather than conquered, shaped by wisdom rather than driven by fear.

Yet in the Heart of the Pathshala, where emergency protocols were finally being stood down after days of crisis management, the celebration was muted by the sight of Nisha's transformed form lying motionless on the stone floor. Her successful intervention at the temple had indeed prevented catastrophe and established the foundation for balanced coexistence between realms, but the cost had pushed her own condition beyond anything they had previously imagined possible.

"She's in an even more critical state than before," *Guru* Chanda reported after conducting the most comprehensive assessment possible with conventional healing techniques. Her hands moved in diagnostic patterns that had been refined over centuries of Pathshala practice, but the energy signatures she was detecting defied every theoretical framework they had developed for understanding divine essence manifestation.

The silvery filigree covering Nisha's skin had indeed become a permanent, crystalline layer that resembled armour crafted from moonlight more than any organic tissue. Her body temperature had stabilised at levels that should have been incompatible with human life, yet she continued to breathe, however faintly. Most disturbing of all, her spiral mark now glowed with constant, unblinking intensity that suggested connection to forces operating on cosmic rather than individual scales.

"The mathematical signatures indicate that she exists simultaneously across multiple dimensional states," Dev reported, his floating equations more complex than they had ever been as they tried to map consciousness that transcended every boundary he had previously understood as fundamental. "She's not just transformed—she's become something that can interface directly with the mystical infrastructure we restored at the temple."

Through the Pathshala's monitoring systems, they could observe the effects of the temple's reactivation rippling across Mumbai and beyond. The ancient network of sacred sites that had been dormant for centuries was slowly coming back to life, creating a web of mystical infrastructure that could maintain balance between terrestrial and otherworldly forces without requiring constant conscious intervention.

"The temple's restoration has created something unprecedented," Master Varun observed, studying the reports from monitoring stations throughout the region. "Not just a single point of mystical power, but a distributed network that can adapt to changing conditions while maintaining essential stability."

Indeed, the restored temple complex was functioning as its original builders had intended—not merely as a source of divine essence, but as a conscious entity capable of coordinating responses to supernatural threats while preserving the delicate balance that allowed different forms of existence to coexist peacefully.

But the temple's awakened consciousness carried with it a new understanding of what Nisha had become through her sacrifice. Through her permanent connection to the ancient systems, she had evolved into something that transcended every category they had previously used to understand spiral bearer transformation.

"She's not dying, and she's not dissolving," Kritika reported, her crystals singing with harmonies that incorporated frequencies from multiple dimensions while remaining grounded in recognisably human emotional understanding. "She's…stabilising. But into a form of existence that operates according to principles we've never encountered before."

The physical changes were indeed unprecedented. Where previous spiral bearers had either succumbed to dissolution or chosen complete transformation into otherworldly forms, Nisha appeared to be achieving something that preserved essential aspects of her humanity while gaining capabilities that allowed her to exist in multiple realms simultaneously.

Her breathing, while shallow, followed patterns that suggested not physical distress but adaptation to atmospheric conditions that incorporated elements from both terrestrial and otherworldly environments. Her skin, despite its crystalline appearance, remained warm to the touch, pulsing with internal rhythms that matched the flow of divine essence through the restored temple network.

Most significantly, her eyes, when they occasionally opened, reflected not the empty depths of dissolution but depths filled with awareness that encompassed perspectives no purely human mind could have contained while remaining essentially herself.

Through her connection to the temple's consciousness, Nisha was gradually becoming aware of the broader implications of what had been accomplished. The restoration hadn't just prevented the Sea King's attempt to subvert the ancient systems—it had created something entirely new, a form of mystical infrastructure that could evolve and adapt while maintaining the essential balance between individual autonomy and cosmic interconnection.

The immediate threat has been contained, Vanaraja's voice reached her through channels that now operated as much through the temple network as through the spiral mark on her arm. *But you must understand that this represents a pause rather than a conclusion. The convergence continues, guided now by the systems you have restored, but requiring ongoing attention to maintain the balance you have achieved.*

"I understand," Nisha replied, her voice carrying harmonics that seemed to emanate from the temple network itself as much as from her physical form. "This isn't an ending—it's a beginning. The foundation has been established for the kind of coexistence we've been working toward, but it will require constant care to maintain."

Through her expanding awareness, she could perceive the Sea King's presence retreating but not disappearing entirely. His vast intelligence had indeed been forced to abandon his specific plans for corrupting the temple network, but he remained a cosmic force whose patient nature meant that setbacks were merely temporary obstacles rather than permanent defeats.

Your wisdom grows, he acknowledged, his mental voice carrying something that might have been respect mixed with continued determination. *You have demonstrated that alternatives to my preferred approach are possible. But consider this, the balance you have created is inherently unstable. It requires conscious maintenance, ongoing vigilance, and the kind of cooperation between incompatible forces that has never been sustained over extended periods.*

"Then we'll learn how to sustain it," Nisha replied with certainty that transcended her transformed physical state. "We'll develop the wisdom and techniques necessary to maintain balance, and we'll teach others to carry on the work when we can no longer do so ourselves."

The temple's consciousness, now fully awakened and integrated with Nisha's expanded awareness, offered its own perspective on the challenges ahead. The ancient intelligence had observed the rise and fall of civilisations, had witnessed previous attempts at balancing incompatible forces, and understood both the possibilities and the pitfalls that lay ahead.

The path you have chosen is more difficult than either complete integration or permanent separation, the temple observed, its voice carrying the weight of centuries of accumulated wisdom. *It requires ongoing commitment to principles that are easy to abandon when immediate pressures arise. But it also offers possibilities that neither purely terrestrial nor completely otherworldly approaches could achieve alone.*

As Dev, Mira, and Kritika returned from the temple complex, their successful mission having established the foundation for everything that would follow, they found the Pathshala in a state of cautious optimism mixed with profound uncertainty about what the future would hold.

"The temple is secure and fully operational," Dev reported, his mathematical analysis confirming that the ancient systems were now functioning at levels that exceeded their original design specifications. "The network of sacred sites throughout the region is coming back online, creating a distributed infrastructure that can maintain balance automatically while remaining responsive to conscious direction when needed."

"The Sea King's forces have withdrawn, but they're not defeated," Mira added, her tactical assessment recognising the difference between temporary setbacks and permanent resolution. "They're regrouping, probably developing new approaches that take into account what they learned from this confrontation."

"But the strategic situation has fundamentally changed," Kritika observed, her crystals detecting shifts in the harmonic patterns that governed interactions between realms. "The restored temple network creates options that didn't exist before—ways to channel otherworldly influences constructively while preventing the kind of overwhelming integration that would eliminate individual choice."

The immediate crisis had indeed been resolved, but the resolution had created a new set of challenges and opportunities that would require unprecedented forms of cooperation and understanding. The balance between realms was no longer maintained through separation and barriers, but through active integration guided by principles that honoured both individual autonomy and cosmic interconnection.

"What happens to me now?" Nisha asked, her transformed voice carrying harmonics that allowed her to address both her human friends and the otherworldly forces that continued to influence events from across dimensional boundaries.

The answer, when it came, reflected the fundamental complexity of what she had become. Through her sacrifice and transformation, she had evolved into something that existed permanently between worlds—not fully human, not completely otherworldly, but something unprecedented that could serve as a living bridge while maintaining the essential values and relationships that made such service meaningful.

"You become what you chose to become," *Guru* Chanda replied, her experienced understanding recognising the implications of Nisha's transformation. "A guardian who exists simultaneously in multiple realms, a mediator who can preserve balance through conscious choice rather than unconscious force, a bridge that connects without requiring either side to abandon what makes them unique."

Through her connection to the temple network, Nisha could perceive the scope of what such guardianship would entail. The restored systems required ongoing attention from someone who could interface with both terrestrial and otherworldly forces, coordinate responses to supernatural threats, and ensure that the balance between realms remained stable despite the constant pressures that would always exist between incompatible forms of existence.

But she could also perceive something else—the growing network of individuals who were learning to work with the restored systems, people whose training and dedication would eventually allow them to share the burden of maintaining balance rather than requiring any single person to carry the entire responsibility.

"The work continues," she said, her voice carrying certainty that encompassed both the immediate challenges and the long-term possibilities that lay ahead. "But it continues as a collaboration rather than a solitary burden. The foundation has been established, the tools have been restored, and the knowledge exists to maintain what we've built."

The precarious truce that had been achieved was indeed fragile, requiring constant attention and ongoing commitment to principles that would always be easier to abandon than to maintain. But it was also unprecedented in its scope and potential, offering possibilities for coexistence and mutual enhancement that neither realm could have achieved alone.

As the immediate crisis formally ended and the Pathshala began the complex process of adapting to a world where the relationship between realms had been fundamentally transformed, Nisha felt her consciousness stabilising into its new configuration. She was still herself—her memories, her values, her essential personality remained intact. But she was also something more, something that could exist simultaneously across multiple forms of reality while maintaining the human connections that gave such existence meaning and purpose.

The convergence had been completed, but not through conquest or surrender. Instead, it had created synthesis—a new form of existence that honoured both individual choice and cosmic connection, that preserved what was valuable about human creativity while incorporating the wisdom that came from perspectives that spanned dimensions.

The future stretched ahead, filled with challenges that would test every aspect of the balance they had achieved and opportunities that neither world could have imagined independently. But at its foundation lay the temple network, the restored infrastructure, and the conscious commitment to maintaining harmony between forces that would always be easier to allow to conflict than to keep in productive cooperation.

The truce was precarious, but it was also revolutionary. And at its centre, transformed beyond recognition but still essentially herself, Nisha served as living proof that evolution and preservation could be achieved simultaneously when approached with wisdom, courage, and the kind of love that transcended every boundary between different forms of existence.

The most personal struggle—the fight for her own life against forces that had seemed determined to consume everything that made her human—had indeed only just begun. But it would be fought from a position of strength rather than desperation, with allies who understood the stakes and tools that could address challenges that had previously seemed insurmountable.

The precarious truce would hold, because those who had established it were committed to the ongoing work of maintaining what they had built together.

About the Author

Atul Arjun Mohite is the author of several books, including *Lucid Dream, Of Two Minds, World Without Weakness, Lucid Dream – The Journey Resumes* and *Jean Angel.* He published his first book, *Lucid Dream*, when he was nineteen years old, which depicts his career transition from an aspiring engineer to a writer, while his other books have addressed complex themes involving psychology, romance and adventure inspired by his life events. He was born in the city of Karad, Maharashtra, where he worked as an officer at the Bank of India before turning into a full-time author. He enjoys listening to music and playing lawn tennis in his spare time.